NATIVE EARTH

BOOK 7 ZEB HANKS MYSTERY SERIES

MARK REPS

This book is a work of fiction. Names and characters are products of the author's imagination. Any similarities between the good people of southeastern Arizona and tribal members of the San Carlos Indian Reservation are purely coincidental.

NATIVE EARTH

Text Copyright © 2017 Mark Reps

ISBN-13: 978-1545388075

ISBN-10: 1545388075

ALSO BY MARK REPS

ZEB HANKS MYSTERY SERIES

NATIVE BLOOD

HOLES IN THE SKY

ADIÓS ÁNGEL

NATIVE JUSTICE

NATIVE BONES

NATIVE WARRIOR

NATIVE EARTH

NATIVE DESTINY

NATIVE TROUBLE

NATIVE ROOTS (PREQUEL NOVELLA)

THE ZEB HANKS MYSTERY SERIES 1-3

AUDIOBOOK

NATIVE BLOOD

HOLES IN THE SKY

ADIÓS ÁNGEL

OTHER BOOKS

BUTTERFLY (WITH PUI CHOMNAK)

HEARTLAND HEROES

ACKNOWLEDGMENTS

A writer is much like a sheriff. His work defines him and the buck stops with him. However, it is the people who support him that really determine the final outcome.

I would like to thank the late Sheriff Stevens of Graham County and his son, Dr. Stevens. They inadvertently helped frame these books. Thirty years ago, Sheriff Stevens, his son and grandson picked up my wife and me on a remote road we were hiking. His son and I shared the same profession, chiropractic. In a fifteen-minute car ride, while the sheriff's young grandson slept and his son drove, we all became friends. Of course, my writing is fictional in nature.

Over the last 30 years I have continually visited Graham County and the San Carlos Reservation. With each passing year, I find the people to be more and more welcoming as I learn more about the area, hear more local stories and interact with those who have lived in the area their entire lives. I would like to heartily thank the people of Graham County and the San Carlos Reservation.

I would also like to thank Lisa Vehrenkamp for her help in the create endeavors that involve marketing an independent writer. She has continually come up with new ideas, avenues and concepts. Thanks, Lisa.

Finally, I must acknowledge my wife, Kathy, who is indefatigable in putting up with me when I get lost in the process of writing. She also lets me know when my writing is getting off the rails and edits without minimal complaining. Thanks a ton, Kathy.

1

2:45 A.M

The ringing of the telephone stirred Zeb from the underworld where dark dreams dwell. He tried to make the ring tone part of a fantastic escape, but the third ring destroyed that subconscious fantasy and snatched him from an unsettling sleep into grateful wakefulness. Former Sheriff Jake Dablo, now Zeb's chief deputy, had long ago taught him that a good lawman sleeps with one ear open, one eye half shut and the mind always at the ready. Sheriff Hanks grabbed the phone with one hand, made a vain attempt to wipe the sleep from his eyes with the other and glanced at the bedside digital clock. It read a blurry quarter of three. His mind jumped to the old Frank Sinatra standard *One for My Baby* and its famous line, "It's a quarter to three, there's no one in the place except you and me."

Jake had taught him well. Zeb's mind was alert even though it was the middle of the night. If his dream hadn't been so disturbing, he probably wouldn't feel so strange having his sleep interrupted. As a longtime sheriff, he had lost many nights' sleep from late night calls, yet he never quite got used to the feeling that came with them.

On the other end of the line was a woman with a high-pitched voice that reminded Zeb of a squeaking mouse. She was shouting unintelligibly. Zeb's initial thought was that she sounded drunk. The phone call also roused Echo Skysong, who recently had begun spending more nights sharing Zeb's bed. He glanced over his shoulder at her as he pressed the phone to his ear. Her beautiful, dark-brown eyes were wide open and alert. Her vigilance, heightened from three tours in Afghanistan, may have permanently robbed her of deep slumber. They shared a quick smile that carried an air of concern. Zeb placed his hand on the smooth skin of her brown thigh. Echo placed her hand on his back, gently returning a lover's touch.

Even as he was becoming alert, Zeb couldn't make out the woman's utterances. Slowly he began to make out what she was saying. What he was hearing, however, made little sense at all.

"Angus never came home. He always comes home. We had an important dinner date. I just know something is wrong. Sheriff Hanks, you've got to help me. You've got to help me right now."

Zeb thought of anyone named Angus whose wife might be on a hunt for him in the middle of the night. A few came immediately to mind as his brain began revving up to full capacity. There were less than a half dozen men christened with the name Angus in all of Graham County. He recalled a few more with the same moniker that lived on the Rez.

"To whom am I speaking?" asked Zeb.

Echo listened with a highly trained and attentive ear to his every word.

"Lily McGinty." Her response carried an air of indignance and superiority. "I almost singlehandedly funded your last campaign for sheriff. I should think you would recognize my voice. Don't you have caller ID?"

Zeb slipped on his newly purchased bifocals. The name of Lily McGinty popped clearly into focus. "Lily, you woke me from sleep. I apologize for not recognizing your voice. What's going on? You sound upset."

"Angus didn't come home tonight. He called and said he'd be late. He also said he'd be home in time for our monthly dinner meeting at the Top of the Mountain Steakhouse with the head honchos from

Danforth-Roerg. He was supposed to be home by eight-thirty. Dinner was scheduled at nine. I left numerous messages on Angus's cell phone to meet us there, but he never answered and he never showed up."

"Did you call the mine office?"

"Of course I did," said Lily indignantly. "No one has seen him since around eight o'clock."

"Did anyone see him leave?"

"I didn't ask, but I'm certain they would have mentioned something if they knew he was still there."

Fightin' Angus McGinty was a wild Irishmen with a wandering eye. He had married a land wealthy but somewhat crazy Apache isdzan, as the local Rez residents referred to her. His frequent extramarital affairs were no secret to anyone in Graham County, including Lily. Nevertheless, he didn't let them interfere with business. It seemed odd that he would miss an important business meeting with the top dogs from the mining company.

Zeb's senses had come fully around when he was about to ask Lily why she waited until this ungodly hour to phone him. His question was interrupted when a second call beeped in on his phone. His eyes were now fully focused. He recognized instantly that this call was from Byrne Murphy, security administrator for Danforth-Roerg at the Klondyke I mine.

"Lily, I just might have an answer for you. Someone from the mine is calling on my other line. Hang on one second. I'll be right back with you."

"Find out just what the hell Angus is up to. Let him know if he's coming home he'd better have a damn good excuse for his behavior," said Lily.

Zeb clicked onto the other line.

"Sheriff Hanks."

"Sheriff, this is Byrne Murphy, head of security out at Danforth-Roerg Klondyke I mine."

"Yes, Byrne. What can I do for you?"

"We've got a problem, a big problem."

"Does it involve Angus McGinty?" asked Zeb.

"How'd you know that?"

"Just a hunch. What's up?"

"He's dead. At least I think he's dead."

"What do you mean by that?" asked Zeb.

"I mean I think he's dead, but I'm having a little trouble identifying the body," said Byrne.

"Meaning what exactly?" asked Zeb.

"To make a long story short, we had a Caterpillar road roller breakdown while smoothing out a haul route. We were right in the middle of something with critical timing. We needed a working road roller ASAP. The foreman sent the driver along with a safety man to get the Volvo DD140B. When the driver moved the roller, the safety man noticed something didn't look right underneath where the big machine had been sitting. There was a body, flatter than a pancake, laying on the ground. It's awful. In fact, it's downright freaky."

"I can imagine," replied Zeb.

"Do you know how much a Volvo DD140B road roller weighs?" asked Byrne. Zeb didn't have to ask. Byrne Murphy spouted out the answer. "Thirty-two thousand pounds. Most of it is steel."

The sheriff momentarily pondered what thirty-two thousand pounds of steel would do to a human body laid out on rock hard ground. Immediately, even at a quarter to three, he realized there was no way to figure that out without seeing it in person.

"Do you know how much Angus McGinty weighed?" asked Byrne. Once again Zeb didn't need to ask as the weight of Byrne's boss rolled off the safety manager's tongue. "One hundred seventy-five pounds."

"I see your point," said Zeb. "What makes you think the body is Angus McGinty?"

"Well, his Cadillac Escalade is parked thirty feet away from where the body is. Anyone else authorized to be in that area is accounted for."

"I'll call Jake and Doc Yackley and get them out of bed. We should all be there in thirty minutes. Don't move anything and don't let anyone get close to the scene."

"Got it," said Byrne. "Should I call that crazy Injun wife of his?"

"Let's make a positive ID before we call Lily."

"Thanks. She's about the last person I want to talk to at three in the morning. She's probably drunker than a skunk, licking the lizard of some hunky copper miner, a bum from the Rez, or maybe even goin' down on some young snatch with a Brazilian wax. I've heard she digs that kind of thing."

Zeb ignored Byrne's rant about Lily's sex life and clicked his phone back over to Lily.

"Lily, there's been an accident at the mine. Is Angus's Escalade parked in the garage?"

"No."

"You're sure about that?"

"Of course I am. I've already checked ...three times. Did something happen to him? Is Angus okay?" asked Lily. Her voice was full of anger and seemed to lack genuine concern.

"I don't know one way or the other," said Zeb. "I'm headed out to the mine right now. I'll call you when I know what's going on. In the meantime, I'm sending Deputy Kate Steele and Depute Sawyer Black Bear to your house."

Lily's first response upon hearing Sawyer Black Bear's name was to let out a sexy little sigh, or so it sounded to Zeb. Maybe Byrne's crude remarks about Lily's sex life had taken a foothold in Zeb's mind. Zeb thought back to his last campaign which Lily helped finance. More than once Zeb had felt she was coming on to him. A fraction of a second later Lily's ire was back.

"If Angus isn't hurt, you tell him he's going to be a hurtin' cowboy when he gets home," said Lily. "That cheating son of a bitch."

"I've got to run," said Zeb.

"I want answers and I want them ASAP," said Lily.

"Once I know anything, I promise you will be the first person I call."

"Don't forget that I sit on the board of directors of the Klondyke 1," added Lily.

"Right," said Zeb.

Zeb pressed the end call button.

"Anything I can do to help?" asked Echo. "I overheard everything."

"If any calls come directly to the home phone, have them call me on my cell."

"Do you have any idea who would kill Angus McGinty?" asked Echo.

"The list of those who didn't care for him is longer than his list of friends," replied Zeb.

"Have anyone in particular in mind?" asked Echo.

"No, no one specifically."

Echo got out of bed and turned on the hot water to make Zeb a cup of tea. Zeb got on the phone to Kate. She answered on the first ring.

"Kate, call Black Bear and get him out of bed. I want the two of you to go over and keep a close eye on Lily McGinty."

"What's up, boss?"

"It looks like Angus McGinty is dead. We don't know for certain yet, but when we find out, I want someone to be with Lily," explained Zeb.

"Do you think the situation calls for both of us to be there?" asked Kate.

"Intuition tells me something bad is afoot," said Zeb.

"I'll call Black Bear. We'll be out there as quickly as possible," said Kate.

Zeb called Doc Yackley who also answered on the first ring.

"You up already?" asked Zeb.

"Old men take frequent piss breaks," said Doc. "I just finished my three a.m. bladder trickle. What's up?"

"Trouble out at the Klondyke. I think Angus McGinty might have departed the planet the hard way," said Zeb.

"Are you positive it's him?"

"Nope, not yet. I'm on my way out. Can you be ready in ten minutes?"

"Just need to pull up my britches. I'll be standing at the end of my driveway."

"See you in ten," said Zeb.

Zeb also gave Deputy Jake Dablo a buzz.

"Jake, we've got a situation up at the mine. I'm headed out there right now. Sure could use your help."

"I'll meet you there," Jake replied without hesitation.

2

CRUSHED

At three-thirty in the morning a billion stars glittered overhead. A light, cool breeze floated in from the east, announcing an ever-approaching dawn. Zeb, Jake, Doc and Byrne Murphy were all standing over a body that seemed impossibly flat and hardly human.

"Jesus H. Keerist," said Doc. "Every single bone in the body is crushed damned near to powder. Not in all my born days have I ever seen anything like it."

"It's unbelievable what a big machine can do to a body," added Zeb.

"Zeb, you've seen just about everything. You ever seen anything like this? I betcha a dollar to a donut you haven't."

"No, Doc, I haven't. I do believe I would recall if I had," replied Zeb.

The men's eyes turned to the machine that had just decimated a human body.

"It's a Volvo double drum road roller, the DD140B," explained Byrne. "It's one hell of a working machine. Much bigger than our regular roller. Angus got a deal on this one from a landfill company up in Phoenix. It's got two seven-foot wide drums that vibrate for extra compaction. We have to build and rebuild roads all the time around here. This is our best baby for that. It always gets the job done."

Zeb and Doc nodded, duly impressed.

"How many people working at the mine know how to drive one of these machines?" asked Zeb.

"I got thirty or so DMV qualified drivers. Another dozen or so could drive one if they had to and another few hundred who would love to give it a try, just for the hell of it."

"Can you get me a list of names of those who are qualified to drive the road roller?" asked Zeb.

"I have that on file," replied Byrne.

"You'd better also give me a second list of people you think could drive one if they had to."

"Sure thing. Be right back," said Byrne, heading toward the fore-man's building.

"Wait a second, Byrne. One other quick question," said Zeb.

Byrne stopped, turned and faced the sheriff.

"Most of your big equipment is expensive, right?"

"Yes, Sheriff Hanks, outrageously expensive," replied Byrne. "We've got millions invested in our equipment."

"Do you have a security camera that monitors your big machines when they aren't being used? I mean in case somebody tampers with them, tries to steal them or something like that?"

"Right there, behind ..." Byrne stopped in mid-sentence and uttered four telling words. "Son of a bitch."

"What do you mean by that?" asked Zeb.

"Look," Byrne said, pointing to a camera. "Any damn fool can see that somebody has tampered with that. I don't know how I missed it before now."

Zeb stared into the semi-darkness. He saw nothing obvious.

Byrne traipsed over to the camera with Zeb, Jake and Doc on his heels. The camera was mounted on a metal tripod about five feet off the ground.

"Right here, look."

Zeb shrugged his shoulders.

"This thing is supposed to be on a rotating swivel. The swivel allows it to cover a one hundred eighty-degree field of vision. It gives us a view of all parked equipment. Someone took it off the rotating bracket. Look down the lens line. It's pointed directly at the body."

"Is it still working?" asked Zeb.

"I can check. I'll get the iPad. I can bring up the last twenty-four hours of security footage."

"Jake, why don't you go along with Byrne."

Jake was two steps ahead of Zeb's directive. No sense letting Byrne tamper with any potential evidence in case he was somehow involved. Zeb watched them walk away. He noticed Byrne moving along with a slight limp.

Zeb turned to Doc who had donned a headlight helmet. He was beginning some preliminary autopsy steps. He closely examined what was left of the body of Fightin' Angus McGinty. The remains were flattened paper thin. Zeb looked at them with the absurd thought that he could almost peel them off the ground. The image in his head was grotesquely cartoonish.

"I once saw the body of a man who had accidentally fallen through an industrial cheese slicing machine, the kind that takes a thousand-pound block of cheese and cubes it into half-inch bite-sized pieces. Minced him into a million pieces. You could hardly tell it had been a human until you saw a bunch of the pieces all laid out together," said Doc. "That was some nasty business."

"I bet it was," replied Zeb.

Zeb ran his hand across the road roller as though it were a living being. Based on what it had done to McGinty, it was indeed a monster of a machine.

"Any ideas on what happened?" asked Doc.

"In my professional opinion he got run over," replied Zeb.

"Probably more than once. He was squished flat as a June bug against a windshield on a hot summer night. It's like he got a rub down with a gigantic rolling pin," added Doc.

"I see time of day has no bearing on the dark cleverness of your tongue," said Zeb.

"I gotta have a touch of the gallows humor. Otherwise stuff like this would stick with me and I wouldn't sleep like a baby," said Doc. "You know how it is with PTSD sometimes. It's the image that sticks with you, not the actual event."

"You sleep like a baby, Doc?" asked Zeb, flashing to the moment he found his wife's body.

"Sure do. At my age, I wake up crying every few hours because my diaper's wet."

"Damn it, Doc. It's the middle of the night and you nab me, hook, line and sinker," replied Zeb, pushing the image of Doreen, his wife, away with all the power he could muster.

"Experience," said Doc with a wink.

Jake and Byrne returned from the office. Byrne stood in the background with the iPad in one hand and some papers in the other. Jake went right to work roping off the part of the crime scene that included Angus's Escalade. When Jake was done roping off the surrounding area with police tape, he opened the driver's side of Angus's luxury SUV. He flashed his light on the steering wheel. The first thing that caught his eye was the keys in the ignition. He also noted a piece of paper taped to the dashboard.

"Zeb, get over here," said Jake. "I want you to see this."

Zeb took a few steps toward the Escalade. Jake was still shining his light on the dashboard and the piece of paper taped to it. The writing was in magic marker. The message was simple and direct. "Dinner meeting at 9 with Lily and Danforth Execs." Zeb looked at Doc who returned a puzzled gaze.

"Wonder why he was worried about forgetting the meeting?" asked Doc.

"Angus is, was, a busy man. Probably the dinner wasn't high on his list of priorities," replied Zeb.

"I'm fairly certain he didn't care much for kissing company ass," said Doc.

"Did you know Angus pretty well?" asked Zeb.

"Angus and I bent elbows together more than once. He didn't like to waste his precious time with political crap. You and I both know how these kinds of dinners go. It's all about the dog and pony show. Nothing ever really gets done at them."

Zeb glanced over at Doc. The old country doctor had more horse sense than most men had common sense. If he rendered an opinion that quickly, there was likely something to it.

Byrne walked over, interrupting Zeb's private thoughts.

"Want some light?" asked Byrne. "We got all the light you want."

"Thanks," replied Zeb. "Have them set the lights up thirty feet or so back from the body. Do you have something they can cover their boots with so they don't mess with the crime scene?"

Byrne Murphy called some technicians to bring in some heavy lighting and boot covers. Ten minutes later the place was lit up like it was high noon at the OK Corral.

"Thanks. The lighting gives us a lot better look at the crime scene," said Zeb.

"To answer your question, the camera is still working," said Byrne. "It's going to take a while to pull up specific security footage. I put a call in to my tech guy, Rhett Brock. He's an independent sort. He more or less runs the show when it comes to our electronic security. Rhett has his own set up with that stuff. He's the secretive kind. I think he believes that if he is the only one who knows exactly how the security camera system works, Angus can never fire him."

"Were you able to get hold of him?" asked Zeb.

"Yes."

"Is he on his way?" asked Zeb.

"Like I said, Rhett's an independent guy. He said he'd get here after he had a cup of coffee," said Byrne.

"By the time he gets here, we might be back at the office. I'll take the iPad that has the video on it. Is that the only place the video of the crime scene would be?" asked Zeb.

"As far as I know."

Zeb shouted instructions to enlarge the crime scene area to include everything within thirty feet of the security camera.

"I suppose you have no choice but to designate it a crime scene?" asked Byrne. He was half hopeful that he would hear something other than what was blatantly obvious.

"Do the mines have some other name for it?" asked Zeb. "I mean do you have some official name for a possible crime scene, other than crime scene?"

"No, but if you're designating this a crime scene with a death involved, as head of security I've got to shut the whole damn business down right now. We've got federal, state and local regulations we are required to follow. If we don't play by the book, we can get slapped with huge fines, long shut downs and, worst of all, government types snooping over everything, including our books. A crime scene opens us to every kind of potential trouble."

Zeb curled his lip. He knew the drill all too well. It seemed the primary duty of politicians and career bureaucrats was to make it difficult for anyone to do business.

"I truly am sorry, Byrne. You know I don't have any choice in the matter," said Zeb. "I really wish I could help you out, but I can't."

"Can you at least give me some parameters on the size of the crime scene? Can I assume this immediate area where Angus's body was found is the crime scene?"

"Once I have a little better idea on the facts, I'll map it out clearly for you," replied Zeb.

"Corporate is going to have their undies in a bunch if we have to shut down for more than a day or two. When word gets out that we have a crime scene with a death involved, we're going to have the feds sniffing our rear ends like dogs in heat. We've had enough trouble with those bastards over the last five years to last a lifetime. One federal mine inspector in particular has been a thorn in our side."

"Who's that?"

"A guy by the name of Thorman Wright. Angus had serious issues with him. They threatened each other. I had to pull them apart to keep Angus from pummeling him. Angus would rise from the dead to fight him if he comes around and does the inspection."

"What caused that kind of bad blood?" asked Zeb. "Spot inspections?"

"Spot inspections because of that crazy fucking wife of his. Lily has carried on with Thorman since the first time he inspected the mine. She'd screw him and expect him to look the other way for minor, maybe even major, infractions. If he didn't play ball, she'd go after him with a horsewhip and threaten to tell his wife. It happened more than once."

"I guess that could make for bad blood on many levels," said Zeb.

"Believe me, it did," replied Byrne.

"Let me get everyone on my team out here ASAP," said Zeb. "I can probably narrow down the hot spots considerably in a few hours, and you won't lose too much running time. Can we keep the crime scene to ourselves for the next few hours?"

"Hell yes," replied Byrne.

"Since nobody at the state and federal level is working at this hour anyway, it should keep both of us from getting in too much hot water. How's that sound?" asked Zeb.

"That will work," replied Byrne. "I appreciate whatever you can do for me and so will the company come next election. I'll send the government boys a fax to make it legit. They probably won't even see it until this afternoon."

"I can't promise to stick to an exact schedule. It all depends on what we find," said Zeb.

"If this thing goes south and we shut down for an extended time, I might have to temporarily lay off five hundred hard working men and women," said Byrne. "That'll piss off the board of directors, Lily McGinty, my employees and most of the businesses in town. If it goes on for too long, I'll lose some of my best workers."

"You're getting ahead of yourself, Byrne. Don't jump to conclusions," warned Zeb. "Maybe this is going to be straightforward, and you'll be mining copper by the second shift this afternoon. What is company protocol when a job site death occurs?"

"We're required by federal and state statutes to shut down all but the essential operations until we can prove the mine is safe to operate," said Byrne. "An employee killed by any piece of equipment involved on an ongoing job is one of those circumstances. But that's not the worst of it."

"What do you mean?" asked Zeb.

"All employees have to pass through the area where Angus was found in order to get to our primary work site." Byrne pointed to a road that led to where the miners were currently working. "That specifically shuts us down cold."

"Follow the rules to the letter of the law. If Thorman Wright is as much of a bugaboo as you say he is, you'd better send everyone home. For the time being this area is off limits to everything and everyone, men and machines."

"We got women employees too," said Byrne.

"And women," added Zeb.

Byrne walked away, cell phone in hand, and began barking orders. From the sound of it, his levels of anger and frustration were going to get worse before they got better.

"Zeb, want to come over here?" asked Jake. "I think you're going to want to see this."

Doc and Jake were leaning over the annihilated body of Angus McGinty. Using a flat stick, Doc pulled what remained of Angus's right hand out of a small area of soft, wet, sandy mud. The big Volvo road roller had apparently leaked some hydraulic fluid, allowing Angus's right hand to be pushed into the softened earth.

"What've you got?" asked Zeb.

"Don't know for sure," replied Jake. "But I'd say Angus had something in his right hand when this situation happened."

"Or maybe the killer placed something in his hand," added Doc.

"Still playing amateur detective, eh, Doc?" asked Jake.

"Keeps my interest level up where it should be," replied Doc. "Even an old man needs to keep learning."

Zeb bent in for a closer look. In the twisted, crushed right hand of Angus McGinty was what appeared to be an amulet of some sort.

"Doc, can you use your delicate surgical skills to remove that thing so we can see what it is?" asked Zeb.

"I can give it a try. Can't guarantee it won't crumble to bits when I do," said Doc. "There's not much to work with. It's in piss poor shape."

The old country doctor gently bent back what remained of Angus's right hand. With the gentlest of touch, he opened it ever so slightly. It opened easily considering the mangled shape of the body part. Doc gingerly removed what appeared to be a snake's head, a feather, a wedding ring and a penny. Doc shined the light of his helmet on what he had just removed from the dead man's grasp and noted the copper penny was a 1909 SVDB.

"Everything seems in remarkably good shape considering they were just crushed by thirty-two thousand pounds of steel," said Zeb.

"When she's soft and wet, old Mother Earth can be mighty forgiving," Doc said.

"What've you got?" asked Jake.

Doc poured water over what was left of the snake and rubbed his handkerchief over the ring to clean it. The feather shed the water, but Doc did his best to clean it as well.

Zeb leaned in to examine each item. The design on the snake skin told him it could only be from a diamondback rattler. The feather was a wing feather of an eagle, hawk or maybe even an owl. It was difficult to tell considering the dirt, mud and wetness. The ring was definitely a wedding ring. The penny was unusual, in mint condition and quite clean considering the circumstances.

"The ring is a wedding ring. That's obvious. The old penny, is it valuable?" asked Zeb.

Doc, an avid coin collector, examined the coin.

"This particular penny is worth at least a grand in ideal condition. And this one is in near perfect condition even after being run over."

"Why the hell would he be carrying that around?" asked Jake.

"I know he's a copper coin collector," said Zeb. "Lily might know more about why he'd have that specific coin with him. Maybe he was going to give it as a gift to one of the company executives. I know Angus liked to show off like that."

Jake took some notes.

"When you put the rattlesnake skin and the feather together, it appears like it could be a bad luck talisman," said Zeb.

"What do you mean?" asked Doc.

"When you want to possess someone with bad luck, you give them an object or objects that will bring evil upon them. Each object has a specific significance. I can't say for certain, but I'd guess the rattlesnake had something to do with death or poisoning. When you do the autopsy, check for poison, especially rattlesnake venom. The feather, well, it depends on what kind it actually is. The coin and the wedding ring ... hmmm ... those are real stumpers."

"I suppose your old pal Jimmy Song Bird taught you that stuff about the snakes and the feathers?" asked Doc.

"He did, but it was a long time ago. He wanted me to understand evil and how it works," replied Zeb.

"Looks like it did what it was supposed to," added Jake.

"Native American, maybe Apache, black magic?" asked Doc.

"I'm going to have to give Song Bird a holler on that one," said Zeb.

"You do that. I know this is what I hear called bad juju. Just plain, old-fashioned evil," said Doc.

"You wouldn't be wrong about that, Doc," replied Zeb.

3

THIS GUN FOR HIRE

DAYS EARLIER

"One hundred thousand dollars. Is that correct?"

"My usual fee."

The woman quoting the amount of her compensation called herself Charlotte. The woman asking about the payment called herself Abby.

"Cash money, right?" asked Abby.

"We could use an offshore account. But considering the time-frame you have in mind and considering this is the first time we've worked together, payment has to be made in cash," replied Charlotte. "Don't take it personally, it's just business."

"Then you disappear from Graham County. Got it? It has to be that way. After you have completed the job I hired you to do, you can never have any contact with me again. If you do, I will pay twice that amount of money to make certain you disappear permanently. I will have you killed if I even hear you're in the area again. Count on it."

Charlotte eyed the woman who called herself Abby. What she saw was a hippie-garbed, beautiful young woman with a lusty persona. Charlotte took her warning with a grain of salt. A hired gun doesn't threaten easily. Charlotte paused, locking eyes for a long second with Abby. She wondered if Abby was acting as a liaison for someone else or of her own accord. Professional go-betweens were becoming more common in her trade. These days practically no one did their own bidding.

Abby shoved an unmarked envelope across the table with a hand gloved in latex. A solitary fingerprint absentmindedly left behind could be disastrous. She wasn't about to end up in prison by making a simple mistake.

Charlotte didn't even bother to glance around the room as the money exchanged hands. She nonchalantly slid the packet back and forth on the table top between her hands.

Six other patrons were in the Copper Pit Blues Bar. A young, good-looking couple played a game of three-ball billiards. Four copper miners slouched over cheap glasses of beer, engaged in the grunted conversation of tired men. None even acknowledged Charlotte and Abby. If they had, what would they have seen? Two young women. One a hippie chick in her twenties with long blondish-brown hair. The other a sexy looking motorcycle mama in her early thirties wearing a baseball cap. They appeared to be having a friendly drink and some quiet girl talk. The hippie was drinking a gin and tonic and the biker chick a whiskey, neat.

The bar was dark. It was infused by the odor of all mining town bars—dust, grime, time, cheap beer and sweat. The bored bartender stood at the far end of the bar rubbing a well-worn rag over the inside of an empty glass. Checking his work against the dingy overhead light, he cleaned the one tiny spot on the rim he deemed unsatisfactory. Satisfied, he grabbed another glass and began the process anew. His eyes casually glanced at Charlotte and Abby to see if they were ready for another round. They seemed fine. Compared to the type of women who usually frequented this dive bar, the bartender deemed them a cut above. One in an innocent stoner kind of way, the other in a sexy, tough manner. He went back to the mundane chores of his work. The TV on the wall was playing a painful rerun of the previous season's Arizona Cardinals playoff loss.

"Feels like a hundred G's," said Charlotte.

"You can count it. Go ahead," said Abby. "I guarantee it's all there."

"If we can't trust each other, both of us are out of business. I learned that lesson a long time ago," replied Charlotte. "Only one person ever made the mistake of double-crossing me. I doubt you're the type of person who would make such a foolish mistake."

They clinked glasses. Neither smiled. Both understood the situation. In another time and place they might have developed a friendship, maybe even a relationship. Each recognized something attractive in the other.

"Where do you want the deed done?"

A touch of irony danced momentarily in Abby's mind before she answered. Charlotte caught the hesitation. It was obvious to her the thought had crossed Abby's mind. Maybe she had been given specific orders as to where the killing should take place.

"At the Klondyke 1 mine, of course. How could it be done any other way?"

"When?"

"By the end of the month. Preferably on pay day. Let the workers have a day or two off so they can enjoy themselves."

"Do you want him to suffer?"

Abby pretended to be thinking. The answer to Charlotte's questions was already etched in stone.

"Yes. Make the moment marking the end of his life arrive slowly. Kill him painfully. He has to pay for his evil ways."

"Egregious suffering. I can do that. It's sort of my specialty," replied Charlotte. "Do you want him to know it was you who had him killed?"

This was a foregone conclusion. However, when speaking to Charlotte, Abby acted as though the thought had never crossed her mind. Charlotte was a pro. She knew hatred and revenge played major roles with this kind of killing. Of course Abby wanted the person she had put a hit on to know who his judge and jury were.

"Hmmm ... good question."

The false hesitancy was almost laughable, but the gritted determination of the answer was anything but.

"Yes, tell him it was greed that ended his life."

"Shall I mention the name Abby or do you want me to say someone else?" asked Charlotte.

"He won't recognize the name. Just tell him he is dying for the sin of greed. Tell him that he has to die for what he has done to Mother Earth."

"All right. I can do that. Not a problem."

"If you can, whisper it in his ear, sort of sexy like. Then punch him in the face, maybe break his nose in the process. I want maximum pain."

"You are a bad girl ... a bad, bad girl."

Glasses once again clinked. This time accompanied by sadistic laughter.

"As you wish, Angus McGinty shall die a slow, cruel death at the Klondyke 1 copper mine."

"Nothing could make me happier than sending him to the boneyard after immense suffering," said Abby.

"Like I said, consider it a done deal."

"Did you know that son of a bitch has ruined everything he's ever touched? He has no one who loves him. Even his dog hated him. He has spent an entire career, an entire lifetime, destroying everything he encounters."

"I get it," said Charlotte, using her voice to calm the ever-increasing hatred in Abby's voice.

"Killing him where he has destroyed the earth, overseen the death of a dozen workers and the maiming of countless others falls under the heading of poetic justice. Someone needs to make a statement here. Wouldn't you agree?"

The hired killer nodded. Charlotte was strictly apolitical. Her professionalism allowed her to care only about her work and her payday. Yet she listened to the woman who had just hired her and played along as though she cared. It was all part of the job. After all, a hired killer needed good, reliable references. Charlotte also felt a sexual tension between them.

"Have you ever done any mining work?" asked Charlotte.

"I know something about it," Abby replied. "I know that copper mining destroys Mother Earth and all that is sacred about her."

Charlotte had never done labor of that ilk. Abby's philosophy was little more than dust blowing in the vast, desert wind to her. Hard work, like mining, was beneath her. That was work for plebeians. Women with IQs over 150 weren't bred to do manual labor. They were blessed with strong personal philosophies and born to accomplish far more difficult tasks, such as killing without leaving any trace of evidence in their wake.

"Poetic justice. Yes, that is the correct way of putting it. His vices need to be punished with extreme pain. It's only natural. One more thing."

"Yes?" inquired Charlotte.

"Make certain it looks good enough to throw that damn Sheriff Zeb Hanks off the trail. I don't care much for him either. I want to screw with his head too. Give him plenty of false leads to follow."

"Want me to kill him? It'll cost you more, but it can be done."

"No. I want just the one killing. That's all that needs be done for the time being. I can't stress enough the importance of making absolutely certain the Graham County Sheriff's Office can't put any of this back in my direction or anywhere near me. That, too, would be the death of you."

Charlotte chuckled to herself. Abby had no idea who she was dealing with. Charlotte knew everything about Abby, including who she really was and why she wanted so desperately to see Angus McGinty dead. It had nothing to do with the copper mine, Mother Earth or any of the other excuses she had offered.

"Don't worry. I've already got plans for that. I'll lay down more than a few red herrings. Sheriff Hanks is not that smart. I've been studying him. I know I can lead him astray. In fact, it's already in the works."

"Don't underestimate him. I know people who have dealt with

him. He's no fool. Beneath that easy-going cowboy façade is a heart of stone and a mind like a steel trap. When I was a kid, there were rumors of him killing a child molester and tossing his body into a rattlesnake pit."

"Let me worry about Sheriff Hanks. I'm getting paid. I guarantee you'll get your money's worth." The newly hired killer slipped the money into the pocket of her hoodie. "I guess this is goodbye."

Both women simultaneously reached to the center of the table and held the other's hands.

"It was fun while it lasted," said Charlotte. "Are you certain our paths can never cross again?"

"It's far too dangerous. You know that," said Abby. "Today is the end of our interaction."

"If I were a betting woman, I'd say our paths will cross again," said Charlotte.

"It can't happen. That's just the way things must to be," replied Abby.

Charlotte stood and took a pair of steps that led her closer to the woman who had just hired her. Abby grabbed the hired killer's hands and kissed them. To Charlotte, the kiss felt like a blessing.

Abby noticed something on Charlotte's right wrist. It was a tattoo of a woman riding on the back of a dragon that was clad in a kilt. In another time and place she might have asked about it. Buy familiarity was dangerous here.

"Just do the job you were hired to do."

"No need to worry. I have a hundred thousand reasons not to let you down."

With that Charlotte walked out the front door of the Copper Pit Blues Bar.

From across the room the woman playing pool caught Abby's eye. Abby nodded and gently tipped her head toward the exit door. The woman put away her pool cue. Abby left money on the table for the drinks, got up and departed through the side door. The pool player followed her out the door. Together they disappeared into the darkness of a moonless night.

4

THREE WEEKS AGO

"You've cheated on me for the last time."

Lily's shrill screaming voice hackled the hair on Angus's neck like fingernails digging into the blackness of chalkboard.

"This time you leave and never come back. I'll keep the house and anything else I want. I've already talked to a lawyer in Phoenix. Her firm says our pre-nuptial agreement is full of holes. The trust we set up was never properly registered, making it null and void. The deed to the mine property that I signed over to you was never properly registered with the state. Basically, the ball is in my court. For once in this relationship I call the shots. In short, asshole, you're screwed."

Angus McGinty poured himself three fingers of Old Darby WhistlePig Rye Whiskey. He drank it neat. Like all men of big desires, he wanted the best bang for his buck. He downed the whiskey in a single swallow, then poured himself a follow-up triple shot.

"Fuck you and that goddamned horse your old Aunt Nell gave us when we got married."

Lily Pherson McGinty picked up a glass ash tray and fired it with all the acumen of a Randy Johnson fastball directly at her husband's face. It caromed off his forehead, hit a lamp, knocked it over and flew through a window, leaving a small, angulated hole in its tempered glass. Blood trickled down Angus McGinty's face, temporarily blinding his right eye. Knowing fresh blood to be the anxiety trigger that sped up Lily's congenitally weakened heart, he made no attempt to wipe it away. In his own heart of darkness, he half-wished she'd pop her cork right then and there.

For a long moment they stared at each other, sharing the boiling hatred of twenty-five years of an unhappy marriage. Alcoholism, drug abuse, cheating and stealing from each other had brought them to this low point. Worst of all, with the ugly remark about Aunt Nell's horse, Angus had crossed a line he could never cross back over. The gift of a wedding nag had been a tradition on Lily's side of the family for over two hundred years. In some ways, it was more important and carried more value than the mine she had inherited and placed in Angus's trust.

"I should just put a bullet in your brain and bury you under ten tons of rock," said Angus. "It would serve you right."

"I should slit your throat, cut your balls off, stick them in your mouth and sew it shut," growled Lily.

"Go ahead if you've got the guts, which you don't. Your whole family is nothing but a gang of weak and brainless cowards. They're a bunch of half-bred, Irish-Injun, good-for-nothings that have been mooching off us for years. If I hadn't hauled your ass off the reservation and turned our land into a big time copper mine, you'd be a third-generation gutter snipe or, even more likely, six feet under by now," shouted Angus.

"You are lower than the fetid rats I used to shoot for fun at the dump when I was a kid," screamed Lily.

He poured himself another generous dose of WhistlePig. She grabbed her bottle of Nolet's Reserve Dry Gin. She chugged it down like it was tap water.

"You rotten, junkyard dog. That stuff costs me seven hundred dollars a bottle," yelled Angus. "Drink it with the little class that I thought you had when I married you."

Lily boiled over as she poured the rest of the bottle on the birthday present Angus had given her when she turned forty, a Fereghan carpet from central Persia. The one-of-a-kind rug had cost him over one hundred thousand dollars at a Sotheby's auction.

Jumping from his Dragons chair, Angus raced across the room, grabbed Lily by the neck and walloped her across the bridge of the nose with a closed fist. Lily fell to the floor, face down in the gin-soaked carpet. Angus jumped onto her back and shoved her face into the spilled Nolet's gin.

"Drink it, bitch. Drink every single drop."

Suddenly the combination of the 160 milligrams of OxyContin he had taken an hour earlier blended with the Old Darby WhistlePig. His head began to swoon. Ten seconds later he was lights out, jumbled in a heap on top of his wife.

A solid two hours elapsed before either moved. Then, just as Angus's consciousness returned, he puked all over his wife. The contents of his stomach falling on her bloodied face snapped her back to awareness. Lily wiped it off as though it were nothing at all.

Angus and Lily exchanged an all too familiar glance. They'd done it again. They had pushed each other's buttons just a little too hard. Angus got up, helped Lily to a chair and handed her a wet rag to clean herself.

"I am so sorry," he said. "It was the booze and the drugs. I was in a bad mood. It was a lot of things all rolled up into something that isn't really me."

As crazy as his words would have sounded to anyone but her, Lily believed every word that passed through his lips. She understood all too well that when Angus had a bad day, he had a really bad day. These last ten years he seemed to always take it out on her. Even after all that, she believed he loved her more than any of his earthly treasures.

"What the hell just happened?" asked Lily.

Angus looked around. He opened a new bottle of Nolet's, poured Lily a glassful and handed it to her.

"Thanks, I need it," she said, touching her nose gingerly.

"Broken?" asked Angus.

She examined it again with her fingers. "No, I don't think so. It just hurts a little. You've hit me harder."

"I'm so sorry," said Angus.

"My plastic surgeon is on speed dial in case it is, so don't worry," replied Lily.

Angus popped a pill and offered one to Lily. She swallowed it in a gulp then refilled his whiskey glass.

"We did it again," said Angus. "One of these days one of us is going to kill the other."

Lily cast a sad, sideways glance toward the Persian rug she had damaged.

"I'd better call the cleaning lady from the Rez and get her over here. She keeps quiet for cash."

"Right," said Angus. "Always best to keep this as private as possible."

A long moment of contemplative silence passed between them as they stared into each other's eyes. Lily into the darkness of Angus's face and Angus into the heterochromia eyes that had attracted him to her. Lily's eyes, one green from her Irish lineage and one brown from her Native genes, created a mystery about her that drew Angus in.

"Now tell me what's really wrong, honey?" asked Lily. "What triggered your temper this time?"

Angus slugged down his whiskey, poured another, took another pill and slouched back into his Dragon's chair.

"The price of copper is headed down the shitter," he said, head hung low.

"We can ride it out. This has happened before," replied Lily. "What's so different this time?"

"China and Chile are dumping cheap subsidized copper on the market, and our government isn't doing a damn thing to stop it. They are allowing copper to be sold on the open market, here in the US, for less than it costs us to produce it," said Angus.

"Have you called Senator Russell?" asked Lily.

"I talked with his staff. They're in the process of drafting a bill to put on the Senator's desk by the end of the week. They promised he would introduce it next week. But, to be honest with you, I don't believe it will go anywhere. The copper lobbyists are making more money from the Chinks and the Chili Beans than we can ever pay them."

Lily walked over to her husband and put her arms around him.

"We've been through worse. We'll survive. We always do."

"It feels different this time," said Angus. "I feel doomed. I dream almost every night that the Sword of Damocles, held by a single hair, is hanging over my head. It's like an ever-present peril is just waiting, waiting, waiting, torturing me at every turn."

5

BAD NEWS

PRESENT DAY

K ate and Black Bear pulled down the long privacy road through the coded gate after being recognized on the security camera system. The exterior of the house was well lit. Even in the pre-dawn darkness the opulence of McGinty Manor was obvious.

"Damn, that's some kind of crib the McGintys built for themselves," said Black Bear.

"You've never seen it before?" asked Kate.

"No, I haven't. It makes the mansions in Rapid City look like shacks on the wrong side of the tracks."

"The McGintys own the tracks around here," said Kate.

"I see that."

"Rumor is they spent five million on the original house, added on and then spent almost that much on furnishing it. Wait until you see the inside," said Kate. "They've spent a lifetime collecting rare items from all over the world."

"Where did all the money come from?" asked Black Bear. "I can't believe running a copper mine pays out that kind of money."

"Lily's family, or should I say her crazy aunt, a crazy aunt whom everyone says she takes after, died twenty-five years ago when Lily was a teenager. She left Lily the land and mineral rights to twenty thousand acres of land that, once upon a time, nobody wanted. Her aunt was a lady of the evening, a good old-fashioned whorehouse madam, or so the story goes. She won the land in a poker game way back when people did crazy things like that. More than one rumor says she killed for it."

"Did she?" asked Black Bear.

"Nothing was ever proven."

"Go on with your story. It's intriguing."

"When copper was discovered on the land, Lily had already married Angus McGinty. Together at first, then mostly under his direction, they turned the land and the minerals buried beneath it into what people around here call real money."

"I guess that's what you'd call having a lucky star shining over your head," said Black Bear.

"Depends," said Kate. "Too much, too soon, too fast mixed in with a little bit of mental instability. Well, let's just say not everything is smooth sailing when it comes to Lily and Angus McGinty."

Black Bear wondered what he was about to step into as he and Kate exited the vehicle and approached the porch. Lily, adult beverage gripped in her hand opened the door. She began shooting questions at the deputies in rapid fire succession.

"Was Angus hurt? What happened? How bad is it? Is the mine in trouble? Was there an explosion? Do we have to shut down production? What did Sheriff Hanks tell you? Tell me everything."

"Why don't we step inside and sit down. We'll discuss what we know," said Kate.

Black Bear slipped behind Lily and held the front door open with an extended arm which she casually brushed against.

"Can I get either of you a cocktail?" she asked. "Something else to drink? A cold beer perhaps?"

Black Bear glanced at the clock. It was nearing 4 a.m.

"We're on duty," replied Kate.

Lily glanced in Black Bear's direction and inquired furtively, "Maybe some other time?"

Kate could have sworn she saw Black Bear blush as he ignored Lily's rather indiscreet advance.

"About Angus, your husband," responded Black Bear.

"Yes, yes, Angus. What happened to him? Was he drunk? Was he screwing one of those trollops that work in his office?"

"We believe he may have been involved in an accident," said Kate.

"Well was he or wasn't he? My lord, that's hardly a difficult question to answer. Either he was in an accident or he wasn't," barked Lily. "Which is it?"

"It's not quite that simple," replied Black Bear. "Mrs. McGinty, why don't you have a seat?"

Lily sat down on a lush settee and patted the seat next to her while eyeing Black Bear lasciviously. Black Bear remained standing, keeping his distance.

"We haven't been able to identify the body yet," said Kate.

"I knew it. It was an explosion, wasn't it? He was never careful around anything that went boom. Jesus, he was reckless when it came to explosives. I warned him a million times..."

"No," said Kate. "There was no explosion."

"Is he dead?

"Someone is dead," said Kate. "We haven't positively identified the body yet."

"Why do you believe it could be Angus?"

"His truck was parked near where the body was found."

Lily took a deep drink of the alcohol. Her gaze floated off into some far distant place. For a long moment both Black Bear and Kate knew she was not in a present state of mind. Gradually Lily's mind seemed to clear and she had questions.

"I take it there was significant damage to the body and that's why you couldn't identify the remains as Angus?"

"Yes, ma'am," replied Black Bear. "There was a tragic accident that severely damaged the body of the deceased."

"But not an explosion?" pressed Lily.

"No," said Kate. "There was no explosion."

"Did somebody fall into a vat of sulfuric acid?" she asked.

Neither Kate nor Black Bear responded.

"I've been around long enough to know that it's usually someone getting blown to bits by explosives or falling into a vat of chemicals that makes identification difficult. We've had a few of each over the years. Terrible way to die," said Lily. "You're certain it wasn't an explosion or sulfuric acid?"

Black Bear glanced over Lily's shoulder where a display case held original toy replicas of every type of modern and ancient mining equipment.

"Yes, Mrs. McGinty," said Kate. "I know you're familiar with the copper mining business at all its levels. I can assure you that this was not a typical accident."

"Nor was it sulfuric acid or some other type of caustic chemical," added Black Bear.

"Then what the hell was it? What's the big mystery? I'm on the damn board of directors. I believe you are obliged to let me know what just happened at my company. Technically, the entire mine was once meant to be my personal property. I have my rights, especially since this involves my husband."

Kate knew that Lily had inherited the land where the Klondyke 1 mine was located. She also knew that many years earlier Danforth-Roerg had purchased a fifty-one percent interest in the land and its mineral wealth for a fantastic sum. The money had made the McGintys fabulously wealthy.

"Someone, the person we can't identify, was run over by a Volvo DD140B road roller," said Kate.

Lily let out an involuntary chuckle. She quickly placed her hands over her mouth.

"I'm sorry. I didn't mean anything by that. It's just that a road roller of that size and magnitude would squash a body thin as computer paper. My lord, what a horrible image that conjures up. Something right out of the Road Runner and Coyote cartoons."

Lily paused and gathered herself before continuing in the soberest of fashion.

"Do you think the dead person suffered?"

"It's impossible to know just yet if the person was alive or dead when they got run over," said Kate. "Sheriff Hanks and Doc Yackley are out there right now. Byrne Murphy..."

"Murphy, that idiot couldn't find his ass with both hands," interjected Lily.

"...and they are following company protocol."

"We all know what that means. They're bringing in all kinds of dumbass political appointees and government lackeys who don't know shit from shinola about running a mine. Then they are going to shut us down cold for God only knows how long. That's what they're doing, right?" said Lily.

Both Kate and Black Bear made a mental note that Byrne Murphy and state inspectors put a bee in Lily's bonnet.

"Everyone is simply following procedure," replied Black Bear. "When we figure out exactly what happened, the mine can re-open. It sounds like you know the drill better than we do."

"Fuck yes, I know the drill. Idiotic federal and state regulators have shut us down ten times in the last five years. They've cost us millions of dollars. I bet our competitors overseas don't have to deal with this kind of bureaucratic bullshit. Our own damn government is driving us out of business. Don't they realize over five hundred jobs at the Klondyke mine are at stake? Don't they know how it will have a ripple effect on another five thousand people in the area? They just don't have a clue, the assholes."

"It could be your husband that is lying out there on the cold ground," reminded Kate.

Lily lit a cigarette and poured herself another drink, a stiff one. She paced back and forth across the large living room, alternately puffing on her cigarette and tipping back a drink from her glass of hard liquor.

"I'm going to the mine even if I have to drive out there myself."

Kate and Black Bear exchanged a look that said that wasn't going to happen.

"Well then, I can see by the looks on both of your faces that Zeb ordered you to keep me here. That isn't going to happen. So, am I to drive out there with you or can I drive myself?"

Lily's words were more of a demand than an actual question.

"It might be best if we drove you since you've had something to drink," said Black Bear.

Kate knew Lily was headed to the Klondyke mine come hell, high water or a drunk driving ticket.

Lily plopped the newly lit cigarette into the freshly poured drink. It sizzled ever so briefly as she placed the ash laden drink next to a spotlessly clean art deco ashtray.

"Let's go have a look. If it's Angus, I'll know it right away," she said.

"Ma'am," said Black Bear. "The body is in pretty rough shape. I'm not sure you will want to look at it right now if you don't have to. Perhaps it would be best to wait until we have a positive identification."

"I've been married to the son of a bitch for twenty-five years. If I can't tell it's him, who can?"

"Yes, ma'am."

"You're mighty polite, young Deputy Sheriff Black Bear. Your mama must've brought you up right."

"My mother would appreciate hearing that," replied Black Bear.

"I've been noticing you don't look much like you're Apache. Where you from?"

"Pine Ridge, South Dakota, ma'am."

"Lakota?"

"Yes, ma'am."

"Is it true what they say about the Lakota?" asked Lily, suggestively sweeping her long, dark-brown hair away from her face.

"How's that, ma'am?"

"That they believe the dead go to the Milky Way when they die?"

"How do you know about that?" asked Black Bear.

"I may drink a lot but I also read a lot," said Lily. "I am not an uneducated woman."

"Actually, my people have always called the Milky Way by a different name. We call it the Sky Road. To find your path into the next world you must have the proper tattoos on your physical body. When you get to the Sky Road, it is necessary and essential to show the tattoos to the old woman, Hihankara."

"Hihankara? That's the Lakota version of Saint Peter?"

"I suppose that's one way of looking at it. Hihankara means the Owl-Maker. Like I said, she will admit only those who have the proper tattoos."

"What happens to those who don't have the tattoos?" asked Lily.

"They will be pushed back to Earth where they will eternally wander as ghosts."

"Sort of like the Catholics believing you don't get to heaven if you haven't been baptized in Christ. You believe in that Lakota bullshit?"

"I do," replied Black Bear.

"Care to show me your tattoos sometime?"

Black Bear ignored her drunken query.

"I think if that dead body is my husband, Angus, they probably flung the gates of hell wide open when they heard he was on his way."

"We all have our own eternal destiny," said Black Bear. "You have yours. Kate has hers. I have mine. The person who is dead out at the Klondyke has theirs. Such is the way of life and the journey of death."

"You have those tattoos, don't you?" asked Lily.

She was clearly drunk. Black Bear answered her repeated question as politely as possible this time.

"Yes, ma'am, I do."

"Mind showing them to me?"

Black Bear responded only to get her off the subject. She was taking passage from this existence to the next far too lightly, at least in his mind.

"I can't, ma'am. Only the Owl-Maker can see them."

"Superstition, that's what it sounds like to me. Nothing more than old Indian superstition. Right out of a bygone era. Seems to me you're living in the past with that kind of thinking."

"Ma'am, you are entitled to your beliefs," said Black Bear.

"I suppose I am, aren't I?" slurred Lily. "I suppose I am. Right now I'm entitled to get my ass out to the Klondyke 1 mine."

"Shall we go?" asked Kate.

Lily led them out the front door and hopped into the back of the sheriff's vehicle, making certain not to hit her head. She knew the drill from having been arrested a few times.

"Please put on your seat belt," said Black Bear. "For your own safety."

"Yes, sir," replied Lily, struggling to keep her eyelids open.

In the back of the deputy sheriff's vehicle, Lily lit another cigarette. Neither Kate nor Black Bear bothered to tell her it was a non-smoking vehicle, but she was polite enough to crack her window.

Overhead the Milky Way, or the Sky Road as Black Bear knew it, lit up the night sky, exposing billions of temporary, ongoing or final destinies. A final journey that Fightin' Angus McGinty might just be taking at this very moment.

6

KLONDYKE 1 MINE

K ate, Black Bear and Lily pulled into the mining yard. Night became day as commercial grade lights lit up the equipment overflow parking lot.

"Is that where it happened?" asked Lily. She didn't wait for an answer. "Pull the hell over there and let's see what's going on."

"Sheriff Hanks said it was quite brutal," said Kate. "Maybe you should think twice about looking at the dead body. If it is your husband, it could be terribly traumatic."

"Now just how in the hell am I going to know if it's him or not unless I have a look? I've seen dead bodies before. It's just not that big of a deal."

Kate had killed one man and been exposed to several dead bodies. She knew the bravado Lily was spouting was merely a way of covering up her fear of the possible reality that lay ahead.

Sheriff Hanks approached the vehicle. As Lily tried to fly right by him, Zeb grabbed her firmly but gently by the arm. In an effort to escape his grasp, she squirmed and twisted her arm. Zeb tightened his grip and attempted to distract her from the horrible scene with a direct question.

"Is this Angus's wedding ring?"

He held it directly in front of her eyes. Lily instantly recognized it despite the damage to it.

"Yes. Hell yes! That's his ring alright. Did you take it off the hand of the dead man?" asked Lily.

"Yes, but it's by no means proof positive that the dead man is Angus," said Zeb.

"You think he lent someone his wedding ring and that person ended up underneath a road roller next to my husband's truck? For God's sake, Zeb, that's crazy talk and you know it. Don't try and protect me from the truth."

Lily once again attempted to extract herself from Zeb's grip. Zeb didn't loosen his hold. Zeb thought back to finding his wife, Doreen, dead with a sword through her heart. He knew all too well that Lily seeing her husband of twenty some years flattened thin as paper, every bone in his body crushed, might be more than she could handle. Zeb wanted to save her from that. When she drunkenly ripped her arm from his grip, Zeb realized she was a woman who was experienced in escaping a firm grasp.

"Zeb, I'm going to have a look. I have to know if that dead body is Angus."

Zeb reached toward her. This time she grabbed him by the wrist and pushed his hand away.

"Don't," she said. "Don't try and stop me."

"It's really bad, Lily," said Zeb. "It's for your own good that you don't see him. Please trust me on this one."

"Dead is dead," replied Lily. "How bad can it be?"

Zeb, Jake, Kate and Black Bear surrounded her as she stormed toward the presumed remains of her husband.

Lily stared hard at the dead man. With the realization that there was no doubt it was Angus, she doubled over at the waist. The contents of her stomach erupted all over the corpse. Zeb grabbed her as she passed out, lost her balance and fell forward. Black Bear rushed to help pull the widow away from the scene. Together they laid her down on a blanket.

"I guess her reaction passes for a positive ID on the body," said Jake.

"And creates a highly compromised crime scene," added Zeb.

"Can you even imagine what's going through her mind?" asked Kate.

"Maybe," replied Jake. "I've been in some bad places, but not exactly like this one."

"I can't imagine the thought of him lying there like that will ever leave her mind," said Kate.

"It won't," replied Jake. "The sight of what she's just seen has burrowed itself deep down into her consciousness. It's there to stay."

"It's the seed of PTSD," said Black Bear.

"Get another ambulance out here to take her to the hospital," said Doc Yackley.

"I'm on it," said Black Bear. "I'll call the ambulance."

"I'll call ahead and have them admit her and order a sedative," said Doc.

"In the meantime, we've got to get moving on this investigation as quickly as possible," said Zeb. "We don't want people out of work because of a mine shutdown, and we sure as hell don't want the economy of Graham County to take a huge hit."

Zeb, Kate, Jake, Black Bear and Byrne Murphy, the safety director, huddled under the lights in the early morning coolness.

"Can you think of anyone here at the mines who would want Angus dead?" asked Zeb.

Byrne didn't have to think long. "Hell yes. He was not well liked by many. You were either on his good side or you weren't. If you weren't, he made life miserable for you. And chances were good that you weren't going to be on his good side. Trust me, he made life a living hell for many people."

"What did he think of you?" asked Zeb.

"We got along okay," replied Byrne. "We never had any real problems between us. I learned early on to keep my distance, my head down and to always do exactly as he ordered."

"Of the men and women on this list of people who could drive or wanted to drive a road roller, do any of the names stick out as having a significant hatred of Angus?"

Byrne scanned the printout. "Half of them, maybe more. Yes, definitely more than half."

"That seems like an awfully high number," said Zeb.

"Well, Angus thought that the road roller drivers weren't really miners. He thought of them as road builders. He was always taking short cuts, not building new roads and not reinforcing ones that needed updating. He cut the number of road building crew members in half in the last year. He found any excuse he could to fire one of them, and then he'd leave the position vacant. We are damn lucky we haven't had any major road accidents. Damn lucky."

"Any of them ever threaten his life?" asked Zeb.

"This is the mining business, Sheriff Hanks. A day doesn't go by when someone isn't threatening someone else's life. These are hardscrabble men and women. If you say the wrong thing or push them the wrong way, you're going to hear about it and probably end up in a tussle. Hell, I break up two, three fights a week. But these guys and gals will fight in the afternoon and drink together that night like nothing even happened. It's the nature of the beast, Sheriff."

"Do you have any one person that you think is more likely than the others to have done this?" asked Zeb.

"I know of a couple of guys on this list who hated Angus's guts and made no secret about it."

"Might they go so far as to run Angus over with a road roller?"

"Who knows what a man might do when he is pissed off enough?" said Byrne.

"Who are the two you are thinking of? It'll give us a starting point," said Zeb.

"Toohey Blendah, he's Apache. He always thought he owned at least half and maybe more of the mineral rights to this land."

"How's that?" asked Zeb.

"This goes back some time. Damn near three decades. Toohey and Lily are first cousins. Lily and Toohey's aunt and uncle owned the land. They had no children. About two years before Lily inherited the land from her aunt, Bina Blendah Pherson, Bina was on trial for killing her husband, Nev. She was acquitted. If Nev had been alive when Lily's aunt died, Toohey would ultimately have been co-owner of the land by inheritance. But, as it turned out, Bina loved Lily and didn't care for Toohey. All Toohey got was a decent, well-paying job, which he hated. Toohey curses Lily and Angus every day he gets his hands dirty. He could handle a road roller drunk and blindfolded. It's about all he does well," explained Byrne.

"He has the necessary skill," said Black Bear.

"He has motive," said Kate.

"A longstanding one," added Jake.

"Was he working tonight when Angus was killed?" asked Zeb.

"No, but he lives within walking distance of the mine. He could have sneaked in and out really easily," said Byrne.

"He had the potential and proximity to do it," added Kate.

"Jake, check on Toohey's whereabouts around the time of the murder, say between six p.m. and three a.m." said Zeb.

"Got it," replied Jake.

"You said two people, Byrne. Who was the other one that is high on your list?" asked Zeb.

"Cowboy Bob Shank. He's an equipment operator. He was on duty when the murder happened. He was the one who was sent up to get the road runner, and he was the one who found the body."

"Any particular dispute between Cowboy Shank and Angus?"

"Cowboy was pissed off because he was routinely passed over for promotions. Angus knew Cowboy was great at his job. But, for some reason that no one ever quite understood, Angus had it in for him," said Byrne.

"Anybody speculate on why Angus might not have liked Cowboy?" asked Zeb.

"The Klondyke spits out about as much gossip as it does copper. Ask ten men and you'll get ten good reasons," said Byrne. "All of them based on equal parts truth, rumor and innuendo."

"Byrne, I need to talk to my deputies alone. I know you've got some things that need to get done immediately. If I need to talk to you, how can I contact you?"

Byrne handed Zeb a business card. Zeb pointed at it.

"Is this number your cell phone?"

"Yes."

"I'll be talking to you sooner rather than later," said Zeb. "So please stick around in case I need to talk to you face to face."

"I'm not going anywhere, not with this going on. I'm chest deep in paperwork already," said Byrne, walking away.

"Black Bear, you take Cowboy Shank. Check into his story and possible alibi," said Zeb.

"Roger that," replied Black Bear.

"Kate, I want you to check out Lily McGinty. She heavily funded my last campaign, so I have a conflict of interest. But I do know from personal experience that she and her late husband had a volatile, if not violent relationship. When you start digging, I think you're going to find a lot of reasons pointing to her as the primary suspect. She had a lot to gain by her husband's death."

"There is another angle we need to pursue," said Black Bear.

"Yes?" said Zeb.

"Do any of you listen to Rez Talk Radio?" asked Black Bear.

None of them did with any sort of regularity.

"Well every night at supper time they have environmental hour. I know Echo and her family listen in. Lately it's a three-hour discourse that invariably turns into a tirade about the destruction of the land, excuse me, Mother Earth, caused by the corrupt business of copper mining. From my understanding of what I hear, and I certainly do not have all the facts, radical environmentalists have begun to organize against Danforth-Roerg, specifically the Klondyke 1 mine," added Black Bear.

"How do you know that?" asked Zeb.

"Growing up with a mom who was highly active in AIM and other protests movements, I learned all the key buzzwords. The inner sanctum of all protest groups knows how to make the most of mass media without paying for it. All you have to do is listen, and you will know exactly what they are up to, that is, if you can interpret their hidden messages."

"One of these nights let's listen to the program on the radio together and maybe you can teach me a thing or two," said Zeb.

"My pleasure," replied Black Bear. "Although you might enjoy it more with Echo. She's certainly able to read between the lines of what is being said."

"I'll do that," replied Zeb.

"Do these eco-freaks have any money backing them?" asked Jake.

"The rumor mill is that the Democrat, Frank Tuttle, who is running against Senator Russell, is helping them. He is allegedly getting them the money they need from back channels. They need organizational people to help them push their agenda."

"So we've got a political hot potato in the oven too," said Zeb.

"That's right," replied Black Bear. "God only knows what path that will lead us down."

"Has anyone considered old fightin' Angus McGinty might have done himself in?" asked Kate.

Everyone suddenly shut up. They all had the same thought. Had Kate lost her mind?

"As in suicide?" asked Zeb.

"Yes, as in suicide."

"Care to extrapolate on that one?" asked Zeb.

"My uncle ran a Volvo heavy equipment dealership. I worked for him in college. I can drive anything made by them and drive it better than most anyone."

"So," said Zeb. "What do you know that could possibly make this a suicide?"

"The automatic kill switch on the forward gears allows the machine to run ten feet before it automatically stops. It's a built-in mechanism on some of the newer machines, but not all of them. It's there for drivers who work by themselves and have to hop off their machines for a short period and move something. They can slow the road roller down to a very slow crawl, anywhere from one foot to fifteen feet per minute. They can do that without putting it in idle or turning it off and then having to worry about starting it up again. The machines get too hot and restarting them can be a real headache, causing lots of lost work time. I checked and this machine has the automatic kill switch. Therefore, it is possible that..."

"My God," said Zeb. "You don't think?"

"Do you believe Angus McGinty jumped off the roller, laid underneath a slowly moving machine and very painfully allowed himself to get run over?" said Jake.

"I'm saying we can't automatically rule it out," said Kate.

"That is mighty damn gruesome," said Black Bear. "The way he was run over he would have had to lay down and feel the roller slowly crush him to death. That is sick, sick, sick. No human being in their right mind would do such a thing."

"I don't know if you could say Angus was ever in his right mind," said Jake.

"Kate, double check your theory and triple check to make certain this particular machine has that specific function on it," said Zeb.

"I already have checked and double-checked the road roller," replied Kate. "But I can check it again."

"Check it one more time," said Zeb.

Byrne walked toward them from a nearby building.

"I'm going to have to call the feds within the hour," said Byrne. "Protocol demands that I do."

Sheriff Hanks noticed the sheepishness in Byrne's voice. Obviously calling the feds in was what he had to do. On the other hand, Zeb could see that Byrne felt doing so was disloyal to the workers not to mention the potential economic harm he might be causing the locals and the company. Zeb felt Byrne was asking for permission as much as making a statement of the facts.

"Call them any time is my official response," said Zeb. "Off the record, please wait until the very last minute."

His answer seemed to quell Byrne's anxiety about potentially bending the rules.

"Is that good news or bad news?" asked Byrne.

"It's complicated," replied Zeb. "You'd better plan on being shut down for at least three days. That's the best I've got to offer right now."

"The shit is going to hit the fan," said Byrne, shaking his head from side to side. "I am personally going to be the object of a lot of blowback."

"Then you'd better learn to duck real fast," said Zeb, walking toward Doc and Kate.

Byrne nodded. He understood things were out of his control. Having a set of rules that must be followed would blunt the anger that would certainly come his way.

"Kate, can you run a piece of equipment that can dig down six inches and remove the remains without disturbing them too much?" asked Zeb.

Kate looked around the equipment yard. She pointed to a vertical digger.

"I think so, if I can use that digger over there."

"You have my permission," said Byrne. "That is, if you know how to operate it properly."

"Easy peasy," replied Kate.

"More importantly, Doc, can you do any kind of decent autopsy with the remains flattened out like they are?"

"Hell yes...well, maybe...I'll do the best I can. Kate, can you dig down one foot below what's left of the body?"

Kate's eyes ran from the vertical digger to the body.

"Shouldn't be a problem. Besides the vertical digger, I need a backhoe, a forklift, a four by eight piece of one-inch plywood and a flatbed truck, if you want it done right," said Kate.

"You got them," said Byrne. "Deputy Steele, I'll operate the backhoe. I don't want any part of moving the body. You'll have to drive the forklift."

"Roger that," replied Kate.

"If we can load the remains onto a flatbed and secure it by surrounding it with sandbags, we should be able to get it to the autopsy room at the morgue in fairly decent shape. Old Angus should be no worse for being moved," said Doc.

"The dark humor just rolls right off your tongue, doesn't it, Doc," said Zeb.

The aging Doc Yackley, eyeballing what lay in front of him, either didn't hear or pretended not to.

"Aren't the feds gonna be all over your shit if you do that, Zeb?" asked Doc.

"As things sit right now, this is my case. Someone higher up the food chain may overrule me later. But, as the chief law enforcement officer in Graham County, this falls under my jurisdiction. I don't have any hard and firm evidence that indicates I should turn the investigation over to the feds at this point. It is strictly my call. If they question me, the truth is I'm being as efficient as possible. I'd like you to get right on the autopsy and get as much of it over with before the feds start hootin' and hollerin'."

"What do you know that you aren't telling me?" asked Doc.

"All depends on what you find. Whatever you discover, I'd sure like to have the information before anyone else does. Too many cooks spoil the pot."

Before the sun crept over the mountain tops, what remained of Angus McGinty was on its way to the basement of the hospital where the Graham County morgue did its official business. As the truck rolled down the road, Byrne Murphy was talking to the federal government officials. They had obviously read his fax sooner than he had anticipated. Ninety minutes later when Thorman Wright from the United States Bureau of Mines arrived on the scene, the first thing he wanted to do was get at the body.

"First," said Byrne with a cockeyed smile. "There is some paper-work that is required by the company. We find it imperative to keep in compliance with federal and state regulations."

Thorman's face turned eight shades of angry red. Beaten at his own game, he quickly figured somebody was up to something. They wanted him outside the inner circle of knowledge. He immediately suspected Sheriff Hanks. His suspicions would only broaden as the day went on.

7

ZEB'S OFFICE

ONE HOUR LATER

W hen Helen Nazelrod arrived at the sheriff's office at her usual time, she was shocked to see everyone already hard at work. It took her about one half a second to figure out something was dramatically out of the ordinary. Intuition and thirty years of experience told her that it was likely something very bad. A second clue to exactly how bad things were occurred when her eyes fell on Zeb drinking a cup of black coffee. As far as she knew, Zeb had not had as much as a sip of coffee in his hands for over two years. Helen kept close track of such matters that concerned her nephew's health.

"I take it there was big trouble last night," said Helen.

"At the mines," replied Zeb.

"Which mine?"

"Klondyke 1."

"Whatever happened was so terrible that you are going to ruin your health and wreck your stomach by drinking black coffee?" she asked. "Besides, you react just the opposite to most people when it comes to caffeine. It makes your thinking cloudy and unclear."

Zeb put down his coffee. This was going to be a tough case to plead as he knew Helen was right.

"I need it today. One cup. Just one cup," he replied. "I've been up since three and working ever since. Before that I was having a bad dream that just wouldn't let me go."

"If you are so tired that you're going to make yourself ill, perhaps you should go home and get some rest. There is nothing that can't wait until you get a few hours of shut eye. You've got the best staff a sheriff could ask for. Let them run the show for a few hours."

Zeb smiled at her concern. She was the one constant throughout his entire life. During childhood Zeb had always found refuge with his Aunt Helen. Solace came easily at her house when his dad was on a bender. Zeb's mother was smart enough to have young Zeb stay with Aunt Helen until it was safe to come home.

Helen thought of Zeb as a son. She gave him every bit of love and care that she gave her own children. She kept a close eye on his health and just about every other aspect of his life. All the stress of having a drunkard for a father, she believed, had given Zeb somewhat of a delicate constitution. There were many ways in which she watched over Zeb, but few were ever spoken of directly, coffee being the exception rather than the rule.

Zeb lifted the half empty cup of take-out coffee from the Town Talk, dumped it in the sink and tossed the Styrofoam cup into the trash. Helen smiled and made him a cup of chamomile tea. One problem solved, she got down to office business.

"Who died?" asked Helen.

"Angus McGinty," replied Jake.

"I take it he's the connection to the Klondyke mine?" asked Helen. "Did somebody kill him? It wouldn't surprise me in the least."

"Do you know Angus?" asked Kate.

"I've seen how he treats people," replied Helen. "He's a mean man, excuse me, he was a mean man. I don't mean to speak poorly of the dead, but he had a cold, hard streak in him that was obvious to everyone whoever met him. He even sent his own daughter away because it was more convenient than having her around."

"Where'd you run into him, Helen?" asked Kate.

"I saw him lose his temper at his wife a couple of times when we were out to eat. He even lashed out at the friends they were eating with and their children. I couldn't stand to see it. Then he shouted at the waitress. I saw it other times too. Once right here in this office when he came in to pay a parking ticket. He jumped all over me. I ignored him. Just about anybody could be the object of his wrath when he was in an angry state of mind. He had a nasty temper."

Helen looked as though she had more to say on the subject when the phone rang. She resumed her daily routine and answered the phone, keeping an open ear to the chatter about the killing at the Klondyke.

Zeb turned back to his team.

"Let's review potential suspects," said Zeb. "Starting with Toohey Blendah. Byrne seems to think there was a longstanding dispute between the McGintys, who were making many millions of dollars from owning the land the mines are on, and Toohey. He believes half the money was ... is legally his."

"For years I've heard Toohey rant and rave about how badly he got screwed in the mining deal, especially when he was drinking," said Jake. "Back in my drinking days, I tended to agree with him. But, then again, I was in the middle of a seven-year long bender myself."

Black Bear shot Kate a puzzled look. It was news to him that Jake had once upon a time been a drunk. She gave him a look that told him he would get the details later.

"Maybe I ought to go out and talk with Toohey. Find out just how big of a chip he has on his shoulder and is it big enough to make him commit murder," said Zeb. "Jake, sift through the notes from Angus's murder at Klondyke i. Look for any inconsistencies in the reports."

"Zeb, I think Helen is right about you and coffee. Remember, I was sheriff and taught you how to run an investigation. I've done a few in my day. I know what to do."

"Sorry. I guess I am a little wound up. Could be the coffee screwing me up. Could be that I keep waiting for the feds to walk through the door, throw me off this case and threaten me with interfering with a crime scene, conspiracy or some federal crap. Could be that I'm just plain tired and not thinking all that clearly."

"My guess is that all of those things are true," said Jake.

"Don't worry," said Black Bear. "The feds won't want this case. It's too messy. They won't want to waste the manpower. There's no glory in this case for them. The papers are going to talk about people being laid off, money being lost and the copper industry being dealt a blow. They won't want that kind of publicity."

"You sound pretty sure of yourself," said Zeb.

"When I was a kid up on Pine Ridge, the feds used to cash in on just about anything that was easy and gave them good public relations. They wanted nothing to do with difficult cases that brought trouble. They prefer easy headlines to hard work."

"That's a bit cynical," replied Zeb. "Not that I disagree with you."

"It's my mother in me. She understood all too well how the feds worked. My mother was arrested forty some times, and my old man worked with government law enforcement. Let's just say it tends to bring out a bit of my sarcastic nature. On the flip side, she taught me how important it was to know how to deal with White people in power."

"None of us care much for federal interference," said Jake. "You can be as derisive as you want about the feds, but never forget what your mother taught you. We have to deal with them so don't create enemies...unless absolutely necessary."

Silence flooded the room, leaving Black Bear wondering exactly what Jake meant by "unless absolutely necessary."

"Kate, didn't you handle the last serious accident with injuries out at the mines?" asked Zeb.

"Yes, but it was different. No death was involved. The U.S. Department of Labor Mine Safety and Health Administration led the charge on that one."

"How were they to deal with?" asked Zeb.

"They were bureaucrats," replied Kate. "Generally speaking, they were slow, inefficient and created mountains of paperwork. It took them months to work things through their antiquated system just to come to an obvious conclusion. They seemed actively disinterested in doing much, other than following what seemed to be arcane rules and regulations. If the answer fell into their laps, I'm not certain they'd recognize it."

"I think you should run point on them. Try and keep them satisfied without having them interfere with our investigation," said Zeb. "Lead them down some bureaucratic paperwork path that keeps them occupied, if you can."

"I can do that. I have a pretty good idea about how they operate, but I can't predict how they'll react."

"I trust you can take care of them," said Zeb.

"That leaves me with Bob 'Cowboy' Shank," said Black Bear.

"He hates Indians, even calls them Injuns," said Jake. "You'll need a thick skin to deal with that guy."

"I've got buffalo hide for skin when it comes to those sorts of folks," said Black Bear.

"Good. You'll need it."

"How come the Cowboy hates the People?" asked Black Bear.

"He hates a lot of stuff. Indians just happen to be on his list."

"Lots of rednecks hate Indians. I'll kill him with kindness," said Black Bear. "By the time I'm done with him, he'll claim Native heritage. The redder the neck on the White man the easier it is to make them want to be an Indian."

"Good luck on that," said Zeb. "Kate, since Lily was my primary campaign donor, I would like you to check her out thoroughly."

Jake chuckled.

"What's that supposed to mean?" asked Zeb.

"You're sending Kate into the lionesses' den. Lily will probably try and seduce her just like she tries to seduce everyone who crosses her path."

"I've got no interest in that," said Kate. "I don't roll that way."

"There's more than one kind of seduction," added Jake.

"Kate, keep it in mind. Lily knew I had no interest in her. Still she hit on me a thousand times when she was funding my re-election campaign. Don't fall for any of her nonsense. She's sneaky, smart, clever and devious. Any questions?"

"Can I have a minute of your time after the meeting is done?" asked Black Bear.

"The meeting is over," said Zeb. "I would like preliminary investigative reports tomorrow. I'm headed over to talk to Doc right now and see if he has anything."

Black Bear approached Zeb as the others departed, looking sheepish.

"What's the problem, Deputy Black Bear?"

"Uh, uh," stammered the new deputy.

"Is there a problem?" asked Zeb. "Spit it out if there is. I've got work to do."

"Sort of. No. I mean yes there is a problem."

"Let's hear it," sighed Zeb.

The sheriff's mind took him to a bad place. A conflict with one of his deputies and anyone involved in the murder case would only complicate things.

"I've slept with Lily McGinty."

"When?" asked Zeb.

"Yesterday, the afternoon of the murder," confessed Black Bear.

Zeb shook his head. He gave Deputy Black Bear a cold, hard scrutinizing stare.

"Please tell me she seduced you and it wasn't the other way around."

"She seduced me."

"Never give anyone else a different answer to that question should it come up," said Zeb.

"Right," replied Black Bear.

Where did this happen?"

"In her Range Rover."

"Where?"

"In a pull-off, halfway up Mount Graham."

"Anyone see you two together?"

"No, not that I know of."

"You sure of that?"

"As sure as I can be. I was trying to be somewhat cautious."

"Damn it," said Zeb. "I don't need this kind of crap from you or anyone else."

"I'd apologize, but it's water over the dam."

"Angus was last seen about the time he left work around five-thirty. What time was this little rendezvous?"

"Between four-thirty and five. I got back to my truck at ten after five."

"Has this been a regular thing between the two of you?"

"Half dozen times, give or take."

"This does present a conflict," said Zeb. "I can't have you as much as looking at her during the course of the investigation without another deputy being present. Don't talk to her on the phone, text her or much less sleep with her. Let's keep this between you and me for now. I suspect Lily knows how to keep her mouth shut."

"Unless she wants to use me as an alibi," said Black Bear.

"Damn it all, Black Bear. I don't know how things work up north, but you've got to use some discretion around here."

"From this point on I promise I will be overly cautious," replied Black Bear.

Black Bear's gaze returned to Zeb's disappointed eyes. His mother had given him that look a thousand times before. Zeb had the look down, but he was no match for Black Bear's mother.

"I'll talk to Doc and get an approximate time of death. I know that the time you were with her is going to fall within that general time frame. There may be no getting around what you two have been up to."

"I know," said Black Bear. "I'm willing to stand up and take my punishment like a man."

"Your punishment is as likely to be a venereal disease as anything," said Zeb.

Black Bear glanced downward toward his private parts with a frown on his face.

"I guess I'd better see the Doc."

"I'd do it sooner rather than later," advised Zeb.

As Black Bear turned to leave, his junk began to itch. He felt very uneasy as he passed Helen's desk.

"Are you all right, Deputy Black Bear?" asked Helen.

"Let's just say I've been better," replied Black Bear.

Helen's phone rang and Black Bear disappeared out the door.

8

THORMAN WRIGHT

The hairs on the back of Zeb's neck stood erect as Helen gave him some news he didn't want to hear.

"Mr. Thorman Wright is on his way over. He said you knew who he was. He sounded upset," said Helen. "Really upset."

"When he gets here, I'll see him right away," replied Zeb. "Don't worry about being too nice to him. I imagine he's on the warpath."

"Why?" asked Helen.

"I had the remains of Angus McGinty removed from the scene of the crime before he and his people had a look at them."

"You didn't follow federal guidelines, did you, Zeb?"

"I don't think I broke any federal guidelines, but there is the possibility I might have. My decision to do what I did would fall into a gray area."

"What are you talking about, Zeb Hanks?" asked Helen, scolding him as she had when he was a child.

"Well, I don't exactly know what the federal guidelines are in this specific case. You could say the question of my precise authority is up for debate."

"Hardly," replied Helen. "Zeb Hanks, you know the law as well as any sheriff in the state. I don't think you should be so blasé about something that might put you in hot water."

"I had to think on my feet. I needed to get things done as quickly as possible so no evidence would be destroyed. I also needed to make sure the feds wouldn't throw a monkey wrench into the works. Right or wrong, I'll have to live with my decision."

"Why didn't you just wait until Mr. Wright got there. You most certainly could have avoided trouble with the federal government," replied Helen. "And, knowing you, I would bet my last dime you could have figured out a way to remain in control."

"I want the mines to be shut down as short a time as possible. The feds would have taken days to move the body. Heaven only knows what else they would have done had I not moved the actual crime scene, lock stock and barrel."

"I guess in terms of finding the best answer in the quickest way," said Helen, "that you believed you were doing the right thing."

Zeb knew in the back of his mind that he had stepped outside the normal boundaries of proper protocol. Still, he was glad to hear Helen backing him up. She was the face of the Graham County Sheriff's Office. Nothing that happened there didn't go through her at some time or other. More often than not, it went through Helen first. He needed her to have the right answers when people walked through the sheriff's office door.

"The Klondyke mine feeds a lot of families and pays a lot of taxes that keep the school running and the streets fresh and clean. You could even make the argument they pay our salaries, in a manner of speaking. I work for the good people of Graham County who work that mine, not the regional version of federal bureaucrats who take their orders from Washington, D.C. This truly is a local matter."

"I understand your point," said Helen. "But my best guess is that Mr. Wright is going to think you were dead wrong in doing what you did."

Zeb and Helen giggled at her accidental pun. Under these circumstances any relief from the tension that Thorman Wright would bring with him was wholly welcome.

"I'll straighten it out with him," said Zeb. "It's my problem, don't make it yours."

"He said he'd be here in five minutes," said Helen, glancing at the clock in Zeb's office. "That was six minutes ago."

A commotion erupted in the reception area as the outer door opened and promptly slammed shut.

"You'd better get that," said Zeb. "I assume Mr. Wright isn't used to waiting."

Helen hurried out of Zeb's office. A moment later she returned with Mr. Thorman Wright. He greeted Zeb by handing him his business card.

"Have a seat," said Zeb, pointing to the large, well-worn chair that sat directly in front of his desk.

Thorman Wright, Regional Director of the US Department of Mine Safety and Health Administration, took a seat. He spared no effort in hiding the look of disdain on his face. Zeb rested his elbows on his desk and leaned forward. Thorman opened a briefcase on his lap.

"Sheriff Hanks, I don't want to get off on the wrong foot, but what were you thinking when you moved the body of Angus McGinty?" asked Thorman.

"You must know something I don't," said Zeb.

The government man's eyes widened and his jaw dropped.

"That being what?" asked Thorman.

"That a positive and conclusive identification of the remains have proven to be those of Angus McGinty."

"No, I don't have that information, but I assumed you did."

"Assume nothing," replied Zeb. "I am waiting on the ID of the remains."

"Why move the body?" asked Thorman. "That can't be a regular procedure of your office, can it?"

"The working conditions for Doc Yackley, our local medical examiner, were less than ideal. I had to make a call based on the odds."

"What odds?"

"The weather calls for a thirty percent chance of rain today. I didn't want the rain to destroy any evidence."

Thorman pulled a smart phone from his pocket and opened his weather app.

"I don't know where you get your weather forecasts, but it hasn't rained in seventeen days. It shows here that the National Weather Service has no forecast of rain in the near future."

"I must've misread the forecast," replied Zeb. "I tend to be overly cautious when it comes to these things."

"Did you ever think of putting a canopy over the body?" asked Thorman.

"I didn't have access to one," replied Zeb.

"You didn't think of it, did you?"

Zeb ignored the caustic remark.

"I wanted the body moved to the morgue so Doc Yackley could identify the remains more quickly and efficiently. I wanted it done without the chance of destroying evidence."

"You shouldn't have moved it," said Thorman.

"I oversaw the crime scene. It was my call. To the best of my knowledge, I didn't break any federal rules or regulations."

"But you must admit that you did break generally accepted standards," said Thorman.

"There were what I considered special circumstances," said Zeb. "Based on those I made an appropriate judgment call."

"I'd call it poor judgment and will be reflecting so in my report," said Thorman.

Zeb nodded, bit his tongue and in his head said, "reflect away." He knew it was pointless to argue with or to waste his anger on someone like Thorman. The government man was a mere cog in the wheel of a large bureaucracy that moved forward under its own weight. The worst that could happen was a reprimand which would be worth less than the paper it was printed on. Helen had long ago created a file, now several inches thick, that contained Zeb's federal and state reprimands.

"Should we go to the morgue and see what Doctor Yackley has found?" asked Thorman.

"Do you want to ride with me or follow me?" asked Zeb.

"I'll follow you," said Thorman, wearing a distrusting look on his face.

9

SURVEILLANCE VIDEO

Doc Yackley was finishing the preliminary results of his autopsy. Zeb knocked once on the hospital morgue door before he and Thorman entered.

"Doc, this is Thorman Wright of the US Department of Mine Safety and Health Administration."

Doc looked over the rims of his glasses and nodded, "Thorman Wright."

"Doctor Yackley," replied the bureaucrat.

"You two know each other?' asked Zeb.

"We've met," replied Doc.

"Have you found anything that would be of interest to us?" asked Thorman.

"Yup," replied Doc, placing a fine, razor-edged scalpel along the body. "For a middle-aged man, Angus had an old man's arteries, but I'm fairly certain that isn't what killed him."

Thorman sighed audibly. Zeb grinned.

"Nope, clogged up arteries didn't bring an end to his existence in this vale of tears. I think getting squished flatter than a pancake by a Volvo DD140B road roller is what took him on the journey to meet his maker," stated Doc.

Zeb smiled. Thorman frowned.

"Did you find anything that you weren't expecting to find?" asked Zeb.

"Yes and no," replied Doc.

"Meaning what?"

"Well, I think he was doped up when he was killed. I'm running the tests now."

"Any idea what he was doped up on?" asked Zeb.

"Alcohol and OxyContin for certain. But the preliminary tests also show Rohypnol in his system," said Doc.

"It certainly sounds like somebody doped him up," said Thorman.

"Or he self-medicated. I can't give you an answer to that one," replied Doc. "He had some strange ways of dealing with life."

"Did you prescribe OxyContin or Rohypnol for him?" asked Thorman.

Doc continued working steadily on the remains. He glared over the rim of his glasses.

"I'll take that as a no," said Thorman.

Doc gave him no response and went back to work. Someone knocked on the autopsy room door.

"Enter," said Doc.

It was Byrne Murphy with a laptop in his hands. Jake Dablo was with him.

"Doc, Zeb, Thorman," said Byrne. "I've got something here that you're all going to want to see."

Byrne set the computer on a table and pressed the on button. Seconds later his screen was open and running video of Angus McGinty's death.

"This is security surveillance video from last night. I think you are going to find it a little odd," said Byrne. "Perhaps in an enlightening way."

The security video began with a pair of headlights flashing across the Volvo D140B that had flattened Angus McGinty. An unseen hand turned off the headlights. The only remaining light on the big machine was a pale, yellow umbra from an overhead security light. It offered little clarity to the scene of the crime.

"What good is this video? I can't make out anything," said Thorman.

"Hold on," said Byrne. "You will."

An image entered from the lower right hand corner of the video. It was a person whose face was concealed by a mask. They carried something large on their shoulder. With a heave, they tossed what now looked like a human body ten or so feet in front of the Volvo roller. It landed flatly, but was clearly moving, if only minimally, as it lay on the ground.

"What the hell?" said Thorman.

Zeb and Doc kept their eyes glued to the computer screen.

Jake reached past Byrne and pressed the pause button. "It's Angus McGinty. It's obvious that he's still alive." Jake pressed the play button before anyone had a chance to respond.

The person who had dropped the body jumped up onto the road roller and turned on its headlights. The person then stepped down and ambled over to the security camera. Using great precision, they honed the center of the lens to focus directly on the face and body of Angus McGinty. The camera bounced around some. Suddenly a bright light was shining on the semi-conscious Angus McGinty. Jake hit the pause button again. Thorman exhaled disdainfully. Doc and Zeb's eyes turned to Jake.

"The killer was taping a second camera to the security camera. Apparently, there was a variable intensity flashlight on top of the second camera, hence the jiggling," said Jake. "Both cameras and the flashlight were taped together with duct tape."

"Jake and I looked our security camera over closely. You can easily see the sticky remains of the tape," said Byrne.

"Dreaded duct tape," said Thorman. "A thousand and one uses."

"The killer wasn't dumb enough to leave the flashlight or the second camera behind, were they?" asked Zeb.

Jake shook his head.

"The killer left neither the flashlight nor the second camera at the scene," said Byrne.

This time Byrne pressed his pointer finger down on the play button. Zeb, Jake, Doc, Thorman and Byrne all watched in horror as the killer staked a barely conscious Angus McGinty to the ground. When Angus was splayed out like an animal ready to be gutted, the killer dumped a bottle of water on Angus's face. He woke with a sluggish, drugged start. Realizing his predicament, Angus made a vain attempt to fight against the restraints that bound him tightly to the ground. The killer looked back toward the flashlight and pointed at Angus. Reaching into a pocket, the killer walked within a few feet of the security camera and held up a piece of official stationery emblazoned with an elm leaf. It read simply, "ANGUS MCGINTY DESTROYER OF NATURE." In the background, Angus continued a beleaguered and useless struggle.

"Stop the video," shouted Zeb. "What's that?"

"What's what?" asked Byrne.

"What's that on the killer's wrist? It looks like a tattoo. Can you back the video up and zoom in on it?"

A close-up view showed what looked like a woman riding on the back of a dragon. The beast of lore was wearing a kilt.

"Weird tattoo," said Jake.

"Not really," said Byrne. "Back in Scotland it's well known. It's the symbol of the MacMhuradaich clan. They're the black sheep of the MacCurdy clan."

"That means nothing to me," said Zeb.

"The MacMhuradaich clan is a covert clan of assassins. I should say *allegedly* a clandestine clan of assassins. It's rumored that the killers are mostly women. They've purportedly been in business for over a thousand years, but who knows if it's true?" explained Murphy. "When I was a child and behaved badly, my mom used to tell me if I wasn't good the MacMhuradaich clan would come and snatch me from my bed while I slept."

"Do they truly exist?" asked Zeb.

"I believe they do but who knows for certain? Who wants to

know? A clan of killer women that has lasted a thousand years in secrecy. Bloody frightening if you ask me."

Zeb looked at Jake, Doc and Thorman, all of whom appeared either stunned or in disbelief.

"Sounds like a tall tale to scare kids," said Jake.

"Or control your enemies using psychological warfare," added Thorman.

Everyone gathered parked the concept in their minds as the video moved forward.

Calmly, the killer climbed aboard the Volvo DD140B road roller, started it up and slowly drove the large water-filled barrel that made up the front of the machine onto Angus McGinty's feet. They halted the monster machine only after the roller had crushed everything beneath Angus's knees. The security camera showed a grotesquely surreal image of Angus silently screaming in pain. The killer jumped down from the machine and knelt on the ground next to Angus. They pulled out a cell phone and took some pictures. Finally, the killer cupped their hand behind Angus's ear and appeared to say something. The words seemed to turn Angus's pain to anger as he shouted at his nemesis.

The killer got back on the road roller, shoved it into gear and drove another foot or so forward. This time Angus was crushed to the waist line. He had literally become half a man. Angus was lapsing in and out of consciousness. Any ray of hope he was holding onto, even the chance of life itself, was hanging by the tiniest thread. At this point, death was certainly the best option for Angus McGinty.

Once again the killer halted the big machine. As before the killer jumped off the road roller, whipped out a cell phone and, based on the number of brief flashes of light, snapped a half-dozen pictures. The killer walked exactingly around Angus. In the process of doing so, they placed an object or objects in his hand before using the cell phone to take more pictures.

Zeb ordered Byrne to once again stop the video feed.

"Somebody wants proof of death," said Zeb. "It seems certain the killer was placing the feather, coin and the snake's head in Angus's hand. The wedding ring was likely already on his finger. Start the video again."

This time when the killer climbed aboard the road roller, mercifully they drove right over the top of Angus McGinty. Once the driver had flattened the dead man, the machine was put in reverse and rolled over Angus again. The process was repeated a few more times until the body of Angus McGinty was as flat and thin as a year-old newspaper.

The killer got off the machine and took a few more cell phone pictures. They slowly moved toward the video camera where the flashlight and second camera had been placed. Apparently, the killer was removing them. The security camera remained focused directly on Angus McGinty's remains as the perp disappeared like a cat's shadow into the darkness of the oncoming night.

"Looks like the killer headed in the direction of Toohey Blendah's place," said Byrne.

"Toohey Blendah?" asked Thorman.

"First cousin to Angus's wife. He lives near the edge of the mine property," said Byrne.

"There is a half dozen houses in that exact direction," said Zeb.

"Plus an access road," added Jake. "And a horse trail."

"The direction of the departure doesn't really tell us much of anything," asserted Zeb.

Thorman quickly input some information into his laptop computer.

"You never know. I never discount anything quite so quickly," said Thorman.

"Good for you," growled Zeb. "You shouldn't."

"Sheriff Hanks, do you have any one person whom you have in mind as the killer or perhaps more than one primary suspect?" asked Thorman.

"We're just beginning our investigation," replied Zeb. "Let's run the video one more time."

Thorman visibly changed as he watched the video again. Blood drained from his face. His demanding attitude quickly became acutely passive.

"If you would be kind enough to keep me apprised of everything you find," said Thorman, "I would greatly appreciate that."

"Of course," replied Zeb. "I take it you're leaving the Graham County Sheriff's Office in charge of the investigation?"

"Yes. You have a leg up. You're in charge, at least for now. I'll be available with limited federal resources if you need them. This looks like a vengeance killing to me. It appears to be a local matter," said Thorman.

Zeb looked at Byrne who was shaking his head in disbelief. In the past, when it came to the Klondyke 1 mine, Thorman Wright had done anything and everything possible to make his life a headache. Now, with the murder of a high ranking Klondyke mine management official, who also happened to be the largest individual private shareholder in the mine, Thorman was just up and walking away, leaving things to be handled locally. The foul air that accompanies dishonesty permeated the room. Zeb sensed it, was even glad for it, even though he didn't yet know what Thorman's motive really was.

"Thorman, I can promise you that I will keep you up to snuff with what's going on in the investigation," said Zeb.

Thorman extended a hand to Zeb and merely said, "Good." He handed Zeb his card, the second time he had done so, and headed out the door. With the door halfway between open and shut, Thorman Wright stopped, pivoted, stuck his head back in Zeb's direction and said, "Sheriff Hanks, please call me tomorrow so you can bring me up to date."

"What the hell is that all about?" asked Byrne. "He lives to make our lives miserable. Now, when he could make our lives a living hell, he just up and walks out the door? He must have an ulterior motive. He must know more than he's letting on."

"He may indeed have something up his sleeve," said Zeb.

"Or maybe he's just following some obscure federal rule," added Jake.

"But the fact that he doesn't appear like he's going to interfere with our investigation, well, that's a good thing. Let's use that fact to our advantage," said Zeb.

"Let's get some coffee," said Doc. "I'm a little tired."

"I think we could all use a little pick me up," said Jake. "I'll give Kate and Black Bear a ring and have them meet us."

"I'm going to call Song Bird and ask him to meet us at the Town Talk. We need to talk to him about these."

Zeb held up four plastic bags. One held a snake's head, another the feather, the third a gold wedding band and the fourth the 1909 SVDV copper penny.

10

FOUR THINGS

S ong Bird was seated in his usual spot, the most distant back corner of the Town Talk. The back of his shoulders squarely addressed the front entrance. It was his habit to place himself away from other customers. The medicine man's ancient fingers firmly enveloped the cup of dark black coffee he had ordered "from the bottom of the pot." His eyes floated in the images rising from the steam of his brewed drink. He barely looked up when the others came through the back entrance.

Zeb, Doc, Kate, Jake and Black Bear made their way to Song Bird's Table. Greetings were briefly exchanged among the gathered. Zeb got directly to the point as he placed the four plastic evidence bags in front of the medicine man.

"Song Bird, I need to know if a rattlesnake head, a feather, this specific coin and the gold band hold any special meaning."

"This must be important," said Song Bird, looking around the table. "Maybe we should call Helen. She has a better memory than all of you combined."

Indeed, Helen had a mind like a steel trap, but crime solving was not her cup of tea. The group chuckled at Song Bird's remark.

"What have you got for me that is such a big deal that it takes all of you to come and ask questions?' asked Song Bird.

"Murder. Vicious, well-planned and documented," replied Zeb.

"Who?" asked Song Bird.

"Angus McGinty."

"The rich man from the copper mines? The man that no one cares for? The man whose wife cheats on him at every turn? The man who abandoned his only child to a fancy boarding school at the first sign of trouble?" asked Song Bird.

"You obviously know him," said Zeb.

"I know of him. Toohey Blendah's family often came to me for spiritual healing regarding the injury he felt Angus McGinty created in his spirit. It is no secret that Toohey despised Angus McGinty. I worked for years to help him cure himself of his animosity. I think we all know that Toohey chose to hang onto his hatred toward Angus."

"He's on our short list of suspects," replied Zeb.

"I doubt he's a killer," said Song Bird. "Toohey is full of hatred and anger, but he does not have the will nor the spirit to end the life of another human being."

"That doesn't take him off my short list of suspects," replied Zeb.

"I think the worst thing he ever did was to insult Angus by referring to him as a litsog goshe. Another time, when his dander was up, he called Angus a chaa," said Song Bird.

Black Bear chuckled.

"What does that mean?" asked Zeb.

"Toohey thought Angus was a yellow dog, a coward, or a beaver with big teeth," explained Black Bear.

"I guess he really didn't like Angus McGinty," said Zeb.

"You catch on quickly," said Song Bird. I guess I haven't been wasting all these many years instructing you in the ways of the Apache."

Zeb smiled. When the sheriff was a boy and Song Bird was teaching him, he always kidded Zeb that he was a slow learner. But Song Bird also knew that once Zeb learned something he owned the knowledge forever.

Song Bird drank his dark coffee to the bottom of the cup. He gently raised the empty cup to just above the center of his forehead, signaling for more.

"We have some items that were found in Angus's hand. Most of them were put there by the killer."

"How was his spirit taken?" asked Song Bird.

Zeb described what they had seen on the security camera video.

"Evil took him away. If you live like we assume Angus McGinty did and carry wretchedness in your heart, your spirit is condemned to wander the earth looking for its body, perhaps for all eternity," said Song Bird.

Sawyer Black Bear interrupted the conversation, speaking to Song Bird in Athabascan. The conversation went on for several minutes before Jake spoke up.

"Mind letting us in on what you're saying?"

"Deputy Black Bear seems to think that whoever killed Angus McGinty wanted much more than to merely take away his life," said Song Bird.

"Why do you think that?" asked Zeb, turning in Black Bear's direction.

"It's very complicated," said Black Bear. "It has multiple parts."

"Go ahead," said Zeb. "I'll try and keep up."

"I could clearly see that the killing, or perhaps the manner of the murder, scared away the federal man from the mines," said Black Bear.

"Maybe it did. I hadn't thought of it quite like that," said Zeb.

"Did you notice how quickly he stepped out of the case?" asked Black Bear.

"Of course I did. He may have good reasons that he doesn't want to share with us," said Zeb. "I think he wants us to handle it. He wouldn't have backed out of the immediate investigation if he didn't have some legitimate reason. The man goes by the book—page, chapter and verse. I'm certain he was relying on the rules for his decision."

"I watched him closely. He was scared by something," said Black Bear.

"What do you think scared him?" asked Zeb.

"I'm not sure," said Black Bear.

"Kate, did you bring the surveillance video in or is it in your vehicle?" asked Zeb.

Kate reached into her satchel and pulled out the iPad she had taken from the crime scene.

"Let's show it again so Song Bird can see it," suggested Zeb.

Song Bird watched intently. When the video finished, he and Black Bear conversed again, this time in Lakota.

"Enough already," said Jake. "Nothing should be spoken in a language we don't all understand."

"Let them talk it out," said Zeb.

Ten minutes later Song Bird and Black Bear returned to speaking English.

"It's the elm leaf," said Black Bear. "That's the stickler. Song Bird and I can't agree on its meaning."

"We'll talk about the elm leaf in a minute," said Zeb. "First let's have a little chat about these."

He handed Song Bird the plastic bag with the rattlesnake head. Song Bird examined it thoroughly before speaking. He took another long drink of coffee which left coffee grounds on his lips. He wiped the grounds off with a swipe of his finger, opened the bag and placed them on the snake head, approximately where the eyes might have been. Then Song Bird bent forward and smelled the snake. He put it back in the plastic bag, sealed it up and gently placed it in the middle of the table.

"It's the head of a rattlesnake," he said.

The others present already knew that but sat quietly, waiting for more information.

"The rattlesnake is a malevolent creature of the underworld. In my opinion someone is making a statement by using only the head. We all know the old saying about chopping off the head of the snake. I think the snake is symbolism about killing Angus McGinty. Angus was the head of the mine and killing him is like cutting off the head of the snake. Also, by planting these items on Angus, the killer believes Angus McGinty was evil, perhaps the devil himself. That is all I have to say about that."

The old medicine man lifted his coffee cup to the waitress who seemed to have found a pot that was even blacker than the last. The pale, redheaded young woman promptly filled his cup. He thanked her by removing a black obsidian stone from his pocket and placing it in her hand.

"I like that girl," said Song Bird. "She knows how I like my coffee. She must have some Apache blood running through her veins."

The others glanced at the waitress whose skin was as pale as the winter snow on top of Mount Graham. She was anything but Apache, yet Song Bird showed no signs of being facetious.

Zeb handed Song Bird the bag with the feather in it. Black Bear slid closer for a better look.

"This is a Mexican hawk feather," said Song Bird. "You might call it a chicken hawk."

"Is there any special meaning you can give to it in light of it being found in the dead man's hand?" asked Zeb.

Song Bird and Black Bear exchanged a few brief words in Athabascan. Jake cleared his throat, unhappy at being left out of the private conversation.

"The hawk is the protector of mother earth," explained Song Bird. "I think the killer is implying that the hawk will protect what Angus McGinty had destroyed. Remember the letter called him the destroyer of nature."

The explanation made perfect sense to everyone. Whether or not this knowledge would move the investigation forward was quite another question.

"And the wedding band?" asked Zeb.

"Means nothing to me. It could have simply been on his finger."

"Wrong hand," said Zeb.

"I can find no significance in its meaning," replied Song Bird.

Temporary quiet consumed those seated around the table until Black Bear spoke.

"I think the penny has significance," said Black Bear.

Zeb handed Song Bird the 1909 SVDB penny.

"I don't know. Might be valuable as a collector's item," said the medicine man.

"It is very rare and very valuable," said Black Bear, pulling out his cell phone. "Here we go. Only 484,000 were minted in San Francisco, hence the S."

"And the VDB?" asked Zeb.

"The designer of the coin was Victor David Brenner. SVDB literally means minted in San Francisco and designed by Victor David Brenner," said Black Bear.

"Interesting," said Song Bird.

"Any ideas to the meaning of it ending up in Angus's hand when he was crushed?" asked Zeb.

His question was met with silence. He offered up his own explanation.

"I know that Angus was a collector of many things. Certainly coins, valuable copper coins, could have been one of them," said Zeb. "I have a vague recollection of seeing some rare coins displayed in his private office at his house."

"The stationery the letter was written on had an elm leaf emblazoned in all capital letters, as though it were a logo," said Jake.

"Does ELM hold significance to this?" asked Kate.

"Although Song Bird and I don't exactly agree on this, I believe ELM is an acronym for Earth Liberation Movement. They are a radical group that shows up wherever they feel Mother Earth is being desecrated," said Black Bear.

"Are you two still in disagreement about that one?" asked Zeb.

"Elm is significant because it designates a place," said Song Bird. "I read that in the White Eye's Bible, Hosea to be exact."

"Maybe you're both right," said Zeb.

"And maybe we're both wrong," added Black Bear.

"ELM signifying the Earth Liberation Movement seems to make more sense in light of everything," said Zeb.

"I understand how ELM might feel that way about the copper mine," said Kate. "It's not a pretty sight."

"It was Apache land until the McGintys sold it for profit," said Song Bird.

"Sacred land?" asked Zeb.

"All the land of Mother Earth is considered sacred in some way or other," replied Song Bird.

Kate Googled the group that went by the acronym ELM. It was her first chance to use the newly set-up wi-fi network at the Town Talk.

"They're active in almost all fifty states, as well as several foreign countries," she said. "They're known for creating civil disobedience on a mass scale. Nothing here indicates a history of significant violence."

"My home on Pine Ridge was a hot bed of radicalism," said Black Bear. "Every White radical from Abby Hoffman and Timothy Leary to Bernadine Dohrn came to visit Russell Means, Leonard Peltier, Dennis Means and Clyde Bellecourt. They all suffered from the same delusion."

"What delusion was that?" asked Jake.

"That being on an Indian reservation protected them from the FBI and possible arrest by any agent of the federal government. As we all know, that is not true. My mother's house was the underground railroad of the late sixties to the mid-eighties for people involved in radical social change."

"I take it you interacted with some of these people?" asked Zeb.

"I was a kid," replied Black Bear. "But I paid attention."

"Does anything you know about how ELM operates and how the sixties radicals operated ring a bell?" asked Zeb.

"Yes. In the end, they wanted any kind of publicity they could get. I think showing us the video and the letter with the elm leaf across it was a message. The Earth Liberation Movement wants us to know it was them."

"Or someone else could be using ELM as a red herring?" asked Kate. "Remember, murder isn't the modus operandi of ELM."

"Good point," said Zeb. "We can't count them out, but we can't count them in. We do have to look at them."

"Do we have money in the budget to hire Shelly Hamlin, the computer expert we've used before?" asked Kate. "She could get deeper inside information on ELM much faster than we could."

"Excellent idea. I'll pay for what the county won't," offered Zeb, knowing that well over a million dollars from Doreen's estate was sitting in his bank account gathering as much dust as interest.

"We need to get rolling," said Zeb.

"I'll give the grieving widow a call this morning," said Kate.

"Cowboy Bob Shank is my next stop," said Black Bear. "Has anyone contacted Tribal Police Chief Rambler Braing? He might have more information considering Toohey and Lily are both San Carlos Apache by birth."

"I'll have a chat with him," said Jake. "He should know the history between Lily and Toohey."

"We've got our work cut out for us. This is a particularly brutal murder, especially by Graham County standards. I want the son of a bitch who did this behind bars ASAP. You all have your marching orders. Let's roll," ordered Zeb.

11

SENATOR RUSSELL

7 DAYS AGO

"I don't have a lot of time to speak right now, Senator Russell. I'm busy putting out fires."

"Yes, you do, Angus. Your fires will have to wait. We've got a legislative vote coming up this week that will cost you millions if it doesn't pass," said Senator Russell.

"You assured me that it was a done deal," replied Angus McGinty.

"I said it passed my committee without objection. However, we've got some real environmental crackpots in the US Senate who will fight me tooth and nail on this. And that's just the tip of the iceberg. Fortunately, when it comes down to the nitty-gritty..."

"Sounds like nitty-gritty is another word for cash," interrupted Angus.

Senator Russell let Angus's words pass in one ear and out the other.

"...I can horse trade with the environmental whack jobs. The real problem lies with the international donations that are pouring in for the opposition side of this bill."

"Let me guess, what you need is some real cash in the form of a private donation to your favorite charity? Is that correct, Senator Russell?"

The sardonic nature of Angus McGinty's remark slid off the senator like water off a duck's back. Anyone who rose to the level of the US Senate was familiar with the scorn directed at them when they pleaded their case for cash.

"Here in D.C. the wheels of industry have to be heavily greased to get anything done. The opposition to the bill has a strong agenda. It includes legislation that either drastically reduces the amount of water available for copper mining or heavily taxes the water. Their goal is to make it prohibitively expensive to mine copper. Either way they've got us by the balls. Those nut jobs are perfectly happy destroying good, high-paying American jobs by allowing significantly increased imports of copper from China and Brazil. From their perspective, it's not only cheaper to import copper but better for the environment. We both know they're wrong. Their thinking is short term. It's practically anti-American," said Senator Russell.

"Senator, you know that those foreign governments have been flooding the US market with copper for years. Foreign copper is artificially propped up with tax credits, bribery, cash subsidies and God only knows what else. You know the details better than I do. I expect you to honor our personal agreement. I also expect you to get your esteemed colleagues in the upper house of Congress to fight like hell for previously signed international trade pacts. You must not allow this bill to be undermined."

"Angus, there is nothing I can do unless..."

"How much do you need?" asked Angus.

He did little to hide the disgust and resignation in his voice. Cash donations, both above board and otherwise, were a part of doing business with the elites in federal government. Nevertheless, it stuck in his craw like a sideways chicken bone.

"I'd say a hundred grand should get the ball through the net."

"I can drop it off tomorrow at State Senator Devon Dawbyns's office."

"That should solve your problems. The bill should fly right through the Senate," replied Senator Russell.

"This better be a done deal the second this money leaves my hands and ends up in your coffers," said Angus.

"It will be," replied Senator Russell. "Perhaps you and your lovely wife would like to join me for cocktails when I'm in Phoenix during recess?"

"I'm sure she'd like that. She's a big fan of yours."

"She is a lovely woman. As long as she votes for me and stays as beautiful as she is, I think all will be well between us."

"I don't want any last-minute surprises," said Angus.

"Trust me, there won't be any eleventh-hour pitfalls on this bill," replied Senator Russell.

"Goodbye, Senator."

"Goodbye, Angus."

Neither man suspected that the next day an environmental coalition would gather enough votes to stall the copper bill.

12

LILY MCGINTY

W hen Lily McGinty answered Deputy Kate Steele's knock on the mansion door, she appeared anything but the grieving widow. Lily was colorfully dressed. Disco music pounded in the background. She gripped a cocktail in one hand and a cigarette in the other.

"Kate, my dear, do come in."

Kate stepped over the threshold to the entry. Over Lily's shoulder Kate saw a handsome, significantly younger man slipping out the back door. He was shirtless and carried his shoes in one hand. Angus hadn't even been dead for twenty-four hours. Kate reminded herself that her job was not to judge but to get information.

"Is this a good time to talk?" asked Kate.

"Of course," replied Lily. "Just having a little hair of the dog." She smiled as she lifted her glass ever so slightly. "Want one? First one's free."

"I'm on duty," replied Kate. "Maybe some other time."

"Is this the official sheriff's office visit where you want to find out if I killed Angus?"

"This is just an informational interview," said Kate. "We're just filling in some gaps."

"Am I a suspect?" Lily instantly answered her own sarcastic question. "Of course I am. How exciting. The spouse is always the prime suspect in a case like this, isn't she? Who wouldn't suspect the rich widow who drinks too much, spends too much money and has affairs she doesn't bother to hide all that well? I've seen enough movies and watched enough CSI to know that much."

"That's television," replied Kate. "This is real life. There is a difference."

"Really? Hard to say by the way small-minded people think and act around this town, don't you think?"

"I wouldn't know about that, Mrs. McGinty," said Kate, shifting her weight from her right foot to her left.

"My manners," said Lily. "I must have left them somewhere. Do come all the way in."

Lily closed the door gently behind Kate and led her into a sunken living room that dominated the central wing of the first floor of the grand mansion. Lily was well-kept for a woman who drank as much as she allegedly did. Kate assumed Lily worked with a personal trainer. It wasn't difficult to spot the plastic surgery that had obviously enhanced her breasts, cheeks and lips. Botox, no doubt, had removed any aging lines in the 45-year-old's face. Lily's teeth were perfectly straight and white. Her hair looked like it had been professionally done, a bit mussed probably by the young man who had sneaked out the back entrance. Kate glanced around the excessively opulent living room and wondered if all wealthy people lived this ostentatiously.

"Water? Lemonade? Soda? I won't tell anyone if you have an adult beverage. If you want one, just name your poison," said Lily. "I really detest drinking alone. It makes me feel, well, like I'm living the life portrayed in the movie *Days of Wine and Roses* or *Leaving Las Vegas*."

"I'm fine, thank you," replied Kate.

Kate was a bit leery of the integration of the word poison with an offer of a drink by a primary suspect. She sized up Lily in a quick glance before beginning her questioning.

"When was the last time you saw your husband?" asked Kate.

Lily let a tiny giggle slip through her collagen plumped lips.

"Oh, I am so sorry. I didn't mean to laugh. It's just that the last time I saw him was at the morgue. He was so obviously dead and frightfully flattened that it was almost cartoonish, now that I think of it. It was all quite heinous, no doubt about it. But it was also a caricature of life inside of death."

Kate thought she perceived a touch of sadness, loneliness in Lily's eyes. Kate took Lily's laughter as a spontaneous reaction. Often the deputy had witnessed unusual reactions from those dealing with some grim reality. The alcohol in her system also probably increased the likelihood of the ill-timed reaction. Kate knew from experience that grief was a difficult emotion to handle. She once again reminded herself not to judge Lily.

"It's okay," said Kate. "Strange situations cause unusual reactions. You're not the first person I've interviewed who had a seemingly inappropriate reaction to the circumstance. Now, other than the morgue, when was the last time you saw your husband?"

"Do call him Angus, please, would you Deputy Kate?"

"When did you last see Angus?" asked Kate.

"I saw him at the mine," said Lily.

"Yes, of course," replied Kate. "How about other than that."

"The night before last," replied Lily. "He was always an early riser. We went to bed and watched some TV. I fell asleep first. He must have turned off the TV. He was gone to work before I woke up and got out of bed the next morning."

"Did you talk with him yesterday?"

"Technically no. I called his cell phone and left him numerous messages. We were supposed to have dinner at the Top of the Mountain Steakhouse last night at nine o'clock with some executives from Danforth-Roerg. I called him to remind him but we never talked."

"Do you know where he was? I mean do you have any idea where he was when he wasn't answering his cell phone?"

"No, I don't. I called the main office at the mine. His secretary told me he had left around eight o'clock to pick me up for dinner with the executives from Danforth-Roerg," said Lily.

"Did he call you to say he was on his way by any chance?"

"No. I never heard from him, even after I left numerous messages. Wait a minute, I did talk with him briefly in morning."

"What did you discuss?"

"We talked about an upcoming social event. We chatted around eleven. I wanted to make sure his calendar was open and that he would agree to go."

"What sort of social event?" asked Kate.

"It was a fundraiser in Tucson for a kill-free animal shelter."

Lily inhaled a deep drag from her cigarette. She exhaled the smoke like a fire-breathing dragon, through her mouth and nose. No sooner had the smoke departed her lips than she took a long drink from the glass of what Kate took to be gin.

"When you last talked to him, what was his mood?"

"Normal. Normal for Angus that is. He was pissed off about something at the mine. He always was. I don't know who it was or what it was about that time because I only listened to that crap with half an ear. If the mine wasn't operating at one hundred fifty percent efficiency, he was angry at someone or about something. That man could make a new enemy every day and he usually did."

"In your opinion, he wasn't well liked?"

"Ha! He was hated by most and loathed by the rest. He didn't care what people thought of him. If that machine that ran over him had a mind of its own, it would have wanted to crush him. He was only interested in making more and more money," said Lily.

"Did he have any friends?"

"None. No close ones anyway, at least that I ever knew of. He only had mining acquaintances and business contacts. Considering we've been together twenty-five years, I'd say he didn't make friends easily."

"About his enemies?"

"Angus thought a nemesis was hiding behind every bush, lurking under every rock, tucked away in every corner. New ones were after him every day."

"Did anyone ever threaten his life?" asked Kate.

"I'm certain someone must have along the way."

"Any idea who might have threatened his life?"

"Like I said, I only listened with half an ear to the part of him that was always angry and often downright paranoid."

"Was he ever fearful because he believed he had enemies?" asked Kate.

"No. He always believed he was stronger, tougher and meaner than anyone out there. He was brought up to believe rage and strength were one and the same," replied Lily.

"That's a tough way to live," said Kate.

Lily lifted her glass. "Cheers to that."

"He had a good side, too, didn't he?" asked Kate.

"Heavens yes. He was generous with me to a fault. He donated huge money to local and regional charities. You can talk to our tax accountant about which ones, if you're interested. Until recently he gave more money to the reservation than you could shake a stick at," replied Lily. "He wasn't all bad. Angus was just full of rage, a rage that, for the most part, was out of his control."

Kate made a note of Lily's curious statement about Angus and his rage.

"Why did he quit giving money to the reservation?"

"He didn't care much for the tribal council or Police Chief Rambler Braing. On top of that my cousin, Toohey Blendah, who is a tribal member, got Angus's goat. He thought they had all recently pooled their resources and were conspiring against him and his hopes for opening a second mine near the Rez. You must understand that it takes a tremendous amount of water to run a mine. The tribe has sovereign rights to the water. He needed water and lots of it to open the new mine, the Klondyke 2. I think he was going to contact Senator Russell and try to usurp the local tribal authority. Angus viewed the tribal council as his main enemy. His attitude was basically screw them if they're going to try and screw me. I know that was the main reason he cut off his charitable funding to the Rez. If the tribal council agreed to allow the water to flow to the Klondyke 2, he may have even started his charitable funding right up again. That was his nature, kind and giving but full of rage if you crossed him."

"What was his conflict with Toohey Blendah?"

"His conflict with Toohey goes back to the opening of the Klondyke 1. I'm sure you know all about that."

"I don't know all the details. I've heard that Toohey thought he deserved the rights to the copper on the land as much as you did," said Kate.

"Oh, that inheritance mess. Terrible business. Toohey and I had always been close as kids. How was I to know our aunt would leave the land to only me and that he'd be left high and dry? It was a legal matter that I had no control over. I got lucky, Toohey didn't. Such are the paths of our lives."

Satisfied with her explanation, Kate asked, "What was Angus's conflict with Rambler about?"

Lily sipped from her glass, thinking before answering.

"Angus backed someone else for Tribal Police Chief. Angus was angry because the guy he backed lost. My husband didn't care much for losing. He claimed Rambler rigged the election."

"Elections are nasty events," said Kate.

"Tell me about it," replied Lily.

"What can you tell me about the conflict between Angus and the tribal council?" asked Kate.

When Lily described her dead husband's grudge against the tribal council, it seemed to be specifically about the potential for using tribal water for Klondyke 2, the second Klondyke copper mine that was in the planning stage.

"Did Angus have any specific enemies on the council?"

"He hated them all," said Lily. "As far as he was concerned, they were going to stop him from making his second fortune. Angus was certain Toohey was somehow influencing them."

"Was Toohey influencing the council?" asked Kate.

"In my opinion he was. Recently Toohey got a rather large sum of money from somewhere. I have no idea where he got it. He certainly didn't make enough to do what he did," said Lily.

"What did Toohey do?" asked Kate.

"He hired a high buck law firm out of Los Angeles. He was attempting to get what he believed to be rightfully his."

"That being specifically what?" asked Kate.

"The mineral rights, past, present and future, from both Klondyke mines. Angus could have paid him off for a few hundred thousand dollars. However, that wasn't his nature. He chose to make it a slug fest rather than settle like a gentleman. We've spent twice what a settlement would have cost on legal fees. Angus hated Toohey with as much gusto as one man can muster against another. I think Toohey might have felt the same level of hatred toward my husband."

Another half hour of conversation proved to be little more than Lily ranting about Angus's bad side. She gave plenty of reasons why someone, almost anyone who had dealings with him, might want to kill him. The longer they spoke the more Lily drank. She was quickly becoming drunk. Kate decided to end the informational interview. She would return and, hopefully, catch Lily in a more sober state of mind.

"Thank you for your time, Lily," said Kate.

"Perhaps you'll come back when you're off duty and have a drink with me?"

"I might just do that," replied Kate. "My time is a little taken up by my recent marriage…"

"I heard you married Josh Diamond. Congratulations."

"Thanks."

"You two going to have children?"

"Probably," replied Kate.

"Think about it before you do it. Pregnancy is hard. Raising a kid is even worse."

"Do you have children?" asked Kate.

"Not anymore," replied Lily.

"I'm sorry,"

"No, that came out wrong. My child, Ela Sorcha McGinty, is an adult," explained Lily. "Sorcha means Earth Princess."

"It's a beautiful name," said Kate.

"My so-called earth princess just turned twenty-one and received the trust fund her father set up for her when she was born. If he had died a few weeks ago, I would have dissolved the trust and let her live with her crazy friends of the earth or whatever they call themselves. She's a real piece of work."

"I'm sorry to hear that," said Kate.

"Not your problem, nor mine anymore," replied Lily with a sneer.

As Kate walked to the patrol truck, she pondered how different the rich are. Angus and Lily hadn't attended her wedding ceremony but sent her and Josh a voucher for an all-expenses paid, week-long vacation at a high-end resort on the Caribbean island of Saint Bart's. It dawned on Kate that it was likely Angus had his staff take care of the details, and Lily probably never even knew about the gift.

On the drive back to Safford, Kate considered the possibility of Lily being the murderer. She remained high on Kate's list of suspects. But this case was just unfolding and, from what she had just learned, Angus McGinty created more enemies than most men. Something stuck in her head about the way Lily described her only child, Ela. She pulled off the road and wrote herself a note to check into Angus and Lily's daughter, Ela Sorcha, the Earth Princess.

13

COWBOY BOB SHANK

B lack Bear knocked on the front door of the run-down house belonging to Cowboy Bob Shank. When no one answered, Black Bear banged on the loose screen door with a closed fist. While slamming his fist on the door, he noticed the doorbell. He pressed it twice. A heavy metal tune blared from speakers inside the house. Black Bear recognized the band, Metallica, as well as the song, *Master of Puppets*. He was impressed by Cowboy Bob's taste in music. Black Bear placed his right foot against the loose screen door, closed his fist and once again pounded on the edge of the door. This time he got a response.

"Hold your stinkin' horses."

The gruff, grunting voice shouted during a pause between the Metallica song and Kid Rock's *Devil Without a Cause*. The bellowing utterance came from an upstairs window.

"I'm dropping the kids off at the pool and having a little trouble. I'll be there shortly. Sit down or let yourself in. Beers in the fridge if you want one, Deputy Black Bear."

Black Bear glanced toward the upstairs bathroom window. Cowboy Bob Shank stared back at him, a diamond earring reflecting in the sun from his right ear lobe. Cowboy tipped his hat to the deputy and went back to business, which Black Bear could see involved reading a comic book. The sheriff's deputy let himself in, gave the downstairs a quick once over and grabbed a Corona Light from the fridge. He considered it a good sign Cowboy had decent taste in beer along with a righteous musical ear. Commonalities always made for easier interviews. By the time Black Bear had downed the front half of the Corona, the upstairs toilet finally flushed, twice.

Cowboy Shank paraded down the stairs, buckling his belt and grinning like a cat who had just eaten the proverbial canary. At the bottom step, he reached into his pocket, pulled out a set of partial dentures and slipped them into his mouth. Black Bear noticed one of the front teeth was gold.

"Deputy Black Bear, I've heard a lot about you. Good to finally meet you."

"Bob ..."

"My friends call me Cowboy. I'd prefer you did the same. It would be better if we were on a first name basis."

"Okay, Cowboy, pleased to meet you."

Black Bear stuck out his calloused paw. Cowboy wiped his damp, large hand on his pants and they shared a hard grip. Very quickly the handshake turned into a mano a mano wrestling match. Thirty seconds later they called it a draw when neither man had buckled at the knees. Cowboy realized he had encountered Black Bear before.

"You don't remember me, do you?" asked Cowboy.

Black Bear eyed him up and down.

"I think I might have seen you at Kip's Tavern."

"Hell no. That's not what I'm talking about. Think harder."

Black Bear searched the deepest recesses of his mind. Something about Cowboy looked familiar.

"Think Pine Ridge," said Cowboy. He broke into a grin. Cowboy broke into an ear-to-ear smirk.

Then it dawned on Black Bear.

"The gay rodeo," said Black Bear, smiling. "You were drunk as a skunk, and I picked you up for driving recklessly."

"And with an expired license, outdated license tabs and a couple of unpaid tickets," added Cowboy.

"I decided to give you a break when I figured out you'd come to town for the rodeo," said Black Bear.

"When you saw that I had the championship belt for winning the bronco busting event, you drove me to my motel."

"I always admired the bronco busters. Besides, a White boy like you wouldn't do very well on a Saturday night in the Rez jailhouse, especially with the fancy belt."

"Who knows. I might have done real good," grinned Cowboy.

Cowboy cracked open a Corona Light and guzzled it down.

"Light beer?" asked Black Bear. "You on a diet?"

"Got to keep my figure," said Cowboy, rubbing his protruding belly.

"I'm here to ask you a few questions about your former boss, Angus McGinty."

"I wasn't all that surprised when I heard he got tortured to death," said Cowboy. "I guess he got what he had coming."

"Did you do it?"

Cowboy didn't bat an eyelash as he finished off his beer and opened another.

"Do what?"

"Kill him. Torture him. Run him over with a big roller. Flatten him into a pancake."

"Seriously?"

"I am one hundred percent serious," replied Black Bear.

"I applaud whoever killed that bastard, but I had no part in his death nor was it my idea. I will say I'm a little envious at the creativity of the killer. I tip my hat to the genius who thought of such a vicious way to put down that mangy dog. I don't know that I have it in me to kill another human being, but I surely didn't shed a tear at his demise. Another beer?"

"I'm on duty, so I'm good."

"Just about everybody I know drinks on the job."

"I bet."

Cowboy tipped his head back, opened his throat and guzzled down three-quarters of the fresh beer.

"Tell me about Angus," said Black Bear.

"He was a prick, a dick and I didn't care for him one lick. Angus McGinty screwed me, and not in the good way, every chance he got."

"Why did he have it in for you?"

"I banged his old lady. When I was done, I stole her panties and bra and left them on Angus's desk the next morning."

"You're not gay?"

"I'll bust any bronco that wants to be ridden hard and put away wet," said Cowboy.

The puzzled look on Black Bear's face told Cowboy he had better explain himself.

"I play on any team that will have me," replied Cowboy. "Lily wanted me because she thought I was only gay. She didn't know I was a switch hitter. I do believe her goal was to change my sexual nature by some sort of sex conversion therapy. Weird, huh? You might say that I went along for the ride."

"You are what you are. I learned that a long, long time ago. Is that the only reason he had it in for you?"

"Hell no. I was his best equipment man and he knew it. I saved him more time and money than the next five guys combined. But the rotten bastard kept passing me over for promotions and raises because he was homophobic."

"And you screwed his wife," added Black Bear.

"I've heard you've driven the Lily train yourself," said Cowboy.

"How would you know something like that?"

"Lily and I are not just occasional lovers. We are confidants for each other, sexual soul mates of a sort. We've gossiped many times after sex and over coffee. You know how it goes with women. They want a girlfriend as much as they want what dangles between your legs. As handsome and good-looking as you are, you must have had a hundred lovers or more. You must share special bonds with some of them."

"I make it a rule to never talk about my love life," said Black Bear.

"Nor do I approve of sharing secrets about even the most casual of lovers."

"To each his own. Anyway, Lily and I talked about you the day after the first time you had sex with her. She told me about your hidden lasso love trick. She even made me try it. But you know how it goes, second best is always second best. I don't think I ever got it quite right. However, I'm game if you ever want to share it with me."

"I don't ride the range that way," said Black Bear.

"If you ever want to hop the fence, give me a call."

"Let's talk about Angus McGinty. Which one thing made him hate you more than the other? His homophobia or the fact that you slept with Lily on a part-time basis?" asked Black Bear.

"When it comes right down to it, now that I give it a second thought, it was neither of those things."

"There was another reason you two didn't get along?"

"Yup."

"What was it?" asked Black Bear.

"I helped his daughter out a couple of times when she ran away from home. I suppose she was about thirteen or so when that happened. I know that her coming to me for help got under his skin. I'm certain it was something he could never let go of."

"There must be a story attached to that," said Black Bear.

"There is. Angus and Lily had only the one child, a daughter. Her name is Ela, but she calls herself Earth Princess. She was a troubled child. Really not surprising considering her blood line."

"What sort of trouble did Ela get herself into?"

"The usual. She got a belly button piercing and a small tattoo without telling her parents. They screamed at her, even beat her over that kind of stuff. Every time she'd come running to me."

"Why to you?"

"I got to know her when she came to work with Angus. We joked around some. I listened to her. I think I became a father figure to her because I treated her like a man should treat his daughter. To answer your original question, she ran to me and I confronted her father after what she told me. She trusted me enough to know that I'd defend her."

"What did she tell you?"

"Ela said both Lily and Angus physically beat her. To hear her side of it, they both humiliated her by their words and actions. Mostly it was Angus who was responsible for the abuse. But, according to Ela, Lily never lifted a finger to stop it and in some ways encouraged it."

"Did you report the abuse to Sheriff Hanks?"

"Hell no. Sheriff Hanks had a pretty tight relationship with Angus and Lily. Not only did they fund his campaigns, but he kept the feds off their backs whenever he could when it came to Klondyke business. I didn't trust him to do the right thing."

"You could have trusted him," said Black Bear.

"You haven't been around Graham County as long as I have," said Cowboy.

"Meaning what, exactly?"

"Meaning that things are not always as they seem when it comes to Sheriff Zeb Hanks and his deputies."

"Care to elaborate on that one?" asked Black Bear.

"Nope, I don't."

"It might be helpful to the sheriff's department if I knew what you meant."

"No means no. I've got nothing else to say on that subject."

"Fair enough. How come I haven't seen the McGinty's daughter around?"

"They shipped her off to a Swiss boarding school when she was a teenager. After that she enrolled at the University of California, Berkeley. I would assume she's still there. I haven't heard from her or seen her around in a few years. I would imagine she'll show up for her father's funeral."

"Do you have a picture of her?" asked Black Bear.

"Nothing recent."

"How about an old one?" asked Black Bear.

Cowboy went to a buffet drawer. He shuffled things around for a few minutes before pulling out an old polaroid shot of himself and Ela McGinty. Ela looked to be about fourteen or fifteen. She wore a trendy look of the times, a pair of short cut-offs that accentuated her long legs and a Grateful Dead, tie-dyed T-shirt. She had long, straight, dark hair and a radiant smile.

"When was this taken?" asked Black Bear.

"When she was home after her freshman year in Switzerland. That must be seven or eight years ago."

"She looks like a nice enough kid," said Black Bear.

"She was a great kid, but the same rage that streams through her father's blood runs through hers. If you crossed her, she might just pull a knife and cut you."

"Is she the type that would follow through with the act, once they pulled the knife?"

"As in kill someone with a knife?"

"Precisely."

"Can't make a claim like that about her. What I'm saying is that she has a dark side that ran deep inside her. On the other hand, she is as lovely as the morning dew on a spring day," replied Cowboy. "You don't ever really know what you're getting with any of those McGintys."

Black Bear understood the dual personality profile. He'd seen it in his mother and witnessed it in many of the radicals that hung around the house when he was growing up. Political activists could be nicer than nice, but when push came to shove, they were dogmatic animals with self-serving interests and violent tendencies. Black Bear glanced at Cowboy who was quickly becoming an inside source of information.

"Is Ela political?"

Cowboy shrugged his shoulders. "Don't know. Don't care."

The shrug and the obtuse answer spoke volumes. Black Bear sensed Cowboy knew more than he was letting on.

14

A GIFT

The ever-dutiful sheriff's secretary, Helen Nazelrod, placed a cup of chamomile tea in front of Zeb.

"You've got bags under your eyes and lines on your face," she said. "This might help alleviate some of the stress that is wearing on you."

"Thanks, Helen," replied Zeb without glancing up from the reports Kate and Black Bear had recently submitted.

Helen departed Zeb's office, holding the door open for Kate, Jake and Black Bear. When she passed through, she left it slightly ajar and fiddled with her newly purchased hearing aids.

"We need to get on top of everything that is happening ASAP," said Zeb. "I get the distinct sense the feds are going to come swooping in at any minute. I'm more than a little surprised that they've given me the leeway they already have."

Jake Dablo, former sheriff and most experienced of Zeb's deputies, handed a DVD to his boss and former mentee. Zeb looked at it and gnawed on his lower lip.

"What's this?" asked Zeb.

"Let's call it an early Christmas present from Byrne Murphy," said

Jake. "It might answer the question that is buzzing around in your head."

Zeb popped it in his computer. The others gathered behind him. The disc truly was a gift. It explained why Thorman Wright, US Department of Mines, Safety and Health Administration investigator, had backed off from the case. The contents of the tape clearly shined a light on him that made him a suspect in the death of Angus McGinty.

"Turn it up," said Black Bear. "We need to hear every word."

The tape was time stamped three months earlier. It was clearly recorded in Angus McGinty's office. Present were Angus McGinty and Thorman Wright. Angus McGinty spoke first. He was fingering rapidly through a stack of paperwork.

"What is this shit all about? Why are you nickel and diming me to death? I run a clean and safe mine. I've been in this business for nearly my whole life, and you nitpick more than the next ten inspectors combined. You'd have made a good Nazi SS agent."

"Angus, you've got to follow the rules. I didn't write them. I only enforce them."

"I've had one hundred consecutive accident free days and you pull this shit? You make it look like I'm running a dangerous sweat shop instead of a top notch copper mine."

"Every dollar of every imposed fine is legitimate. You'd better pay them or your business will be in a world of hurt. You don't want to cross the federal government, do you?"

Angus McGinty's face turned beet red as he loosened his necktie.

"Watch your blood pressure, Angus. What's eighty-seven thousand dollars to you anyway? A day's profit?" asked Thorman.

Angus McGinty pulled a knife from his top drawer and jammed it hard into the top of his desk. Thorman Wright took a single step back. Angus left the knife standing vertically in his desk as he maneuvered himself between Thorman and any chance of the mine safety inspector exiting the room.

"I should stick that fucking knife into your heart, if you have one," shouted Angus. "You are nothing but a worthless, government pencil-pushing piece of shit. The world would be better off if you were dead."

"I'm just doing my job," said Thorman. "Just like you are doing yours."

"Screw you, Thorman. You're not one tenth as good at your job as I am at mine. That's why you work for the government. If you didn't have your office to hide behind, you'd be lucky to get a job pumping gas."

Suddenly Thorman made a move for the knife. He grabbed the handle, extracting it from the desk like a man who knew his way around a knife. Angus stormed toward the government man. At the same instant Thorman lifted the knife over his head, preparing to thrust it into Angus's puffed out chest. Angus McGinty stopped dead in his tracks and began to taunt Thorman.

"Go ahead and try to use that knife on me," shouted Angus. "If you don't kill me now, I'll get you later. That you can count on."

"It's either now or later for one of us," replied Thorman.

Thorman jumped at Angus and thrust the knife blade in his direction. In a flash, Angus dove to the floor, pivoted on one hand and used his legs to knock Thorman's feet out from under him. In the process the knife went flying beneath a chair. Angus threw a punch or two, bloodying Thorman's nose. Thorman got in a few licks of his own. As quickly as it began, it was over. Bolting toward the door, Thorman made his escape.

"Asshole," shouted Angus. "Coward."

Nothing else on the DVD was of consequence.

"Well, well, well," said Zeb. "I see why Thorman doesn't want to be involved in the investigation of Angus McGinty's death. He certainly has a conflict of interest. This tape officially makes him a suspect."

"Do you think when Thorman implied he'd get Angus later, it was a legitimate death threat?" asked Black Bear.

"Hell yes," said Zeb and Jake simultaneously.

"He might have been inferring that he could hurt him with fines and other government interference," added Kate.

"He did threaten to use the knife on Angus at some later point. I'd call that a death threat," said Jake.

"We can't prove exactly what he meant, but we can sure as hell ask him," said Zeb. "I'll make a little trip over to Tucson and visit Thorman Wright in the very near future. We know he's not going anywhere. He probably has no idea the tape exists."

"From what I can tell about the man, Thorman Wright is a real government boondoggler," Jake added.

"Keep that to yourself," said Zeb. "Always remember what you taught me. The politics of the Graham County Sheriff's Office are officially neutral and always independent."

Jake smiled. "Of course. You try and remember that when you interview him."

Zeb nodded at the sage advice from his deputy and former sheriff.

"Kate, what did you find out when you talked to Lily?" asked Zeb.

"The ultra-rich live in a different world. The rules are different. Even the playing field is unique to them."

"I don't suppose she confessed to the crime of killing her husband or having his death arranged?" asked Zeb.

"If she is involved, Lily is going to be a tough nut to crack. There is something odd about her. Her emotions don't seem to fit reality. Maybe she handles her grief in a strange fashion. If she did kill her husband or have something to do with it, I suspect murder would amount to little more than a game to her. There is truly something unusual about her. It's something I can't quite put my finger on. It's like she's guilty of something, but murder doesn't seem to be it."

"That's all well and good. You have the beginnings of a psychological profile on her, but did you find out anything concrete?" asked Zeb.

Kate shook her head from side to side. "I wish I could say that I did, but I haven't...yet. I'll talk with her again very soon. I suspect that if I dig a little deeper something will get unearthed."

"Dig into her past. Maybe use our computer expert to hack into her personal life a little," said Zeb.

"I'm not comfortable doing that without a court order," said Kate.

"Fine," said Zeb gruffly. "I'll talk to her and get you the information. That way your hands are technically clean."

"Thanks, Zeb," replied Kate.

"Anyone have anything to add about either Thorman or Lily?" asked Zeb. "Anything at all?" Zeb's eyes landed directly on Black Bear. It was time for him to fess up to everyone.

Black Bear cleared his throat before speaking. "I had a one night stand with Lily," he said. "Several times over."

His statement was news to no one, unless Helen was listening in. She was.

"I can't tell a hell of a lot from that, but I do know she is both distant and clingy. She always called me three or four times right after we had sex. If I didn't call her back, she'd leave a nasty, almost threatening, message."

"What sort of message did she leave?" asked Kate.

"She said the next time that I wanted to see her I should just go fuck myself," replied Black Bear. "She implied that she was going to tell her husband or Sheriff Hanks that I was having an affair with her."

"Well, you did sort of use her," said Kate.

"I always called her back ... eventually," said Black Bear.

"Mighty upstanding of you," replied Kate.

"This is the twenty-first century. You could just as easily say that she used me," responded Black Bear.

"Let's not get caught up in any politically correct bullshit," said Zeb.

Zeb eyed both Kate and Black Bear to make certain they understood his meaning. Both nodded in the affirmative.

"No more sexual contact with her," ordered Zeb. "I suggest you might be nice to her the next time you see her, but it had better not be between the sheets."

"I know how to follow orders," replied Black Bear.

"I need to run out and have a chat with Toohey Blendah," said Zeb. "Jake, I want you to run out to the Rez and have a little chat with Rambler. See what he knows about all of this. He probably knows Toohey quite well. He might even have slept with Lily, for all we know. Who knows if he had any interactions with Thorman Wright. See what he knows, what he thinks. That new copper mine that is going in near the Rez. He might have some serious thoughts on that. He'll have the local angle at least. I've heard there has been quite a bit of backlash because of the water situation and the new mine. Pick his brain. See what you can get."

"Right," replied Jake.

"One last thing. What does anyone know about the funeral?" asked Zeb.

"Nothing," said Black Bear.

"Nada," replied Jake.

"Lily has decided to hold a service at the Kimble Funeral Home," said Kate. "Apparently, she was having trouble finding someone to give the eulogy. She and Angus weren't regular churchgoers. My guess is that Father Delgado didn't really know Angus. No one is offering to eulogize him, not even the big wigs from Danforth-Roerg."

"Bummer for him," said Jake. "But not really all that surprising."

"You reap what you sow," said Zeb. "A good lesson for us all."

"I'm the oldest here," said Jake. "Which one of you is going to speak at the service when my time comes?"

Everyone chuckled except Black Bear who had no history with Jake.

"Oh, I think there are plenty of stories that can be told at your funeral," said Zeb. "I, for one, will be glad to tell quite a few of them."

"Me too," added Kate.

"You planning on passing soon?" asked Black Bear.

Once again everyone had a good chuckle as Helen stuck her head in the door and said, "Who's passing soon?"

"Nobody in this room," replied Jake. "At least not that we know of. But if I did die, would you step up and speak for me at my funeral?"

"I'm not much for that kind of thing, but for you, Jake Dablo, I do believe the spirit would move me."

"We Lakota believe it is bad luck to speak of one's own death," said Black Bear.

"Then don't do it," said Jake.

"Believe me, I won't," replied Black Bear.

15

TOOOHEY BLENDAH

Toohey Blendah was in the middle of a siesta. He was stretched out sideways on a beat-up sofa with a bottle of Tecate resting on his beer belly as Zeb pulled his truck up the heavily graveled driveway. The sound of the engine truck roused the half-sleeping Apache. He cleared the grit from his bloodshot eyes and recognized the sheriff, hailing him over. Even from a distance Zeb noticed the dirt under Toohey's fingernails.

"My friend, the good sheriff of Graham County. It's good to see you," said Toohey. "You are a welcome sight at the Blendah estate. Do you have news about who killed the man who stole what is rightfully mine?"

Zeb noticed a half dozen empty beer cans strewn around Toohey's weather beaten sofa.

"I see you're making the most of the mine shutdown," said Zeb.

"Why not? It's too windy to stack rocks on a day like this and it's too much work walking uphill to hunt elk," replied a grinning Toohey Blendah. "What can I do you for, Sheriff Zebulon P. Hanks?"

"Just doing some follow up regarding Angus McGinty's death," replied Zeb. "Since the two of you are related by marriage, I thought you might have something to say. I was hoping you might even have some inside knowledge of the situation."

"Oh I have lots to say about that stinking corpse," said Toohey, pulling on his long ponytail.

Zeb raised his eyebrows. Maybe this was going to be easier than he thought.

"Yes," said Zeb. "Do tell."

"What do you want to know, Sheriff? I'm an open book," said Toohey.

"Let's start with the day of Angus's murder," said Zeb.

Toohey pulled a handkerchief from his back pocket and dabbed his brow. He sat upright on the old sofa, making a half-hearted attempt to tuck his shirt into his faded jeans. He placed a sun-yellowed cowboy hat at an angle, which kept the sun's rays out of his eyes.

"I was working at the Klondyke the day he got pancaked. Can't say as I find that anything but the nature of the universe doing its work. I guess karma would be the right word for what happened. You know what karma is, don't you, Sheriff?"

Zeb let the remark pass and continued his probe of Toohey.

"You know how to drive one of those big machines, like the one that ran him over?" asked Zeb.

"The Volvo DD140B?"

"Yup, that's the killer machine."

"Hell yes. I can drive one with my eyes shut. I'm probably as good at it as anyone out at the Klondyke, maybe even better. But that son of a bitch Angus never gave me the chance to prove that. Fuck him. I'm glad he's dead and gone. The thieving bastard got exactly what he deserved."

"I take it the two of you didn't get along?" asked Zeb.

Toohey rolled his dark eyes.

"Sheriff, don't treat me like a fool. You know the situation damn good and well. The Klondyke mine should have been mine. I should be the rich man living in a mansion with all that life has to offer instead of the working schmuck that I am. I should have been able to treat Angus McGinty like he treated me and just about everyone else, like shit."

"Okay. I know you two didn't get along and I know the reasons why. But his death won't change anything for you. His wife will inherit his ownership in the mine."

"I can at least tolerate her, somewhat. She's family and family has some respect attached to it," replied Toohey. "Eventually the mine will go to their daughter, Ela. She hates the mine. She will see that it is closed and that the land is once again sacred rather than scarred. Usen may even use the opportunity to see that Ela's scarred soul is healed."

Zeb had seen Ela's picture at the McGinty house during a fundraiser for his re-election run. At first he assumed it was a picture of Lily in her youth. When he commented on the photograph, Lily and Angus had precious little to say about their only child. When Zeb had pressed a bit, he discovered she had been sent to a boarding school in Switzerland. When she returned to the states after graduating, she enrolled at the University of California, Berkeley. He remembered that little fact because the now deceased and former tribal chairman, Eskadi Black Robes, had attended the same university.

"Scarred?" asked Zeb. "Why would you say that Ela's soul was scarred?"

Toohey fired a spitball from between his two front teeth. It landed a few feet from Zeb's boots.

"If you were raised by an asshole like Angus McGinty, wouldn't your spirit be scarred?"

It was an assumption, but no doubt it had some basis in truth. He made a mental note to have Kate ask Lily about the relationship between father and daughter and, while she was at it, mother and daughter. Zeb didn't directly respond to Toohey's statement.

"Did he scar you, Toohey?"

"He pissed me off because he screwed me over so many times. But did he scar me? Sheriff Hanks, I am a man, an Apache man. Angus McGinty was also a man, a White man. Could he have scarred me? Not a chance. He just pissed me off. I knew there was nothing I could do about it. Sometimes you just have to face the reality of the situation and hope that Usen plays a hand," said Toohey.

"Do you really believe God, Usen, would play a hand in Angus's death?" asked Zeb.

"It's just an expression. Maybe karma finally caught up with him. The White Eyes are always preaching about karma."

Zeb let it pass. He was not in the mood for a philosophical conversation with a man who had just downed at least six beers and carried enough hatred in his heart, Zeb believed, to kill a man.

"Did you hate him?"

"Hate is weakness of the spirit. I hate no one."

"Okay. Did you wish him dead?"

"His death affects me not at all. Each man dies his own death. I can't say I'm sorry to see him gone, but his death only means he probably can't piss me off anymore."

Every question was met with intended aversion. Toohey Blendah was a well-rehearsed liar. Zeb had learned a long time ago that men who responded like Toohey did were usually too clever by half. Jake and Song Bird had long ago taught Zeb that these types of men generally dig themselves into a hole or back themselves into a corner they can't get out of. Zeb needed patience if Toohey Blendah was the killer. Still, he fired one last question at Toohey.

"One final thing," said Zeb.

"You want to know if I killed the son of a bitch, don't you?" asked Toohey.

It was precisely what Zeb was going to ask.

"Did you?" asked Zeb.

Toohey puffed his large chest. Zeb had crossed a line. No one was going to accuse him of murder, not on his own property.

"Sheriff, we've talked long enough," said Toohey, pointing to Zeb's truck. "Good day, Sheriff Zeb Hanks. I hope you get your man or woman or spirit being that killed Angus McGinty. I'd like to shake their hand or dance the cha-ja-la for them."

"Cha-ja-la?" asked Zeb.

"Spirit dance. I want to give the killer of Angus McGinty an eternal blessing."

Zeb placed his hat on his head as he slowly ambled to his truck. Toohey's final answer was just obtuse enough to keep him on Zeb's short list of suspects. In the distance, toward the Klondyke mine, matching dust devils swirled tightly down through the adjacent arroyos. He glanced over his shoulder where Toohey Blendah was taking a sip from his can of warm beer. Toohey gave the appearance of a man who was calm and totally at ease. Was he a psychopathic killer who could easily remain composed? Was he the sort of man who could lie directly to the face of a law officer? Or, was he simply not guilty of anything other than righteous anger?

16

REZ

Jake had long held a particular affectation for the Rez. As a boy, he hung around with Apache kids as much as his White buddies. His dad and uncle had taken him hunting and fishing on the San Carlos for as far back as memory served him. When Zeb became Graham County Sheriff, Jake made it clear the Apaches caused no more trouble than anyone else. Jake had warned Zeb that tribal police chiefs tended to keep everything close to the vest and, whenever possible, they kept the Graham County Sheriff's Office out of their business. The arrangement had worked fine in Jake's day. Any legal interaction with younger Apaches was as much social work as it had been sheriff's duties. Today, on the trip to the San Carlos, Jake carried a heavy heart. Angus McGinty had chosen his wife, Lily, from the Rez. Their only child, Ela, had not only lost her father, but she had long been distant to her native roots and the Apache ways. The whole situation was shrouded by a cloud of sadness.

Approaching Tribal Police Chief Rambler Braing's office, Jake noticed an absence of activity. That seemed odd since the police chief's office was often the hub of activity in the town of San Carlos. Jake pulled his truck right in front of Rambler's office. He got out and looked up and down the street. Except for a few stray dogs sleeping in the sun, not much was happening. He walked into the office and rapped on the secretary's desk.

Rambler shouted from his office in the rear of the building, "Back here."

"Where the hell is everyone?" asked Jake, entering Rambler's office.

"Big pow-wow at the church," replied Rambler.

"What's up?" asked Jake.

"All the talk is about the killing of Angus McGinty. Well, not so much his murder as what should happen to the mining property. To be more correct, the topic at hand is should the owners of the new mine, the Klondyke 2, have any water rights from the Rez."

"What's the deal?" asked Jake.

"Besides managing the Klondyke 1, Angus was a minority shareholder in the mine," said Rambler.

"I've heard he owned forty-nine percent of the Klondyke," replied Jake.

"That's what they say."

"So, what's up?"

"Some sharp, liberal Los Angeles lawyer who specializes in Indian rights and treaty abuse has made a claim that not only the water rights to the newly proposed mine, the Klondyke 2, but the mine location itself belongs to the tribe. He's making the claim that Angus's family owns none of the land and needs to pay the tribe for the profits they have taken out of the ground. Some radical group, ELM, the Earth Liberation Movement, filed the lawsuit to have the land returned to the tribe," explained Rambler.

"For the money?" asked Jake.

"Partially. They want to shut the mine down. ELM doesn't want anyone to steal from Mother Earth what rightly belongs to her. In this case, that not only means copper but water. There is also a great deal of concern about the Rez running out of water in the not so distant future."

"I didn't know land had the same rights as an individual," said Jake. "But, then again, I'm no lawyer."

"What complicates the issue is the fact that Ela McGinty, the McGinty's only child, is now next in line to inherit the Klondyke 1 and the land the Klondyke 2 sits on."

"That's pretty much common knowledge," said Jake.

"Ela is also an ELM activist. In fact, when she turned twenty-one, she came into her personal trust fund. It is rumored to be worth millions and, from what I hear, she's using it to fund this particular ELM project."

"I take it ELM is a national group?"

"It is," replied Rambler. "I don't know that much about them, but I'm learning. Google is a wonderful tool for that. I don't know if everything I'm learning is the truth, but it's a starting place."

"What's Ela's connection, other than funding this project?"

"She's president of the Arizona Chapter of ELM and a regional representative on its national board. I pulled that information from their website."

"I don't suppose Angus and Lily cared much for that," said Jake.

"I can't imagine they would," replied Rambler. "Especially when, according to my Google search, the primary objective of the Arizona chapter is to close the Klondyke 1 and all other mines destroying Native American lands."

"Sounds like a poor little rich girl syndrome," said Jake. "Maybe she's getting back at her parents in a weird sort of way. Maybe she feels guilty because her trust fund came from money earned from the Klondyke 1 copper mine."

"Guilt over being rich is usually a White-eyes syndrome. Indians haven't had much of a chance to experience that."

"Do you think Ela got involved with ELM to get back at her parents?"

"I'm not a psychologist. I can't really answer that question with any type of authority," said Rambler. "But human nature, being what it is, would suggest you are correct."

"Do you know Ela?"

"I've never met her. However, I do know one thing about her that strikes me," replied Rambler.

"That being what?" asked Jake.

"Even though she went to boarding school in Switzerland, college in California and has never lived on the reservation, she considers herself more Apache than White. One of her friends told me she is moving to the Rez. She's been spending some time here since she flew home for the funeral the other day."

"Chic rebellion?"

"Probably. She's just acting her age. You know young folks can get their heads full of funny ideas," replied Rambler. "But she does have plenty of Apache blood running through her veins. So I suppose her cause could be more than just righteous indignation."

"I'd like to talk with her to get some idea of who she is," said Jake.

"If you want to meet her, we can go over to the meeting at the church. It starts in about fifteen minutes."

"Let's do that," replied Jake. "Might be interesting. By the way, do you know if ELM advocates violence?"

"Officially they don't, at least according to the information on their website. But other stories on the Internet suggest they advocate aggression in the name of saving the earth," replied Rambler.

"Do you think Ela could possibly be involved in what happened at the mine?"

"Do I think she had a hand in killing her father? Is that what you're asking?"

"Yup," replied Jake. "That's my question."

"Like I said, I've never met her," replied Rambler. "Maybe if we hear her speak at the church, we'll have a better idea of who she is, what she stands for and maybe even what she's capable of."

"Do you know a government worker named Thorman Wright?" asked Jake. "He works on mining business for the feds."

"I've met him. He's a real stickler on the rules. He's spoken to the tribal council on water rights. He informs them on exactly what rules they have to follow if they're going to sell water to the mine. Most of what I know is secondhand, from rumors. You don't think he killed Angus, do you?"

"I don't know who killed Angus," replied Jake.

Rambler finished what he was working on as Jake hit him with another question.

"If the Klondyke 2 moves forward, is the tribal council going to sell water to them?"

"It's up to them," replied Rambler. "I don't think they've made a final decision."

"Any idea which way they're leaning?" asked Jake.

"I would bet it sort of depends on whether or not the proper wheels are being greased," replied Rambler.

"Since Angus is dead and he's the one who would have been handing out the cash, do you think Lily is trying to buy votes?" asked Jake.

"I don't think it's that simple," replied Rambler. "The Apache Nation might be sovereign, but, as a people, we are dependent on the US government as much as anyone."

"You're implying pressure could be coming from higher up the food chain than the mining company," said Jake.

"I'm not implying anything," replied Rambler. "This is the Rez. You might never know how or why certain things happen."

Jake nodded. Truth be told, he didn't have a clue as to exactly whom or what Rambler was referring.

"Got some black coffee?" asked Jake. "I think I'm going to need to be sharp for this little get together."

Rambler poured Jake a cup of dark black mud. As he poured he let out a little chuckle. Jake raised his eyebrows as if asking what Rambler meant.

"I wonder how different the world would be if us Indians hadn't sold you White Eyes Manhattan Island for twenty-four dollars' worth of beads."

17

ELM

The non-denominational Church of Christ the Redeemer was less than half full when Jake and Rambler took seats in the back pew. Jake turned to Rambler and whispered.

"Not a big turnout."

Rambler pointed to the front of the church. People from the local radio station, the one that had been started by Eskadi Black Robes to educate and inform tribal members, were setting up their equipment.

"This is going out live. The radio station came in and asked if they could broadcast from the church. I told them to talk to the church council. The council must have said yes."

"Excuse me," said Jake. "I've got to make a call."

The deputy stepped outside the church and called Zeb to let him know the daughter of Angus and Lily McGinty was going to be speaking about the Klondyke 1 mine incident on Rez radio in about fifteen minutes. Zeb had just picked up Echo for lunch.

"Thanks for the heads up, Jake," said Zeb, ending his call with Jake.

"What's going on?" asked Echo.

"Change of plans. How do you feel about a Sonic burger?"

"I can eat one. Why?"

"We need to listen to the radio while we eat. That might be a little bit difficult at the Town Talk," replied Zeb.

"What's on Rez radio this time of day? Isn't it usually *Trade Time*?"

"What's *Trade Time*?" asked Zeb.

"People have stuff they don't need and they offer it up for trade. Say you needed some firewood and had some old tools you didn't use anymore. You offer to exchange the tools for firewood. Good old fashioned barter. *Trade Time* has the highest ratings of any of the shows on the station. You wouldn't believe some of the stuff people trade. One time a woman traded ten bowling balls, a pair of bowling shoes, a bowling shirt and a bowling trophy for a half dozen ducks and some new lingerie."

"Sounds like somebody gave her husband the boot and decided to find a new man through his stomach and, um, other ways," said Zeb.

"She found a new husband and got rid of the bowling equipment in the same day," replied Echo. "It turned out to be a good deal for her."

Their conversation was interrupted by an announcement from the radio program.

"*Trade Time* on KREZ is going to start a few minutes late today. We are presenting a special report regarding the Klondyke mines. Ela McGinty, daughter of Lily Pherson McGinty and the recently demised Angus McGinty, is a member of ELM..."

"ELM as in Earth Liberation Movement?" asked Echo.

"One and the same. Anyway, Ela is giving a little rally speech on the desecration of the earth by the Danforth-Roerg Mining Company. She's speaking from a church on the Rez," explained Zeb.

"Sort of odd timing, don't you think?" asked Echo. "I mean with her father just having been murdered."

"Death has a strange effect on people."

"Maybe she finally feels free enough to speak in public about what she really feels," replied Echo.

Zeb pulled into the Sonic Burger and hit the order button. He already knew he wanted the #6 and that Echo would choose the #4 special.

"The usual?" Zeb asked Echo. "And hold the onions?"

Echo smiled and nodded. "How about some extra mayo too?"

"May I take your order, Sheriff Hanks?" asked the disembodied voice of a teenager.

"Number six, hold the onions, and a number four with extra mayo, hold the onions on that one too."

"Coming right up."

Echo turned up Zeb's radio. When *Trade Time* disc jockey, Early Bing, reiterated that there was going to be a brief conversation with Ela McGinty, daughter of the largest individual owner of the Klondyke mine shares, the KREZ phones began ringing off the hook. People were mostly complaining about the delay in the *Trade Time* show. However, others asked if they could call in and ask questions after she spoke. The *Trade Time* host announced he would allow questions when Ela was done speaking.

"My name is Ela McGinty. My father died a few days ago at the Klondyke 1 mine. My mother is now the owner of his stock shares, or will be once they are legally transferred. I have several things I want to speak about. I am asking for your help in shutting down the Klondyke 1 mine once and for all. I also want your help to make certain the Klondyke 2 mine never opens. The Klondyke 1 is scarring our Mother Earth and stealing from her what is rightfully hers. The copper should never have been allowed to be dug out of the sacred land in the first place. It is a horrible wrong that must be righted."

"No bones about it, Ela McGinty definitely has an agenda," said Zeb, biting into a Sonic burger.

"She's young and motivated by her beliefs," replied Echo. "Let's listen and see what she has to say. She may have some valid points."

"I am an Apache woman. I am ashamed of what my father has done to strip away Mother Earth, destroy her beauty and rob her of the minerals that were naturally placed on sacred ground belonging to the Apache Nation. I am greatly concerned because the mine has taken billions of gallons of precious water from the Apache Nation. Now that my father is no longer among the living, I am going to use everything in my power to convince my mother to shut down the Klondyke 1 Mine and make certain the Klondyke 2 is never opened near sovereign Apache land. I have hired a lawyer who is an expert in Native people's tribal rights to stop the wealthy mining company from stealing and polluting our water. I speak as an Apache as well as a member of the Earth Liberation Movement. The Earth Liberation Movement is a group of like-minded individuals who wants to save the earth from further destruction and chaos. I, we, need your help. Please come to the radio station and sign a petition that demands my mother return the Klondyke 1 mine to their rightful owners, the Apache Nation. If we work together, we can right this wrong and make the land sacred once and forever more. I thank you and once again remind you to come to the radio station any time in the next week to sign the petition. Power to Mother Earth! Power to the Apache Nation! Power to the People!"

"Right on," added Early Bing. "Every phone line is lit up, so please call back if you get a busy signal. Ela McGinty has promised to answer all your questions. Caller, what is your question?"

"If I sign that petition of yours, will the White man's government come after me and my family?" asked the first caller.

"You have rights," replied Ela. "I have done this before and you are going to have to trust me. They cannot come after you."

"If they do, what are you going to do about it?"

"I will personally put up bail money or hire a lawyer for anyone who is harassed or arrested," replied Ela.

"Okay," replied the caller. "I will be right over to sign the petition. That mine has done nothing but injure good Apache men. My son was killed out there in an accident three years ago."

"How can a petition shut down the Klondyke mine?" asked another caller.

"The power of the people can get things done," replied Ela. "We have solid legal footing to make this happen. We have hired an excellent lawyer to help us. I believe the courts will find in our favor."

"She can't really be that naïve," said Zeb.

"Her heart is in it," said Echo. "Who knows what she can get done? Stranger things have happened."

For the next fifteen minutes, enthusiastic questions came in rapid fire, one after the next. The seeds of a local movement had been planted and appeared to have a good chance of sprouting. After the questions ended, the *Trade Talk* show began. Zeb turned off the radio.

"I have a suspicion we're going to have some outside agitators show up on our doorstep," said Zeb.

"Freedom of speech is a very real thing. It's guaranteed by the Constitution of the United States of America," said Echo.

"I agree with that, but provocative speech that incites people is always trouble," replied Zeb.

"Better to have free speech than not," said Echo. "Why do you think American soldiers keep going to war?"

"I just don't want this turning violent," said Zeb.

"Your job is to keep the peace, isn't it? Just do your job and all will be well."

"I can't control an unruly mob," said Zeb.

"You're getting way ahead of yourself," said Echo. "All she is asking is for people to sign a petition. I will probably sign it myself."

"That's your right," said Zeb. "Since you're dating me, that is going to put some pressure on my office if anyone connects the dots. But if you believe shutting down the mine and having Graham County lose hundreds of jobs is the right thing to do, then go ahead and sign."

"Maybe you'd better talk to Black Bear about how this all works. His mother was very active in the American Indian Movement," said Echo. "She was a major organizer before and after the Wounded Knee incident back in the seventies and eighties."

"And we all know that Wounded Knee was a fiasco and ended poorly for both the Oglala Lakota and the federal government," said Zeb. "Not well at all."

"Some good could also come of this," said Echo. "If Apaches act together as a unified people, we might feel like we have regained our dignity and maybe even have a true voice in affairs that affect us."

"While killing the economy of Graham County."

"Maybe an agreement can be reached," said Echo. "Didn't I read that the mine will only operate for another thirty or forty years at the most?"

"That's one of the rumors that I've heard too," replied Zeb.

"Maybe an agreement involving reclaiming the land and money, of course, can bring this to an end peacefully," said Echo.

Zeb reached over and kissed Echo.

"Thanks for being the voice of reason," said Zeb. "Sometimes I need to hear that."

"That's part of the reason I love you," said Echo. "You know you're not perfect."

Zeb knew that fact all too well.

18

LILY AND ELA

The BMW i8 breezed into the driveway of Lily McGinty's mansion without so much as a tap on the brakes. The driver, Ela McGinty, took one last hit on her marijuana cigarette and tossed the butt out the window. She spoke aloud to herself.

"Feels weird being home."

Dressed like the hippie chick she embodied, Ela bounced up the front stairs and twisted the door handle only to find it was locked tight. She rang the bell. A young man in a bathing suit answered.

"Hey," he said. "Whazzup?"

"I'm looking for my mother, Lily. Is she here?"

"Oh, man, now I recognize you. You're the one in those pictures on the fireplace mantle. Hey, come on in. After all, it's your house."

"Not really," replied Ela. "I lived here in another lifetime."

"Cool."

"My mom?"

"She's changing. We just got done taking a dip in the pool. Hey, want to freshen up with a swim?"

"Who are you again?" asked Ela.

"I work for your mother doing odds and ends. Shame about your old man. Sorry."

"It's all right, we weren't that tight," said Ela.

"Still, he was your dad."

"Maybe," replied Ela.

The young stud looked puzzled. Ela surmised it was the natural expression that hung on his face.

"You in town for the funeral? Heard you live up in California. Cool."

"Yes, yes and California is a cool place."

"I heard you on Rez radio. Nice job. I never thought about it the way you described it. I just thought it was people pulling copper out of the ground for copper pipes and shit like that. You got me thinking, maybe the earth is getting destroyed. Can a white dude sign the petition?"

"Yes, you can. In fact, you should."

"I dig what you're trying to do. I'll put John Adams on your petition."

"John Hancock," interjected Ela, correcting his faux pas.

Her response was met by a completely perplexed expression.

"Who are you talking to, Damien?" Lily's voice came from somewhere in the upstairs catacombs of the mansion she called home.

"Your daughter is here. She's pretty rad. I was talking about signing her petition against the copper mine."

"You might want to reconsider that if you enjoy your lifestyle," said Lily. "Tell Ela I'm getting dressed and will be right down."

"Your mom will be..."

"I heard her, Damien."

"Cool. Drink?"

"Vodka on the rocks," said Ela.

"You want the good stuff?"

"Of course. Better make mine a double."

"You are just like your mother."

Damien made three vodka doubles as Lily made an entrance down the winding staircase. Damien raced the drink over to Lily. She dismissed him with a flick of the wrist.

"I dig it," said Damien. "A little mother daughter time. Cool. I'll be by the pool if you need me."

"I see the local chapter of MENSA is sending out their best and brightest to help you run the place," said Ela.

"He works hard," replied Lilly. "Someone has to do the maintenance around here."

"What's he maintaining other than the pool...you?"

"Don't get catty with me. You may be a woman, but you're also my daughter. Show a little respect. After all, we just lost Angus."

A stony silence hung in the air between mother and daughter. Ela's eyes tossed daggers. Lily carried a defensive posture. They sipped their Kors Vodka, alternately looking at and away from each other. Each waited for the other to speak first.

"I hated that you turned Dad into a monster," said Ela. "He could have been a good and charitable man if it weren't for you."

"That's a load of crap and you know it. I didn't turn him into anything. He was born the way he was and, because of the way he lived his life, his death was fitting," replied Lily.

"Bullshit. You know damn good and well that every time you two got into it, I ended up the punching bag. He hit me so many times when he was mad at you that I couldn't even count them all if I tried."

Lily's mind raced. It was true. Ela had taken the brunt of any anger Angus had intended for Lily.

"Why don't you blame him then? After all, he was the one who hit you," said Lily.

"He would never have laid a hand on me if it hadn't been for you."

"You've got it backwards. I was just trying to protect you. Why do you think I sent you away to boarding school? It was for your safety," said Lily.

"Does a single word of truth ever come out your lying mouth? You sent me away so you could have Dad all to yourself. He loved me more than he loved you. You were jealous of me," said Ela.

"He was a spiteful, bitter, angry man. It was dangerous to have you around. He might have killed you."

"Oh, my lord, the lies you tell yourself," said Ela. "He sent me away because you irritated him all the time with your drinking and drug taking. He wanted to protect me from that. Besides, when he hit me, it was out of love."

Lily looked at her daughter, realizing she had no idea how her mind worked or who she was.

"I won't argue with you about what I know to be the truth. Your father was out of control and you were the object of his hatred. You weren't even his natural child."

There, Lily had finally said it aloud. With the force of a violent sea behind it, her hatred and anger about Ela came storming out. She had wanted to tell someone this awful truth for years. Somewhere in the confusion of letting out a longheld secret came an odd sort of relief. Ela was likely not the biological daughter of Angus McGinty. Lily had slept around so much at that time in her life she didn't know who the real father was. She was, however, fairly certain it wasn't Angus. Even then he was usually so drunk he rarely completed the act of love making. The sexual part of their marriage had been a sham, forced upon her by Angus's impotence.

Ela slowly picked up her drink. She turned away from her mother and, without warning, suddenly spun around and fired the glass of vodka at her mother. The tumbler struck a glancing blow off the top of Lily's head.

"I fucking hate you. You are a liar, a cheat, a drunk and a drug addict. Who could possibly love you? Dad, my one and only real father, Angus McGinty, never loved you. He even wrote me that in a letter. He told me that you would lie to me one day and claim that I wasn't his daughter. I have the letter to prove it. You are evil. I hope you rot in hell."

Ela stormed out the door. Lily checked in the mirror to see if the glancing blow of the vodka glass had mussed her hair. Then she poured herself another drink, slowly walked to the safe and pulled out a copy of Angus's final will and testament. Lily had been shocked to learn Angus had updated his will only thirty days before his demise. She paged through the updated version of his will. Reading it made her blood begin to boil.

19

—————

PREPARATION

Years of experience had taught Zeb there was much to be learned at a funeral. In the best case scenario, the killer would show their face. More likely, some small piece of evidence might be found that could tie loose threads of evidence together.

Zeb gathered his team at the sheriff's office to coordinate assignments for the funeral. Already several threats to blow up what little remained of Angus, or in some other way desecrate the funeral ceremony, had been phoned in. The threats were all anonymous. Most of them sounded like angry diatribes aimed at a man who was already dead. Still, they had to be taken seriously. Zeb knew there would be hell to pay, not to mention statewide publicity, if someone did something crazy at the funeral.

"Who wants to keep an eye on the parking lot?" asked Zeb, holding up a newly purchased Nikon D3300 digital camera. "I've got a half dozen lenses to go with it? What am I bid for the spy job?"

It was quiet for a very long thirty seconds before Black Bear spoke.

"I'm a bit of a camera buff, or at least I have been in the past. I really don't know too many people around here yet, so I'll probably end up shooting everything and anything that looks out of the ordinary."

"That could cover a lot of turf at this funeral," said Jake.

Everyone laughed.

"Good, the camera job is yours," said Zeb. "Take pictures of everything, even the ordinary."

"Anyone specifically I should be looking for?"

"No, follow your gut and your training. Angus had so many enemies that you just never know who might want to throw a monkey wrench into the works. Someone might want to try and mess with Angus in death because they couldn't mess with him when he was alive," added Zeb.

"Got it. Thank Wakhan Thanka for digital cameras," said Black Bear.

"Wakhan Thanka?" asked Kate.

"Wakhan Thanka is Lakota for God. It's a joke. I'm grateful for digital cameras so I don't have to put my hands in messy chemicals to develop the pictures," said Black Bear.

"Clever," said Jake.

"They're proven carcinogens," replied Black Bear.

"Okay. I'll cover inside the funeral parlor with Jake and Kate," said Zeb.

"Sounds good," said Kate. Jake nodded in agreement.

Zeb turned to Black Bear as he thought of one more thing.

"Continue to take pictures at the burial. I would use a telephoto lens and stay on the east side of the mausoleum."

"Can do," replied Black Bear. "I take it the idea is for me not to be seen by anyone?"

"Right," replied Zeb.

"Anyone in particular or everyone in general?"

"Do your best to stay out of sight. People tend to wander off and visit other graves, both before and after a funeral. Be aware others might be around who could see you."

Black Bear nodded. He took it as Zeb's way of advising him to be as invisible as humanly possible.

"The rest of us will mingle at the burial. Keep an eye out for anyone who looks like they don't belong or who is known to have grudges against Angus or the McGinty family. A double tap on the walkie-talkie with hand tap over the heart will be the signal to Black Bear to zoom in on the person we think might be suspicious. So, Black Bear, you're going to have three sets of eyes."

"Roger that, double tap and a hand over the heart is the signal," replied Black Bear. "One question, Zeb? Why all the cloak and dagger stuff? After all, we're in uniform and people will recognize us instantly."

"Angus had so many enemies that we want to get as many camera shots as possible for later. It's what we might see but not recognize that's important at the funeral and burial. Later on we might identify something as important in the pictures you'll be taking," explained Zeb.

"One more question," said Black Bear. "Have you used this method successfully in the past?"

Zeb stared a hole in Black Bear. His innocent enough question tripped Zeb's anger switch. How dare Black Bear question his reasoning in front of the entire department?

"Hell yes. More than once."

"Sorry. I was just asking. I'm new. This is a different style than I have used in the past, that's all."

Zeb realized he had vented for no reason and quickly backpedaled.

"It's good to ask. I'm glad you brought it up. I should have explained my reasoning from the onset. Angus, among his other traits, was a sly dog. He may have even planned for what happened after his death if he was murdered. He may have some hired guns planted among the mourners looking for his killer."

"Do you really think Angus was that clever and forward thinking?" asked Black Bear.

"I know he was. Even though he technically had nothing to do with my re-election campaigns, his fingerprints, through Lily, were all over them. He kept anyone who could possibly beat me in an election from running against me. He knew how to forward think."

Kate and Jake exchanged a look. The backpedaling from Black Bear's question and the confession that there were shady dealings related to his re-elections were unusual. Zeb was never one for backpedaling. That seemed odd. Also, Kate and Jake knew nothing of Zeb's belief that Angus McGinty had some unseen designs on how Zeb's campaigns were handled. Without saying a word, both knew something strange was going on with their boss.

"The funeral is at the Kimble Funeral Home at eleven a.m. Be there a good half hour beforehand. Any questions?"

"Do you expect this ELM group to make an appearance?" asked Kate.

"I suspect they might protest or try and pull something off. They haven't applied for a protest permit, so I can't say for certain if they'll make an appearance. But I can bet that all of you will recognize them if they show up."

Coming from a long line of protestors and as one who believed in the right to protest, Black Bear took umbrage.

"Are you insinuating they will look like riff-raff?" he asked.

"You'll know them when you see them," said Zeb, sounding more like his regular self. "That is what I'm saying. Do you have trouble with that?"

Black Bear said nothing. He didn't care much for Zeb's tone. This was not the time nor place to mix it up about protests, even funeral protests.

20

SERVICE

A small number of people began showing up a half hour before eleven. Black Bear snapped a photo of every single person, their vehicles and license plates. On several occasions he picked up the double tap on the mic with the hand over the heart signal from the others. He made mental notes on these people and which of his coworkers had signaled for the photo.

Shortly thereafter, Lily and her daughter arrived. They were in separate cars and a few minutes apart. Lily got there first. A handsome, well-dressed young man who appeared to be in his thirties acted as her chauffeur. Ela arrived second. She was accompanied by three others, two young women who were practically clones of Ela and a young man who, by his dress and mannerisms, appeared to be from a moneyed background. Black Bear immediately assumed the young man was from higher up the food chain of ELM.

Over the next fifteen minutes another fifty to sixty people entered the Kimble Funeral Home. Some of the men were obviously executives from the mining company. The rest seemed to be a mish mash of mine workers, friends of the family and a few locals who were probably funeral gawkers.

As is traditional in the rural area, everyone was dressed in their best black funereal wear. Black Bear considered how differently the Whites looked at the passage from this life to the next. He pondered where the tradition of darkness in their clothing came from. It seemed oddly juxtaposed when he considered that the people who passed were returning to the light.

Angus's ashes were fittingly inside a burnished copper urn. It had been placed front and center on a table that was covered by a white cloth with gold gilt edging. The vessel was surrounded by four hand-made burning candles. On one side of the table was a large, professionally photographed head shot of Angus McGinty. On the other side was an equally large facial image emblazoned in copper. The artist made a true to life representation by using a technique that perfectly showed the wrinkled lines on Angus's face.

Lily was standing at the end of the table on one side of the urn greeting people. Ela stood on the opposite side. Lily wore a veil; Ela did not.

Zeb and Kate, dressed in uniform, approached Lily.

"My condolences," said Zeb. "I know this is a rough time."

Lily drew close to Zeb. Her actions let him know that he should lean in to hear her speak. She held her hand next to her mouth and whispered a question in Zeb's ear.

"What have you found out about Angus's murderer?"

Though Zeb towered over her, he leaned even closer to answer her somewhat out of place and untimely query.

"We're working on it constantly," replied Zeb. "We should have something soon."

In the next breath, Lily's voice became demanding rather than demure.

"I funded your campaign practically by myself. I expect something done quickly. My anticipation is that you will find his killer very soon. Don't let me down, Zeb. It would be very bad timing."

Zeb knew this demanding side of his benefactress. In fact, he had presumed she would say something at the gathering. He pressed his hands one above and one below her palm, cupping it gently and firmly.

"I won't let you down. I will find out who did this to Angus."

With that he moved on. Zeb walked to one of several picture boards of the late Angus McGinty. He perused them half in curiosity and half in the hope that they might contain a stray piece of evidence. While doing so he considered Lily's veiled threat. What did she mean it would be very bad timing?

Kate followed in line, offering her condolences to Lily.

"I am sorry to hear about your husband," said Kate. "It's a horrible tragedy."

Lily gripped Kate's hands with her own. They interlocked eyes.

"Being a newly married woman, I'm sure you can understand what I'm going through. I hope something like this never happens to you," said Lily. "It's a terrible thing."

Kate's mind wandered briefly to her husband, Josh Diamond. They were only months into their marriage. They were growing closer every day, learning each other's daily ways and secrets. Kate had quit taking her birth control pills. There was much said and unsaid between them about having a child. Kate knew Angus and Lily had been together twenty-five years. She couldn't even begin to fathom all she and Josh would go through over the next twenty-five years.

"I can't begin to imagine your loss," said Kate.

Lily tightened her grip on Kate's hands, practically digging her fingernails into Kate's palms.

"Love is eternal," said Lily. "Angus will always live in my heart."

"Of course," replied Kate. "Best of luck today and in the upcoming days."

"Thank you, Kate. Your words are so kind."

As Kate began to walk away, Lily beckoned her back.

"Yes," said Kate.

"I've found out something that might aid your investigation. Would you stop by the house later today?"

The timing struck Kate as odd.

"Are you sure you want me to stop by today?" asked Kate.

"Yes, absolutely," replied Lily.

"If that's what you want, I'll stop by. What time would work for you?"

"I'm going directly home after the burial. Let's say three o'clock?"

"I'll see you then," replied Kate.

Next Jake offered his sympathy. Lily accepted it graciously.

"It seems Deputy Black Bear is the only officer not making an official visit," probed Lily.

"He's working on other duties," replied Jake.

"You tell Zeb that if he doesn't treat Black Bear right, I just might hire him as head of security for the mine," said Lily. "I have a particular fondness for that man."

"Yes, ma'am," replied Jake, heading off to mingle among the mourners.

Zeb and Kate approached Ela. They introduced themselves, but she seemed to already know who they were.

"How are you doing?" asked Kate.

"I'm okay," said Ela. "It's tough, but I am okay."

"Take care of yourself and help your mother as much as you can," suggested Kate. "I know it may sound trite, but time really does heal all wounds."

"Thank you," replied Ela. "I do appreciate the sentiment."

Zeb eyed the young daughter of Angus and Lily with as much neutrality as possible. She was young and pretty, but something about her seemed insincere. He couldn't put his finger on exactly what was off. He studied her face. It seemed unlikely she was involved, even peripherally, in the death of her father. Ela smiled at Sheriff Hanks as he held his cowboy hat in his hands.

"Please find my father's killer," she said softly. "I won't rest comfortably until you do. I fear that I might be next."

The curious statement sounded alarm bells in Zeb's head. Had she been threatened? Did she know something she wanted to tell him? What would make her say such a thing?

"Could I have some of your time in the near future?" asked Zeb.

"I'll stop by your office tomorrow morning at ten if that's okay," replied Ela.

Zeb shook her hand and nodded, "Certainly. I'll see you then."

Kate and Zeb moved around the funeral parlor as Jake exchanged a few words with Ela.

"Not a huge turnout," said Zeb.

"I guess people really didn't like him," replied Kate.

"I haven't learned much today. Have you?" asked Zeb.

"Not really," replied Kate.

"Ela wants to come in and talk tomorrow," said Zeb. "I think she knows something. What that something is I can't say. She seems a bit fearful that she could be next."

"Not outside the realm of a normal reaction when a family member is murdered," said Kate.

"I suppose," replied Zeb.

"Lily gave me the okay, actually, she invited me to come to her house after the burial," said Kate.

"See what you can find. If you can find anything that links Lily to the murder, no matter how obtuse, it will be helpful," said Zeb.

Jake tapped Zeb on the shoulder, interrupting his conversation with Kate.

"The funeral director is about to say something."

"Friends of Angus McGinty, please be seated," began the funeral director.

Jake took a seat with the fifty or so others whom had gathered at the funeral home. Zeb and Kate stood in the shadows ten feet behind the last row of chairs.

"I have been asked by the family of the late Angus McGinty to say a few words about him. When I'm done, any or all of you are welcome to step up to the podium and say something."

The funeral director cleared his throat, pulled a piece of paper out of his pocket and began reading directly from it. Clearly, he hadn't known Angus.

"Angus McGinty was an important man in the local business community. As the Executive Director of the Klondyke Copper Mine Number One, he oversaw five hundred employees. His business acumen kept many good men and women employed. His unfortunate and untimely death came too soon. While alive he donated heavily to many charitable and political organizations. He was a member of the local Kiwanis Club, Chamber of Commerce, served on the hospital and school boards at various times in his life and was a Freemason. His charming wife, Lily, and his lovely daughter, Ela, will carry on his legacy. Let us bow our heads in a moment of silence for Angus McGinty."

The funeral director neatly folded the piece of paper on which his short speech was written and placed it back inside his black suit. He scanned the audience before asking.

"Would anyone like to step up and say a few words?"

Utter silence ensued. No one even shuffled in their seats. The funeral director, obviously used to this type of reaction, remained still and at ease. He waited an appropriate amount of time before speaking again.

"Please enjoy the pictures of Angus and his family as well as the video the family has put together from family vacations, holidays and birthdays. The burial will be private."

People stayed only briefly. Within half an hour only the funeral director, Lily, Ela, Angus's lawyer and an executive from the mines remained.

Zeb, Jake and Kate headed back to the office. Ela and Lily, who had arrived in separate cars, left in separate cars. Ela and the family lawyer rode together. Lily and the mine executive from Danforth-Roerg paired together in the other car. Both, however, headed to the cemetery.

Lily and Ela's worlds were about to change in unimaginable ways.

21

WHAT'S YOURS IS MINE

"Lily, I'm afraid I have something to discuss with you that you may not want to hear." The president of the Danforth-Roerg Mining Company had delivered all kinds of news in his tenure. Today, however, was different.

"Oh, don't worry about it," replied Lily. "Angus brought me up to date on the copper situation in Chile and China. I will be much easier to deal with than Angus concerning that. My intention is to have a long-term view of copper price fluctuations. I don't really plan on doing much with day to day operations. However, I do plan to remain on the executive board."

"Well, Lily, I am going to cut right to the chase. I know you are a very direct, no-nonsense woman."

"I consider that a compliment," replied Lily, crossing her gloved hands on her lap.

"In recent months Angus came to me with a succession plan. You know forty-nine percent of the company is in his name."

"I am well aware of the numbers."

"Angus was concerned that having so much responsibility for mining operations would be more than you would want to take on.

He said that you had helped him so much and worked so hard that he wanted you to retire in luxury."

"I know I don't like where this is heading," replied Lily. "But it matters not. I have already seen the changes Angus made to his will. I assume that is where this is leading."

"Yes. And your intentions are what?"

"I am going to fight like hell to get the new will suppressed and have the old will re-instated. Angus was a drug addicted alcoholic. He was not of sound mind when he made the changes. In fact, I have security tape of him making notes on the old will and changing it. He made them at home, at his desk. I specifically kept that tape because of this very possibility. The security tape shows him consuming significant amounts of alcohol and taking illegal drugs while he was making those changes. I have already shown the tape to my lawyer. He said it's solid evidence of Angus's state of mind when he changed his will and took from me what is rightfully mine."

"You're going to contest the will even though he left you all the property, mutual holdings and over ten million in cash?"

"Hell yes," replied Lily.

The president of Danforth-Roerg gazed out the car window across the open desert. This was a battle neither he nor anyone at the company wanted. He had no option except to somehow stop Lily from making this a public brawl. Glancing into the side view mirror, he imagined how the meeting between the family business lawyer and Ela McGinty was going. More than that he wondered how Ela, with her rabid radical background, would be reacting. When it was all said and done, he knew Lily would be the proverbial tempest in a teapot.

"Ela," the lawyer's tone was all business. "I have some news for you."

"Yes?"

"I really don't know what you're going to think."

"For God's sake just spit it out. The day has been weird enough as it is," replied Ela.

"A month or so ago your father changed his will. As you know he owns forty-nine percent of the stock in the Klondyke 1 mine. He also has one hundred percent ownership to the rights of the tentatively named Klondyke 2 mine near the San Carlos Reservation."

"I've been made aware of the Klondyke 2 travesty," snarled Ela. "My father had zero respect for Mother Earth."

"You may not be aware of all the particulars involved," said the lawyer.

"What do I need to know other than everything goes to my mother. I don't agree with what my late father and my mother have in mind with the Klondyke mines, but, as I understand it, I have no say in anything regarding that," said Ela.

"Ela, circumstances have changed. The situation is not as you might suppose it to be," said the lawyer.

"What situation?"

"When your father changed his will, he left all his mine holdings, future mine holdings and a substantial sum of money to you. I will be honest with you. I advised against his plan. My suggestion was to put in place a graduated trust that would give you your inheritance over a ten-year period. Your father was a stubborn man. He would have no part of my recommendation. He wanted you to immediately carry on his legacy."

"Does my mother know about this?"

"I believe she's being told right now."

Ela's mind began spinning. She thought of her mother's anger, her father's gift and the goals of ELM. In truth, she thought mostly of herself. The allure of great power and money overwhelmed everything else.

"I don't believe my mother will take this lying down," said Ela.

"Perhaps the two of you can hammer out an agreement that serves everyone."

"Ha! I don't have even a vague recollection of the last time my mother and I saw eye to eye."

"We all need to act like reasonable adults," said the lawyer. "If not for the sake of your family, for the future of the mine."

"It isn't going to happen. My mother will dig in for war. She's probably already devising a plan for battle. I want you to know that my mother cannot, under even the best of circumstances, be trusted," said Ela.

"It's important that there be some middle ground," said the lawyer. "It's best for everyone. Not just you and your mother, but all the workers at the mine, the potential workers at the new mine and the townspeople. The future of Graham County may well hang in the balance."

"You're asking me to play nice while my mother goes ballistic?" asked Ela. "She may even be plotting my demise at this very moment."

"I think you're being a bit dramatic, Ela."

"You don't know my mother."

"I think you should look at this with open eyes," replied the lawyer.

"Even though it goes against the grain of everything I believe in?"

"Your inheritance changes your world. You are now, quite literally, holding the future of many people in your hands. My advice is not to make any rash decisions."

The two black limousines pulled into the graveyard. Lily and the Danforth-Roerg executive stepped out first. Ela and the family attorney departed the other. The casket had been placed on a move-able gurney above the open ground that would become Angus's place of permanent internment. As the Lily and Ela approached the grave, they exchanged an icy glance. A second later the two sets of eyes stared into the hole in the ground. A slight wind, rising from the southeast, brushed their faces.

The funeral director broke the uneasy silence with a cough, followed by a few final words.

"A man enters the world alone and alone he departs. May the good Lord above accept Angus McGinty into his eternal flock."

Black Bear snapped a few long-distance photos while doing his best to keep out of sight of any graveyard wanderers. Lily and Ela didn't stick around for the internment. Each returned to her respective car with the man who had brought them. The small procession of two limousines headed back to the Kimble Funeral Home. At the funeral parlor, the president of Danforth-Roerg and the McGinty family attorney exited their respective vehicles. Immediately they formed a two-man huddle.

"We're going to have a battle on our hands," said the Danforth-Roerg executive.

"Yes, negotiations are going to be tough," said the lawyer. "Given all that has happened, it will take some time. But I do believe ultimately an arrangement can be made."

"What sort of an arrangement?"

"Leave the details to me," said the lawyer. "I'm certain I can arrange something we can all live with."

The two men watched as the limousines carrying Lily and Ela pulled out of the parking lot.

22

MCGINTY MANSION

Kate glanced at her watch. It was only minutes before three p.m., the time of her designated meeting with Lily McGinty. Kate pulled into the arced driveway and parked her police truck. The second she opened her vehicle door she could hear hollering. It didn't sound like a normal screaming match between a mother and daughter. The shrieking was bathed in hatred and dripping with animosity. Kate quickly approached the house. She glanced through the edge of the picture window. Lily and Ela were facing each other while slowly circling the main room. The scene reminded Kate of an old western shootout. However, in this case, neither held a gun. Each woman gripped a knife. Kate could easily hear every word through the open window as she unholstered her weapon and clicked off the safety.

"I told you Dad hated you. He could barely tolerate being around you," shouted Ela. "Why do you think he worked all the time?"

"He was my husband and you turned him against me ... you ... you whore."

Ela made an odd guttural sound before responding with great deliberation.

"Don't make me laugh. You poisoned him against yourself with your constant nagging and bitching and drinking and cheating and lying!"

"We had an agreement about all of that," said Lily. "I didn't do anything he didn't do. Your father was not the saint you've made him out to be."

"He probably wasn't perfect, but at least he wasn't you," said Ela, lunging deftly at her mother with the knife. Lily easily stepped away from the attempted blow.

To Kate, the interaction was as much of a dance as it was a knife fight. Nevertheless, Kate barged through the front door, gun drawn.

"My daughter just tried to kill me," shouted Lily. "Arrest her."

"Why don't both of you put down your knives? There's no reason for bloodshed," said Kate.

"The hell there isn't," said Lily. "This spoiled little brat of a daughter of mine just ruined my life."

"Put down the knives, ladies," said Kate for a second time.

"Not until I draw blood from this piece of shit I once considered my daughter," said Lily.

Keeping the gun in her hand, Kate reached back and, with her open hand, grabbed the night stick that was attached to her belt. The last thing she wanted to do was to shoot Lily or Ela on the day of Angus's burial. Kate sneaked closer to the two women just as Lily lunged. In one quick motion Kate used the night stick to slap the knife from Lily's hand. The wood struck Lily's right hand, making a cracking sound like bones breaking.

Seeing her mother unarmed and injured, Ela flew toward Lily. Kate struck Ela on the back of the right knee. The impact of the night stick caused Ela to crumble to the floor in a heap. In the process, Ela struck her head against a chair. Kate stepped forward and kicked both knives away from the fighting mother and daughter.

"Mind telling me what the hell is going on here?" asked Kate.

Both Ela and Lily began talking so fast Kate couldn't make head nor tails of their hyperbolic gibberish.

"Shut up. Both of you. Lily sit there," said Kate, pointing to the chair with the night stick. "Ela, can you get up to the couch without my assistance?"

Ela was on her knees, but woozy.

"Jesus Christ, why'd you hit me so hard?" Ela asked Kate.

"To save you from twenty years in prison," replied Kate. "Trust me, I did you a favor."

Ela clumsily found her way to the sofa, a safe thirty feet from her mother. Kate tapped on her mic.

"Helen, do you read?"

"Yes, Kate. What can I do for you?' said Helen.

"I am at the McGinty house. I need back up."

"I can send Black Bear right now. He should be there in less than fifteen minutes. Are you good until then?"

"I'm good until then. Wait one second. Send an ambulance. Over and out."

"Do you mind if I have a drink?' asked Lily. "For the pain."

Kate reached into her shirt pocket and pulled out a two pack of aspirin. She handed it to Lily. Lily walked a couple of steps to the bar, grabbed a bottle of water and washed the aspirin down.

"There's an ice pack in the mini-fridge, mind if I grab it?" asked Lily.

"Get me one too," demanded Ela.

"Get it yourself, you little bitch."

"Everyone just calm down," said Kate.

Kate followed Lily to the small refrigerator, making certain she didn't have a weapon stashed there. She didn't.

"Let's all take a minute and chill out," said Kate, handing an ice pack to Lily while grabbing a second one for Ela.

Lily covered her wrist. Ela rubbed her leg and held the ice pack against her knee. For being so vociferous only moments earlier, both were extraordinarily sedate.

Within minutes Black Bear arrived. He raced from his vehicle to the house. From his perspective, except for some apparent bruising, everything appeared to be under control.

"Who won the fight?" he whispered to Kate.

"Bad question to ask," said Kate, pointing at the knives.

"Good old-fashioned Injun fight?" he asked.

"That's not funny," said Kate.

"No, it's not funny, but it's the truth, isn't it?"

Black Bear picked up the knives and placed them away from the women.

"Why don't you take Ela outside and get her side of the story," said Kate. "I'll talk with Lily."

Black Bear politely asked Ela to join him on the porch.

"Can I bring the ice pack? My knee hurts," she said.

Black Bear handed her a couple of aspirin. She chewed them down as they took a seat on the front porch swing.

"Rough day," said Black Bear.

"Fucked up day," replied Ela.

"It's tough losing your father. I'm sorry about that."

"I suppose. We had a different kind of relationship."

"How so?" asked Black Bear.

Instead of hearing about the knife fight, Black Bear got a psychological profile from Ela.

"I got sent away to a very toney boarding school in Switzerland when I was a kid. I was sent away from everything I knew, all my friends, everything I knew and loved."

"That must have been horrible," said Black Bear.

"It was."

"A hundred years ago the government took all the Indian kids in my tribe away from their parents. The Whites made them cut their hair, took away their religion and did everything they could to turn Indian children into White Eyes. We're still recovering from that. In one sense I understand how terrible it was for you, even though I never experienced it myself."

Black Bear's compassion helped ease the pain of the circumstance.

"You seem like you might understand," said Ela.

"Explain it to me and let's see if I do," said Black Bear.

"When I got sent away, I thought it was my fault. I was certain it was because of something I did wrong. When I was older, I became angry and decided that it was only partially my fault. It was difficult for me. I had to have years of therapy to realize I was the victim."

Black Bear nodded.

"My parents have hated each other for as long as I can remember," continued Ela. "God only knows what held them together. Probably the mutual disdain for each other. About the only thing I know for certain was that they taught me how to hate. I have terribly mixed feelings about that."

"You feel bad about the feelings you have inside?" asked Black Bear.

"Yes and no. I don't like to feel hatred. But if and when it rises up and I can use it for something constructive, I feed on it like a shark drawn to blood."

"Do you act out on that rage often?" asked Black Bear.

"Not often. Probably because I've seen so little of my parents. But my hatred toward my mother rose up today when I confronted her about my late father."

"What happened?"

"She was pissed off that my dad left me his ownership in the Klondyke 1 mine and the property for the Klondyke 2. She was so angry she claimed I wasn't even his natural born child. I assume she is laying the groundwork for a legal battle. I assume she wants the mine in her name. I don't even want the damn thing. I hate everything it represents.

Black Bear sensed an opportunity. He opened his iPhone to an image of Angus McGinty's killer holding up an official looking piece of stationery with the ELM logo that read, "Angus McGinty Destroyer Of Nature."

Seeing her father in the background, pegged to the ground like some sort of sacrificial animal, Ela shrieked out a deathly, inhuman squeal. She broke into tears as her mother and Deputy Kate Steele came rushing out of the house.

"What's going on here?" shouted Lily.

Lily made no attempt to console her daughter. She asked coolly, "Are you okay?"

"Hell no, I'm not okay," shouted Ela.

She grabbed Black Bear's cell phone and shoved the image of a staked down and about to flattened Angus McGinty in her mother's face. Lily stared at the image in disbelief and resignation.

Ela flew from the porch swing she shared with Black Bear. Leaping through the air, she grabbed her mother by the hair and pulled her to the ground. She got in a half-dozen face punches before Kate and Black Bear could separate mother and daughter.

Black Bear snapped his cuffs on Ela and put her in the patrol car.

"What the hell are you doing, Deputy?" yelled the bloody-faced Lily.

"She's going to jail for assault," replied Black Bear.

"No, she's not," retorted Lily. "I am not going to embarrass my family by pressing charges on Angus's funeral day. Let her go. Now!"

Kate glared at Black Bear. He quickly realized it was poor judgement on his part to have shown Ela the picture of her father about to be crushed to death. But he did learn two things. The heart beating in Lily's chest carried little compassion, and crocodile tears flowed easily from Ela's eyes.

"Let her go," ordered Kate.

Black Bear hesitated. "I was..."

"Uncuff her," ordered Kate.

Black Bear did as instructed. Ela and Lily walked hesitatingly toward each other. When they were within arm's reach, they simultaneously jumped on each other and began to fight like wild animals.

"Black Bear, grab Ela. I'll grab Lily," shouted Kate.

The deputies separated the women. This time both were placed in handcuffs as they continued to curse and spit at each other. Kate placed Lily in her vehicle. Black Bear helped Ela into the back of his truck. Once the women were secured in the separate vehicles, Black Bear walked over to Kate.

"We should have let them duke it out," said Black Bear. "They've both been holding their hatred in for so long that it might have been cathartic for them to fight it out."

"I don't think so," replied Kate.

"If they don't knock the living daylights out of each other in front of someone, one of them is going to end up dead," said Black Bear.

"Then we're going to have keep them apart until things calm down," replied Kate.

"I don't think that's going to happen," said Black Bear.

"Let's take them into town and let them think about it overnight in a jail cell," said Kate.

"Right."

"I hate to do it today, considering they just put a family member in the ground, but we have to."

Kate did a U-turn. As her vehicle passed by Black Bear's, Ela shouted through the cracked window at her mother.

"You killed my father. I know you did. You'll end up paying for this."

"You're as crazy as he was," shouted back Lily.

"Did you hear that Deputy Black Bear?" asked Ela calmly.

"Hear what?"

"My mother didn't deny killing my father."

Black Bear drove on in silence. Ela was correct. Lily did not deny killing Angus.

23

ZEB'S OFFICE

H elen buzzed Zeb's office.

"Zeb, I think you ought to see this."

"What is it?"

"It's something you're going to want to see with your own eyes," replied Helen.

Zeb pushed his chair back, walked across his office, opened the door and eyed Helen. She nudged her pointer finger twice down the long hallway that led to the county jail cells. Instantly he recognized his deputies and their respective perps.

"What's that all about?"

"Lily was holding a swollen wrist. Ela was limping badly. Domestic dispute is my guess," said Helen.

"I was hoping they would remain civil to each other for at least a few days," said Zeb.

"We don't always get what we wish for. Might I suggest you go straighten that mess out," said Helen. "I think it is one of those situations that requires your input."

"This is bad timing. Did anyone else see what you saw?" asked Zeb.

Helen gave Zeb a puzzled look.

"I mean did anyone see Black Bear and Kate bringing in Lily and Ela?"

"Kate and Black Bear brought them in through the ground floor side entrance, so I doubt it," replied Helen.

Zeb was halfway down the hall headed to the jail cells by the time Helen finished speaking. The women were locked in separate cells as far apart as possible, which wasn't much considering there were only four cells.

"What the hell happened?" asked Zeb.

Kate turned and looked in Black Bear's direction. She spoke first.

"I broke up a knife fight between mother and daughter," said Kate.

"Crap," replied Zeb.

"At least it wasn't a gun fight," said Black Bear.

"Thank God for small favors," replied Zeb.

"I called Black Bear immediately once I had the situation under control. He arrived within ten minutes. We separated the women and talked to them separately," said Kate. "Then..."

"Then I made a mistake," said Black Bear, pulling out his cell phone. "I showed this to Ela. I flashed the ELM letterhead hoping she wouldn't see her father staked out in the background, but she saw him and went crazy. She accused her mother of killing her father."

Zeb eyed his deputies. Black Bear had indeed screwed up. It was the second time he had screwed up on this case already. First, by sleeping with Lily, repeatedly, and now by flashing Ela the image of her father being tortured to death.

"I assume something came out of the debriefing?" asked Zeb.

"I wasn't finished with Lily," said Kate. "I'd like to continue with her now."

"Take her to the interrogation room. Record everything," said Zeb.

"Will do," replied Kate.

"Black Bear, bring Ela to my office."

"Yes, sir."

Zeb was irate with Black Bear. He thanked the good lord that

Echo had been working with him on understanding his emotional reactions. He was learning that instant reaction can bring instant trouble and distrust, especially with a new team member.

Kate waited for Black Bear to remove Ela from her cell before taking Lily to the interrogation room. She got them both coffee.

"Not such a great day," said Kate.

"I've had worse. It's practically nothing compared to days I've had with Angus and that activist slut I used to call a daughter," replied Lily.

"Emotions, both yours and hers, are running high," said Kate.

"Could I get a drink? I mean you must have some booze stashed around the office, don't you?" asked Lily. "I gave the sheriff a case of damned expensive whiskey when he won the election."

"He rarely drinks. The whiskey you gave him is probably gathering dust in his basement. But, no matter, you can't have any alcohol," said Kate.

"Then how about a couple more aspirin? I'm hurting everywhere. My so-called daughter has a nasty right hook and you swing a club pretty good yourself."

Lily held up her swollen wrist.

"Can you move it?" asked Kate.

Lily rotated her wrist in a circle and flexed it back and forth.

"I guess, but it hurts like crazy."

"You want Doc to look at it?"

Lily moved it around some more.

"No. It's not broken. I don't need the hassle. I would take a couple of aspirin, if you would be so kind?"

Kate handed her two extra-strength Excedrin. Lily downed them with her coffee.

"We were talking back at your house..."

"Yes, there were several things about Angus's death that I haven't told you. They are things I think you should know."

"The penny that was found in Angus's hand," said Lily.

"The 1909 SVDB. I understand it's quite valuable."

"I assume it is. He kept fifty of them on display, under lock and key. I remember him asking me about them only a few days before he was killed. He said one of them was missing. I told him he still had forty-nine so why worry? He got upset and accused me of stealing one of them. I guess he has the only complete roll of fifty uncirculated 1909 SVDB pennies in the world."

"Who had the key to the display case?" asked Kate.

"I've got one somewhere, I think. But I couldn't tell you where it was to save my life. Angus gave Ela a key a long time ago. He didn't know that I knew about it. He gave her a set of keys to all his important things when she turned sixteen."

"You think the 1909 SVDB is from Angus's collection?"

"There's an easy way to tell. All fifty coins had the same error. The B in the SVDB has a shadow. Angus called it an umbra B. It was a printing error. He claimed that is what made them extra valuable. All you have to do is compare the one you found in his hand to the forty-nine others in the roll."

Kate made a note. "Okay, I'll check it out."

"I'd bet anything somebody planted it there to make me look guilty," said Lily.

"Does anyone else know about Ela's key?"

"Only Hector Jorgenson, the locksmith. He knew about it," said Lily.

"He passed away last year, didn't he?" asked Kate. "Seems I remember that."

"Yes, he passed. Long before Hector died, Angus had him make one of a kind locks for his collection. The locks all look different in terms of design, but the same key fits them all."

"Makes the coin pretty damning evidence against you, doesn't it?" asked Kate.

Lily pounded the table. "I didn't kill Angus. I swear by all that's holy and unholy. I hated the man at times, but I loved him too. We fought like a street cat cornered by a junkyard dog. But you must believe me when I tell you that I would never kill the son of a bitch. No man alive is worth going to prison for."

A wave of nausea rushed over Kate. She felt like vomiting.

Breaking into a sudden, profuse sweat, she excused herself. She passed by Zeb as she made her way down the hallway.

"You okay?" he asked. "You look sick."

"I'm fine. Just woozy from something. I think I need something to eat. Do you think Lily will be okay in there for fifteen minutes by herself?" asked Kate.

"She'll be fine. The camera is running. I'll be watching. Go get something to eat."

"Where's Ela? I thought you were talking to her?" asked Kate.

"Doc Yackley is checking her out. I want to make sure she doesn't have a concussion. If she has a minor brain injury, anything she says would be inadmissible as evidence. Get a quick bite. By the time you're done, Doc Yackley should be too."

Fifteen minutes later Kate walked back into the interrogation room, feeling better.

"I thought you'd forgotten about me. Actually, I was hoping you had," said Lily.

"You said you had two things you wanted to tell me," said Kate.

"About a month ago, almost exactly a month ago, Angus got a threatening letter. It said his life was in danger if he opened up Klondyke 2."

"Who was the letter from?" asked Kate.

"I don't know."

"Did you see the postmark?"

"I did."

"Where was it from?"

"When am I going to get out of here?" asked Lily.

"Are you trying to make a deal with me?" asked Kate.

"I most certainly am," replied Lily. "You know you don't have enough evidence to hold me. If you think you do, my lawyer will have me out of here within the hour. I am here merely to cooperate. Besides, I need a drink."

"Let me talk to Sheriff Hanks," said Kate.

Lily shooed Deputy Kate away with a sweep of the hand. Five minutes later Kate returned.

"Where was the letter mailed from?"

"Did Zeb agree to my request?" asked Lily.

"He did. First you have to give us the location," said Kate.

"Tucson," replied Lily. "I'll even throw in the zip code for free. It was 85706. I looked it up. It's the zip code for the Tucson airport."

Kate held the door open for Lily.

"I'm sure we'll talk again soon," said Kate.

"Perhaps," replied Lily. "But next time my lawyer will do my talking for me."

24

ELA

Doc Yackley escorted Ela into Zeb's office.

"She's a bit lightheaded from all the action. She took a pretty good knock to the noggin, but she's all right," said Doc. "No concussion. She's got a jim-dandy of a bruise on the back of her right knee. She's gonna be sore for a day or so, but she'll be fine."

"Appreciate it, Doc."

"No problem," replied the grizzled old doctor.

"One more thing," said Zeb.

"Yup?"

"Mind taking a quick look at Lily before you go?"

"Kate left word with Helen that Lily didn't want to see me. She said she was fine. Still want me to have a look?" asked Doc.

"No. I guess we best leave it alone," replied Zeb. "If she's hurt, she'll be in to see you."

Doc tipped his hat. His ancient, bowed legs walked him out the door of Zeb's office. He stopped long enough to chat briefly with Helen before heading back to the medical clinic.

"I think he's the doctor that delivered me when I was born," said Ela.

"There is an almost one hundred percent chance of that," replied Zeb.

"Can I get something to drink, a Gokusen cold pressed fruit juice, an Aquadeco sparkling water or something along those lines?" asked Ela.

Zeb had never heard of either of the brand names, but buzzed Helen with Ela's request. A few minutes later she knocked on Zeb's door with an Arizona brand flavored mineral water.

"It'll do if that's all you have," replied Ela, eyeing the can. "Thank you."

"You're welcome, young lady," said Helen. As she departed, Helen left the door slightly ajar. Zeb considered getting up from behind his desk and shutting it but decided not to. Helen might catch something he may miss.

"Ela, I have some questions for you," said Zeb.

"Of course you do," replied Ela. "I would be glad to answer them to the best of my ability. Should I call a lawyer?"

"I don't think that will be necessary. Your mother isn't going to press any charges,"

"Ha! I should be the one considering charges," said Ela.

Zeb reached into a desk drawer and pulled out an official looking document.

"Okay, what charges would you like to write up against your mother?"

"Perhaps you didn't hear me correctly. I said I *should* be the one considering charges. I have no complaint to file."

Zeb put the document back in his desk drawer and pulled a legal pad in front of him.

"What were you and your mother fighting about?" asked Zeb.

"Why do you need to know if no one is pressing charges?" asked Ela.

"It might help me solve your father's murder. That is what you want, isn't it?" asked Zeb.

"Of course it is," replied Ela. "But the fight between me and my mother had nothing to do with his death."

"How can you be so sure of that?" asked Zeb.

"Well, uh, I can't."

"In that case, your cooperation would be greatly appreciated."

"Oh, okay, I'll tell you."

Zeb poised his pen.

"After the burial, the family attorney told both of us that my father had left his forty-nine percent stake in the Klondyke 1 mine to me," said Ela.

Zeb put his pen on the yellow legal pad and shook his head.

"I suppose your mother was angry when she heard that?"

"She lost her fricking mind. For God's sake, my dad left her ten million in cash, all the properties and personal belongings. She's a rich woman."

"Sometimes a lot is not enough," said Zeb.

"That's true, but it's not the reason behind all this," replied Ela.

"What is the reason?" asked Zeb.

"My mother hates me because my father loved me. She was always extremely jealous of his love for me. I think that's why she went bananas and pulled a knife on me when she found out he loved me enough to leave me his stake in the Klondyke 1 mine and the land on which the future Klondyke 2 is supposed to be built."

"After listening to you on KREZ, I assumed you were against the copper mines. In fact, I thought you had strong ethical beliefs against mining in general," said Zeb.

"As a matter of principle, I am against the mining of Mother Earth. On a more practical level, now that I've given it some thought, I have a fiduciary responsibility to the other stockholders. Being a large stockholder in the Klondyke 1 copper mine and sole owner of the inevitable Klondyke 2, I am rethinking my position," replied Ela.

"Of course," said Zeb.

"After all, my father is deceased and my mother and I have no relationship to speak of," said Ela. "A woman has to look after herself in this world, Sheriff Hanks."

Zeb paused as Ela took a drink of mineral water. Was she bluffing? Was her cause, the Earth Liberation Movement, just BS? Money can change people. However, Ela had only known for a few hours that she was the owner of the Klondyke 1. Like they song goes, thought Zeb, money doesn't sing, dance or walk, but it does talk. In Ela's case, it seemed to be talking loudly.

As Ela stared back into his eyes, Zeb saw Lily as a young woman. Lily had also been idealistic before money, drugs and alcohol ruined her life. Ela softened her face and smiled at Zeb. It was precisely the same smile Lily had used each time she had tried to seduce him.

"Tell me about ELM."

"What's to tell?" asked Ela.

"You're on the national board of directors and you're the president of the Arizona chapter of ELM, right?"

"As of this moment I am. I may have to resign due to conflict of interest," replied Ela.

This time when Zeb stared back at her she had the eyes of a wolf, beautiful and enticing, yet menacing and threatening. Of course, how had he not thought of it before now? Any progeny of Angus and Lily could be nothing short of a dangerous, wild animal.

"Are you moving back to Safford permanently?" asked Zeb.

"No, not to Safford," she replied.

"Of course," replied Zeb. "A young woman with power and money would want to be where more is going on. So, did you opt for Tucson or Phoenix? Maybe even San Francisco?"

"None of the above, Sheriff Hanks."

"Where can I get in touch with you if anything comes up in the investigation?" asked Zeb. "Or if I have any more questions?"

"I bought a house with some land on the San Carlos Reservation. You probably know exactly where it is," said Ela. "Have you noticed the entrance to Casa Cielo when you've visited Echo Skysong's family? I purchased it about a month ago. I was going to use it as a getaway home. Now I think I will finish what had been started, expand it and make it my permanent residence."

The foreboding look in Ela's eyes darkened. She knew about his personal life. Ela calmly grabbed Zeb's legal pad, spun it around and wrote down a couple of phone numbers.

"You can reach me at either of these," she said. "Is that everything?"

"For now," replied Zeb.

"Am I free to go?"

Zeb nodded.

Ela walked out just as Helen entered Zeb's office.

"That young woman has the devil in her, Zeb. Watch out for her."

"Thanks, Helen. I think you've got her number."

25

ZEB'S HOUSE

*Z*eb returned home to the stimulating aromas of true Native American cooking. It was Echo's family recipe for something she called Apache magic stew.

"Is that you, Zeb?"

Zeb laughed for nearly the first time all day.

"Were you expecting someone else?"

"Well." Echo slipped into the living room from the kitchen wearing only a tightly fitting apron that left just the right amount to the imagination. "I just wanted to be sure."

The next half hour was nothing short of dreamland. The stress of a difficult day melted away as Zeb held Echo in an afterglow that lit up the bedroom. Having peered into the satanic, wolf-like orbs of Ela McGinty, Zeb couldn't help but have a closer look into the eyes of the woman he was falling deeply in love with.

"What are you looking at?" Echo asked. "You look like you're searching for something."

Inside Echo was the fear that Zeb could only see and feel Doreen in his lovemaking.

"Whatever you're thinking," said Zeb. "I guarantee that this is one case where you can't read my mind."

"Really?" asked Echo.

"I'm sorry. I shouldn't have let my thoughts from today spill over into our lovemaking. I know that's the wrong thing to do."

"Now you *have* to tell me what you were thinking," said Echo, cuddling against Zeb's chest and smelling his pheromones intertwine with the aroma of their lovemaking.

"I don't want dinner to burn," said Zeb.

"It won't," said Echo. "Quit trying to avoid telling me what you were thinking."

Echo wasn't going to let go of this. Zeb knew better than to try to change the subject or, worse, lie to her.

"I stared down a hungry, rabid wolf today," he said.

"And you were looking to see if that wolf existed in me, weren't you?"

Zeb hemmed and hawed. That is precisely what he had done. How could he have been so transparent? His reaction was instinctual. It was out of curiosity, not concern. When he began to explain himself, Echo pressed a finger against his lips.

"I understand," said Echo. "For years when I was in the military, I searched people by evaluating what I was seeing in their eyes. I was always hoping to see directly into their hearts. I am perfectly fine with your need to check me out that way. Trust me, I understand. Now tell me what's going on."

Zeb gave her the entire lowdown on Ela and Lily. He explained that he felt both had good enough reasons to want to kill Angus McGinty. He also admitted that he didn't have proof enough to validate his gut feelings.

"I have never witnessed the animalistic expression I saw in Ela's eyes before, at least not in a young woman," admitted Zeb.

"I trust you didn't see it in me?" asked Echo. "Even when we ate peyote?"

Zeb laughed. "Hell no."

"Good, because if you did, you would be eating Apache magic stew alone tonight."

Zeb laughed uproariously. Echo could never be capable of having the evil, wolven gaze in her eyes that Ela had.

Echo wanted to talk more about the case. Zeb was hungry and tired. The Apache stew was overwhelming his senses. Over supper he gave her other bits and pieces of the Angus McGinty case and let her know whom else he suspected in his death.

"Ela also knows about us."

"It's not exactly a secret," said Echo.

"She purchased Casa Cielo."

"So what? It was for sale. She's got one quarter Apache blood in her. She has every right to buy it," said Echo. "It's better off with someone living there than vacant."

"I don't like her that close to your family," said Zeb. "My intuition and years of experience tell me there's something not right about her. Not only is something not right about her, something may be seriously wrong with her. She might be dangerous."

This time it was Echo's turn to laugh.

"You think my family can't take care of themselves? Both my dad and my mom shoot as well or better than I do," said Echo.

"Ela's got evil in her eyes, and I think she's sneakier than a hungry coyote," said Zeb.

"No sweat," said Echo. "No need to worry about them."

"You seem awfully certain of that."

"I am."

"How can you be so sure of yourself?"

"After my first tour in Afghanistan, I returned stateside with a touch of paranoia. I gave my parents what now seems like a strange sort of anniversary present, but they love it."

"What did you give them?" asked Zeb.

"You know how their house sits up on a hill and is surrounded by wadis on three sides?"

"Of course."

"I set them up with military grade electronic invisible eyes at the bottom of each of the wadis. I went so far as to put in another set of electronic eyes halfway up the hill. The first set fires off short bursts of sound alarms. It's more than enough to scare just about anyone or anything away. The second alarm triggers a set of floodlights that would give my parents unobstructed vision of anything within a few hundred feet of their house. Only trouble is night critters sometimes set the system off, but I kind of think they get a kick out of that. It gives them a little excitement in their lives. They were both in the Marines."

"Semper fi," said Zeb.

"You want some dessert?" asked Echo.

"I could eat some."

"You're a good man, Zeb Hanks, better than you know."

With that she grabbed his hand and led him back into the bedroom.

26

DEATH ON THE REZ

*Z*eb caught some extra sleep the next morning. By the time he awoke, Echo was already up and gone. As he dressed Zeb noticed Echo had rearranged some things in the walk-in closet. His shoes and belts had been moved to the left. A pair of boots that he rarely wore and an old, well-used belt seemed to be missing. He only noticed the boots because more than once he had stubbed his toe on them. The belt was another matter. It had been a gift from Doreen. It was the first gift she had ever given him. It was thick and black, capable of carrying his professional equipment on it. She had purchased it through a military surplus store. Though it was practically worn out he had kept it. It reminded him of Doreen because she had etched 'You are Z-man' and then signed her name with a series of small hearts on the belt.

He would have asked Echo where it had gone had she not risen early. She left him a note on her pillow that said, "Off to see my parents, I love you, Echo."

He chuckled when he read it. He suspected she was doing recon on Casa Cielo and its new owner, Ela McGinty. He figured she was also checking the invisible fencing she had put up along the perimeter of her parent's house. He smiled at the thought of it all and realized how much he really was falling in love with her, perhaps even tuning into her way of thinking.

When Zeb arrived at the office, everyone seemed to be waiting for him. Kate approached him with a sense of urgency.

"Did you hear?" she asked.

"Hear what?" asked Zeb.

"Lily McGinty was found dead on the San Carlos early this morning by some deer hunters," replied Kate. "One of Rambler's deputies called to inform us a few minutes ago. I would've thought for sure they had called you already."

Zeb looked at his cell phone. There was a message. The ringer was on silent. Echo must have turned it off last night when he came home.

"Found dead? What's the cause of death? Do they know?" asked Zeb.

"She hanged herself," said Kate. "From a tree. With a belt."

The conversation was cut short by Helen.

"Zeb, it's Rambler. He said he left you a message. He needs to talk with you."

"I'll take it in my office," replied Zeb.

Zeb picked up his office landline. He waited for the click on the other end which indicated Helen had hung up.

"Rambler."

"Zeb."

"I just got news that Lily McGinty was found dead on the Rez," said Zeb.

"That's why I need to talk to you," replied Rambler.

"Let's talk," said Zeb. "What've you got?"

"I think it's better if you come out here."

A strange curtness took the place of the usual lackadaisical, laid-back manner Rambler was well known for.

"I can do that. When would you like to talk?" asked Zeb.

"The sooner the better."

"Okay, when would you like me to run out there?"

"How does right now work for you?" asked Rambler.

"I've got a murder case of my own. I've got a meeting with my deputies, and I was planning on talking to one of the suspects this morning. How long it will take?"

"I know you've got the Angus McGinty case. Still, it would be better for you if you came here immediately," replied Rambler.

Maybe Rambler had something that would help Zeb solve the Angus McGinty murder case, and he didn't want to speak about it over the phone.

"Zeb, you there?"

"Yeah."

"It's important."

"I'll rearrange my day. I'll be there in thirty minutes."

"I'll be waiting for you," said Rambler.

Zeb quickly briefed his deputies. He ordered them to carry on with their own investigations into Angus McGinty's death.

"Keep your eyes and ears open to anything that might link the deaths of Angus and Lily McGinty. I'll be back as quickly as I can. Let's all plan on meeting around one," said Zeb.

Kate, Jake and Black Bear all nodded and went to work.

"Helen, I'm headed out to the Rez to talk to Rambler. I suspect he knows more than he told me on the phone. I should be back by one."

"Drive carefully," said Helen.

Zeb smiled, grabbed his hat and was out the door and on his way to the Rez. Thirty minutes later he was sitting in front of Tribal Police Chief Rambler Braing.

"Zeb."

"Rambler. What's up? You sounded serious and urgent on the phone."

"Have a seat, Zeb. I have a couple of questions for you."

"From the tone of your voice, this almost sounds like an interrogation," replied Zeb.

"It is, and unless you want this to get way out of control, you'll want to answer me truthfully the first time I ask."

"Okay, I've got nothing to hide...from you," said Zeb.

"Where were you last night?"

"What?" asked Zeb.

"You heard me. Tell me everything. It's very important. You're not in this one alone," said Rambler.

"What do you mean?" asked Zeb.

"While you're here talking to me, FBI Agent Jesus Ezequiele is having a little chat with Echo."

The hairs on the back of Zeb's head stood at attention.

"Echo? Why?"

"You'll know soon enough. Now, where were you last night?" asked Rambler.

"At home with Echo."

"All night?"

"Yes, all night."

Zeb didn't like the way this was sounding even though he still had no idea what was going on.

"What time did you get home from work?"

"Around six."

"Were you at home all night?" asked Rambler.

"Yes."

"What did you have for dinner?"

"Something Echo made. It's her family recipe. They jokingly refer to it as Apache magic stew."

"Then what did you do?"

"What I do in the privacy of my own home is none of your damn business," growled Zeb.

Rambler leaned forward and spoke, almost whispering.

"I'm trying to help you. For God's sake, let me."

Zeb held his head in his hands.

"Tell me what this is all about and I'll give you every detail," said Zeb.

"Murder. There was a murder out past Dry Rock Creek last night."

Zeb knew it well. Dry Rock Creek led right into the wadi that ran just west of Echo's family home and east of Casa Cielo. Only a week earlier, after a surprise rain shower, Zeb and Echo had hiked through it. He remembered how they had laughed because it was so muddy that her shoes practically got sucked off her feet.

"Who are you talking about? You said Lily McGinty was found dead. Your deputy told my deputy that Lily hanged herself with a belt. Was there a murder, too?"

"Just answer my questions."

"What was the question again?"

"What did you do after you ate supper?"

"We had dessert," replied Zeb dryly.

"And then?"

"We watched some TV and went to bed."

"Both of you stayed home all night?"

"Yes, of course," replied Zeb.

It occurred to him he had slept so deeply that he didn't know what time Echo had risen and departed. He only knew she had left him a note, still sitting on the table beside the bed, telling him that she had gone to visit her parents.

"You're certain of that?" asked Rambler.

Zeb grew angry.

"Not one more word until you tell me what's going on."

Rambler reached under his desk and pulled out a pair of boots. He set them on the desk without saying a word. Zeb knew Rambler was waiting for his reaction. Then Rambler reached under his desk again. This time he slapped a belt on the table. He flipped it so the inside of the belt was facing upward. Etched into the belt were the words 'You are Z-man' and Doreen's name written in tiny hearts.

"Where the hell did you get those?" asked Zeb.

"Where do you think I got them?" asked Rambler.

"How the hell should I know where you got them. Both the boots and the belt were missing from my house."

"Since when?"

"I only noticed this morning they were gone."

"You're absolutely certain of that?" asked Rambler.

"Hell yes, I'm sure of it. Why? What do they have to do with the murder? And who was murdered?"

"Is this your belt?"

"Yes, you already know that, and, yes, those are my boots. Now tell me what the hell is going on."

"You're certain that these boots and this belt are yours?" asked Rambler tapping his finger next to the tape recorder.

"Just as no means no, yes means yes. They're mine."

"Lily McGinty was found hanging by your belt. Boot prints from these boots match exactly those found by her dead body. There was a second set of boot prints as well. It also appears as though she might have been tortured first."

"What the hell? Who set me up?" asked Zeb. "Do you know?"

"I'm sorry, Zeb, but you're my only suspect," said Rambler.

"Why on earth would I kill Lily McGinty?" asked Zeb.

"I don't know," replied Rambler. "But I do know you have a dark side. Your girlfriend worked with Special Forces in Afghanistan. God only knows what sorts of skills she has."

Zeb's fist landed hard on Rambler's desk.

"How dare you implicate Echo? You know she isn't a murderer. You know I didn't kill Lily McGinty. Who is pushing you to go after me and why?"

"I'm just doing my job," said Rambler.

"Agent Ezequiele has his fingers in this, doesn't he?"

"We're done for now," said Rambler, stepping away from his desk and Zeb's cold hard glare. "You can be thankful you're the sheriff of Graham County. Otherwise, I would be obliged to put you behind bars."

The men had been nearly lifelong friends. Rambler didn't want to part with this cloud of suspicion hanging over Zeb. The facts just didn't add up in Rambler's head. He knew in his heart Zeb wasn't guilty of the murder of Lily McGinty. Zeb was capable of many things, but not this.

"Am I free to go?" asked Zeb, holding his temper in check.

"For now," replied Rambler.

As Zeb rose to leave, he wondered who was getting to his tribal cohort. Pressure must be coming from somewhere higher up the food chain. The tribal council might have a hand in all of this. However, the complexity of it all seemed beyond Zeb and Rambler's pay scale.

27

EZEQUIELE

"Agent Ezequiele, I mean no disrespect to you, but I don't really know what you're talking about."

The tone in Echo Skysong's voice was firm. She had worked beside soldiers who knocked down doors in Afghanistan without knowing what or who was on the other side. She had interrogated hundreds upon hundreds of women attempting to gain information about the Taliban or local tribal leaders' actions. Some innocuous looking, middle-aged FBI agent, who seemed more suited to working behind a desk than in the field, wasn't about to set her back on her heels.

"I only want to know what you did last night," said Agent Ezequiele.

"I've already told you everything. When you speak with Sheriff Hanks, I am one hundred percent certain he will tell you exactly the same thing I've told you three times now. I really have nothing else to add."

The FBI agent closed his notebook and switched off his voice recorder. He inhaled a deep sigh and spoke to Echo as though she were an old friend.

"Let's talk off the record."

The tactic was one Echo herself had used many times in the field. Agent Ezequiele rotated his laptop computer so Echo could see the screen.

"Read this synopsis of your boyfriend."

"Aren't all of us a little old to be using the term boyfriend," replied Echo, her eyes remaining transfixed on the agent, away from the screen.

"Your lover, your partner, your paramour, whatever you want to call him. I know that if you read the synopsis that my predecessor, Agent Rodriguez, left behind, you will see that Zeb Hanks is not the man he pretends to be. Nor is he the man you believe him to be."

"I assume you know that I killed Agent Rodriguez when he was about to execute Deputy Sawyer Black Bear," said Echo.

"The official record states that Agent Rodriguez had a mental and physical breakdown and chose to act aggressively and illegally. The whole interaction at Sheriff Hank's office was a shame. The FBI lost a good man. However, your actions were deemed within the confines of the law. You did nothing wrong. The investigation is closed."

Echo had heard nothing nor seen any official report on the incident. She was aware of FBI protocol and assumed the agency had gone over the details of what happened with a fine-toothed comb. However, she was surprised at how little contact they had with her over the incident. She had never received notification they had closed the investigation.

"Agent Rodriguez gathered evidence against Sheriff Hanks over many years. Everything you read in the file about Sheriff Zeb Hanks is this close to proving," said Ezequiele, holding his finger and thumb about one-sixteenth of an inch apart.

Echo read the pages on the computer screen in detail. When she was done, she turned the computer around so it faced the FBI agent.

"Zeb has told me everything that's in this file," she said.

"He confessed this to you?"

"No. That is not at all what I said. Don't try and twist my words. Zeb said Agent Rodriguez had a bone to pick with him and that he was making it his mission to see him behind bars. It was a highly personal thing between Zeb and Agent Rodriguez."

"And you believe every word Sheriff Hanks told you?"

"He told me the truth. I believe every word he said."

"Do you think Agent Rodriguez lied about all of this?" asked Agent Ezequiele, pointing at the computer screen.

"I could not possibly know his personal motivation. I do believe he was a sick man," replied Echo. "That is an opinion you have already corroborated."

"Okay. Please indulge me as we go over a few questions one last time."

Echo nodded and answered each of the agent's questions about what time Zeb got home, what they had for supper, what they did after they ate and when they went to bed.

"Okay. It fits. One last thing. How come you got up so early to see your parents this morning?"

"I'm still operating on military time. I rise early and get things done early. My parents are older, so they rise early too. I knew they would be awake."

She said not a word of why she was visiting them, only that she was.

"Okay. Now we're back on the record. You probably know that I will be in contact with you again," said Agent Ezequiele. "I will be doing a standard follow-up after I chat with Sheriff Hanks."

"Yes, sir," replied Echo. "I'm aware of your protocols."

Agent Ezequiele shut down his computer, got up from his chair and headed for the door. Echo followed him and closed the door behind him. Her parents came out of the bedroom where the Agent Ezequiele had asked them to wait.

"What the hell is going on?" asked Echo's father. "Who was the dead woman they found hanging by her neck so close to our house?"

Echo briefly explained who Angus and Lily McGinty were and that they had been murdered within a week of each other.

"Zeb is a suspect?" asked her mom. "And you are too?"

"Time hasn't diminished your hearing, I see," said Echo.

Her mother pointed to a ventilation grate on the wall between the bedroom and the living room. They all had a good laugh, but Echo could see the concern on her parents' faces. Her mind drifted back to the war. For the first time, she realized just how much her being assigned to a war zone for three years had aged them. She didn't need to stress them out again. The more she could protect them from this the better. She kissed them good-bye and headed for her truck. She hit #2 on speed dial. Zeb picked up after one ring.

"I'll call you back," he said. "I'm just about to leave Rambler's office."

As Zeb was talking to Echo, Rambler's phone rang. It was Agent Ezequiele asking him to have Sheriff Hanks stay until he got there. The FBI agent needed to go over a few things with him.

A gent Ezequiele left the Skysong home and headed down the road over Dry Rock Creek. He stopped at the end of a hidden drive that led to Casa Cielo, recently purchased home of Ela McGinty. He reached across the front seat and grabbed his brief case. He removed a file with overhead photos the FBI had taken of the area using a drone.

Casa Cielo had originally been built by a mid-level Mexican drug lord who had grown marijuana on the reservation for multi-state distribution. It was a beautiful hacienda that was not fully built when the drug grower had been busted, convicted and jailed. The property was abandoned. It ended up being claimed by the tribal council. Before Ela purchased it, Casa Cielo had sat empty for several years.

Ezequiele had a notion to speak with Ela before heading into the San Carlos Police Office but thought better of it. As guilty as he thought Zeb Hanks was of the murder of Lily McGinty, he didn't want to piss him off. If all that Rodriguez had written about Sheriff Hanks' temperament was true, Agent Ezequiele knew he might start a shit storm if he kept him waiting too long.

After twenty minutes of rough road, Agent Ezequiele pulled into the tribal police headquarters. To his surprise, Zeb and Rambler were drinking tea, sitting on a shaded bench and waiting for him.

Rambler stood to greet the FBI man. Zeb leaned back, allowing the shade to hide his face. He observed how Rambler and Ezequiele interacted. Their body language told him exactly what he suspected...they didn't know each other all that well. He breathed a sigh of relief as the men approached him. This time he stood and offered the FBI agent a firm grip of his right hand.

"Agent Ezequiele, nice to meet you," said Zeb.

"Sheriff Zeb Hanks," replied Agent Ezequiele, eying him up and down. "You look like a real cowboy."

"You look like a real live, old-fashioned FBI agent," said Zeb, looking at the man's freshly polished shoes.

Ezequiele was quick on the uptake.

"My shoes might be right out of the J. Edgar Hoover era, but my grandfather and my father shined shoes for a living. I take great pride in keeping my shoes looking sharp," said Ezequiele.

Ezequiele's words humbled Zeb and threw him a bit off balance. Zeb felt bad about the snide remark he had made about the agent's shoes.

"Let's go inside and talk," suggested Rambler.

Agent Ezequiele wasted no time.

"Sheriff Hanks, what was the nature of your relationship with Lily McGinty?" he asked.

"I'm certain you're already aware that she contributed heavily to my campaign the last two times I ran for office," said Zeb.

Ezequiele looked down at his computer screen. He was verifying what he already knew.

"Yes, she and her husband contributed seventy-four percent of the total contributions in your last campaign and sixty-eight percent in the election prior to that one."

"I don't have those kinds of details at my fingertips, but I'd say that seems about right," replied Zeb.

"What did that kind of money buy them, Sheriff?"

Zeb took a sip of his tea before responding.

"Nothing. I don't operate like that."

"I see that on several occasions you or one of your deputies gave Lily McGinty a ride home from Gallagher's Irish Pub and at least once from the Copper Pit Blues Bar."

Zeb held back a chuckle. What sort of interrogation was this?

"True enough. We don't like it when someone who has been drinking gets behind the wheel. If you want to check my records, you'll find at least a hundred instances every year of me or one of my deputies keeping a drunk driver off the road and out of jail. It's a program funded by the federal government. One of my deputies, Jake Dablo, wrote the grant for us. You can ask him about it. It's his way of giving back to the community," explained Zeb.

"Fair enough. Sounds like a good program."

"It is."

"Did you ever have sexual relations with Lily McGinty?" asked Agent Ezequiele.

"No."

"Did she ever approach you and attempt to seduce you?"

Zeb hesitated. Lily was a wildcat. She had put the moves on just about everyone in town at one time or another, but Zeb wasn't about to besmirch the so recently deceased.

"No. I don't recall anything of that nature," he replied. "I do know she had a reputation of being a little on the carefree side when it came to her dalliances."

"Did any of your deputies have a sexual relationship with her?"

Could it even be possible that Ezequiele had heard about Black Bear's tryst with Lily? Zeb chose to lie to the FBI agent.

"None that I know of."

It was an easily covered lie.

"But it's possible?"

"You know the old saying, don't you, Agent Ezequiele? Anything's possible."

"It would reflect poorly on you if I found out later that one of your deputies was having a personal relationship with the late Mrs.

McGinty and that you knew about it and chose to withhold that information."

Zeb said nothing. He was beginning to think Agent Ezequiele had some strange sixth sense.

"I'll take that as you stand by your original answer," said Ezequiele.

Zeb nodded. Certain the FBI man was recording his every word, Zeb chose each utterance with great caution. He knew Black Bear's father had been an FBI man. Maybe Black Bear had already talked with Ezequiele. Zeb decided to take his chances.

"How is the investigation into the death of Angus McGinty coming along?" asked Ezequiele.

The question seemed out of left field. It was too friendly, too easy.

"It's ongoing," replied Zeb. "We're working on it."

"Getting close to anything definitive?"

"Not yet."

"Do you have any reason to believe the same person might have killed both Angus and Lily McGinty?"

"I have no evidence that leads me to believe that. How could I? I only heard about Lily's death a few hours ago. Is there something you'd like to share with me?" asked Zeb.

"Just thinking out loud," replied Agent Ezequiele. "It helps me keep a clear mind."

"Of course," replied Zeb.

"About the boots one of Chief Braing's men found..."

"How did your men find them?" asked Zeb. "Where did they find them?"

Agent Ezequiele didn't give Rambler a chance to answer Zeb's question.

"Where did you last seem them, Sheriff Hanks?" asked Ezequiele.

"In my closet."

"When did you last see them?"

"I can't say for certain. A few days, maybe a week ago," replied Zeb. "How were they found? Where were they found?"

This time Zeb got his answer.

"A homeless man was trying them on outside a dumpster behind the Evangelical Free Church when one of my deputies happened by," interjected Rambler. "The man told my deputy he found them in the dumpster only minutes earlier. He figured since he didn't have any shoes, it was a miraculous gift from God because he needed shoes and there they were, in the church dumpster."

"Do either of you think I am so stupid that if I actually killed someone I would leave a blatant trail of boot prints at the scene of the crime and then leave the boots in a place where they might so obviously be found?" asked Zeb.

Rambler glanced up at Ezequiele who kept typing away on his laptop. When he stopped, he made eye contact with Zeb and pointed at the belt with his chin.

"Yours?"

"Yes."

"A gift from your late wife, Doreen?"

"Yes."

"How do you think she would feel if she knew it was used as a murder weapon?"

It took one hundred percent of Zeb's self-control to prevent him from leaping over to Agent Ezequiele and throttling the agent's throat with his hands. Thankfully Rambler made a move.

"Agent Ezequiele, I believe you've crossed a line that belies every manner of decency. I think it's best we end this right here and now."

Ezequiele looked over at Zeb who still bore every indication of contempt on his face.

"This is only beginning, Sheriff Hanks. I will be in touch very soon."

He extended his hand to Zeb. Zeb shot out of his chair so fast that it flew backwards and tipped over. He stood towering over the much smaller FBI agent. Zeb jutted his right hand so close to the FBI agent that Ezequiele had to use an alligator arm to shake it. As the men exchanged a handshake, Zeb did his best to crush the small hand of the federal agent. When he let go, Zeb pointed his first finger at Rambler who returned a small nod.

Zeb departed Rambler's office and hopped into his truck. His spinning wheels kicked up dust and dirt as he stomped on the gas and headed down the road back to his own turf.

"The sheriff has a temper, doesn't he?" asked Ezequiele.

Rambler said nothing.

"I'm going to talk with Ela McGinty next," said Agent Ezequiele, putting his things in order. "I'll be in touch."

The men shook hands and Rambler walked Agent Ezequiele out of the office.

28

SHERIFF'S OFFICE

"How did it go with Rambler and Agent Ezequiele?" asked Helen.

Zeb had cooled down on the drive back from the Rez after his chat with Rambler and Agent Ezequiele.

"Ezequiele is a weak, little man who uses his badge to play games with people," replied Zeb. "Somehow, he seems to have pulled Rambler onto his team, at least in some small way."

"That doesn't sound good," said Helen.

"It isn't," replied Zeb. "Is everyone here?"

"Kate threw up again. She went home for a bit. She called and said she's on her way back. I'm expecting Deputy Black Bear and Jake any minute."

"When everyone is here, send them all in to see me."

Helen nodded and went back to work. Twenty-five minutes later Kate, Jake and Black Bear were seated in Zeb's office. He was about to shut the door when Kate stopped him.

"Can we have Helen come in for a moment?" asked Kate.

Zeb stuck his head through the door and asked Helen to join them.

"I have something I need to share with all of you," said Kate.

Everyone trained their eyes on her. Helen already had a good idea of what it was. The men didn't.

"The long and short of it is I'm pregnant. I'm about ten weeks along, so the pregnancy shouldn't affect my work for now."

"That's just wonderful," exclaimed Helen. "Congratulations. If there's anything I can do to help, please let me know. If you need anything at all, I would be glad to help."

"Thank you, Helen," said Kate, exchanging a heartfelt hug with Helen.

Black Bear and Jake congratulated her and hugged her warmly. Lastly, Zeb approached her. He spoke quietly.

"I don't know much about pregnancy," he said.

"Neither do I," responded Kate.

"But if you need time, extra help with lifting things or whatever, you've got it. We're family and our family is going to get bigger by one. I want to make sure that nothing about this job interferes with a healthy pregnancy. I want you to have a healthy baby. So, like I said, please let me know if there's anything at all that you need."

"I will," replied Kate at the unexpected, almost fatherly, words from Zeb.

"And, congratulate that big galoot of a husband of yours tonight. Tell him I expect a mighty fancy cigar when the baby is born," said Zeb.

"You got it," replied Kate. "The only thing I ask is that everyone treat me as they always have. I'm not the first deputy sheriff to get pregnant."

"Okay, then let's get to work," said Zeb.

Helen left the room, closing the door ninety percent of the way.

"So, what the hell did you find out about Lily McGinty when you went out to see Rambler?" asked Jake.

Zeb sat back in his chair, lifted his boots to his desk top and gazed out the window toward Mount Graham. The richness of the hues in the blue sky, peculiar to this time of year, reminded Zeb of the color of Paul Newman's eyes. The outcroppings on the edge of the mount looked particularly strong and sturdy, something Zeb knew he would have to be. He thought of Song Bird and how he had shown him the spiritual connection between heaven and earth that lived atop Mount Graham. He looked over at his three deputies and wondered how they were going to take the news that he was a suspect in Lily's murder.

"I'll try to make a long story a shorter one," said Zeb. "But there are some things you need to know. Some if it may crimp my ability to do my job from the way I would normally do it."

"What are you talking about, Zeb?" asked Jake. "Who's grabbing you by the short hairs?"

"For the time being I am a suspect, as a matter of fact the primary suspect, in the murder of Lily McGinty. Rambler talked to me because the alleged murder took place on the Rez. FBI Agent Ezequiele was there as well."

A feather hitting the floor in Zeb's office would have sounded like a car crash at that moment. Jake knew exactly what Zeb was capable of. Kate had a pretty good idea that her boss could cross many lines, but not without purpose and history. She also knew the relationship between Lily and Zeb had been a positive one. Black Bear studied the three of them in silence, keeping a keen eye on each of their reactions.

"As you have already assumed, since I'm a suspect, I didn't get to see the actual physical scene of the crime. But Lily McGinty was hanged near Dry Rock Creek."

"Isn't that near where Ela McGinty just bought that old drug dealer's house?" asked Kate.

"Technically he was a grower and a distributor, not a dealer," said Zeb. "And to answer your question, yes, it is the house Ela McGinty recently purchased. To complicate matters it's just down the road from where Echo grew up and her family still lives."

"You said she was found hanged," said Jake. "With a rope?"

"No. With a belt, my belt. It was a gift Doreen had given me."

"What the..." said Jake.

"Also, a pair of my boots were found in the dumpster behind the

Evangelical Free Church. Prints from those boots were found at the scene of the murder," said Zeb.

"Didn't take Rambler long to call in the FBI," said Black Bear.

"No, it didn't take Rambler long at all. He must have called the FBI immediately after they found Lily's body," replied Zeb. "That bothers me."

"That's not like him. He must have some pressure coming at him from somewhere," added Jake.

"He should have shown you a little more respect on this," said Kate.

"He didn't," replied Zeb. "I don't know why he didn't. It doesn't make sense to me considering our long personal and professional relationship."

"Dollars to donuts they are setting you up because of Agent Rodriguez. I bet they're going after Echo too," said Black Bear. "They protect their own at all costs."

"What makes you say that?" asked Zeb.

"My mother used to tell me horror stories about the FBI. I know what they did and how they did it on Pine Ridge. They've got their sights aimed directly at you, but they're also gunning for anyone linked to you. You need to protect yourself and Echo. They know how to turn Lily's death into something it isn't," said Black Bear. "We all need to keep our heads down."

An electric nervousness hummed through the room. Sweeping winds of paranoia seemed to seep through the cracks in the window sills.

"Who is the FBI agent in charge?" asked Black Bear.

"A guy named Agent Jesus Ezequiele. He said he was working out of the Tucson office. He's an asshole but also has a humble side. I don't know what to make of him," replied Zeb. "I can't quite figure out what makes him tick."

"He sounds like a politician," said Jake. "If he's in on the case this quickly, he's got an agenda."

"We need to find out who he is and what his ambitions are. Is

Shelly Hamlin, the computer expert, still available to us?" asked Black Bear.

"Are you talking about doing a background check and maybe even hacking an FBI agent's private and professional information?" asked Kate.

"What do you think they're doing to Zeb right now, probably as we speak?" asked Black Bear. "We're law enforcement. We have the right to legally gather as much information as possible."

"Legal being the key word here. We need to think this over," replied Kate.

Jake slowly ambled to the door.

"Helen, get Shelly Hamlin on the phone. When you've got her, put her through to Zeb's office, would you please?"

"Right away, Jake," said Helen, signaling him with her first finger to come out of the office.

Jake approached her desk. Helen spoke in a whisper.

"We've got do to do everything in our power to protect the integrity of Zeb and this office."

Jake looked upon the most law-abiding person he'd ever known and nodded his head.

"Yes, we do."

"I smell a rat," added Helen.

Jake lightly tapped his former secretary and longtime friend on the nose.

"Good to know your sniffer still works. Something else is going on here. I do believe someone has a personal vendetta against Zeb, and you can bet the foul odor of mendacity is coming from high places. When you call Shelly, tell her it's vital."

29

ELA

Rambler leaned into the car window of the man who was applying pressure on him. Something wasn't right. Someone above Ezequiele was exerting influence on the agent. Something just didn't fit. Rambler needed to find out why he was being forced to keep Zeb out of the investigation into Lily's murder.

"I think I'll join you," said Rambler.

"I'd like to talk to Ela the first time by myself," replied Agent Ezequiele.

"I don't think you have a full understanding of how things work on the Rez. If you show up without me, you might get shot. If I'm with you, there is a much better chance of you getting what you want from Ela without there being any trouble. I know her a little but, more importantly, I knew her family. I don't want rivers being crossed that can't be crossed back over."

Agent Ezequiele knew his knowledge on tribal protocol was less than it should be. He was smart enough to try and not make a mistake that could be easily avoided.

"Point well taken, Chief Rambler. Let's get a move on and see what Miss Ela McGinty knows."

"I'll ride with you," said Rambler.

As they approached Casa Cielo, Rambler was the first to notice the cameras. They were mostly hidden, one near a wren's nest in a saguaro cactus. The other was in a Mexican Paloverde. He pointed them out to Agent Ezequiele. The security cameras were of no surprise to either man. Whether they belonged to the former owner or the current one was the question neither man knew the answer to.

Rambler got out and dragged open the newly installed gate. Even though someone was in the process of digging ditches around the area so even a four-wheeler couldn't pass, they hadn't bothered to install a lock on the gate.

The dirt road leading to the house had been recently graded. Traversing it was a breeze compared to many of the Rez roads. Over the top of the fourth hill, they reached Ela McGinty's hacienda, Casa Cielo. A dozen men labored putting up an addition that looked to double the size of the five thousand square foot house.

"Somebody's spending some cash," said Agent Ezequiele.

Rambler eyed the workers. Half were Mexican. The other half were local Apaches. He pulled around the entrance and parked one hundred feet away. The workers that saw law enforcement moved to the opposite side of the house.

"Pull up about a hundred feet from the front door. Put the car in park and we'll wait," said Rambler.

"Why?" asked Ezequiele. "We've got work to do. Let's get to it."

"That's not the way it's done around here," said Rambler. "Just hold your horses. We don't want to surprise anyone."

After five minutes the FBI agent reached for the door handle. Rambler placed a firm grip on Ezequiele's forearm and whispered, "Wait."

"Do you mind if I ask exactly what we're waiting for?" asked the FBI agent.

"First time on a Rez?" asked Rambler.

"I've driven through many of them," replied Ezequiele.

"You ever stop at somebody's house?"

"No, why?"

"Custom dictates we stay back a distance until we're invited in," replied Rambler.

"What if no one invites us in?"

"Then nobody is home," replied Rambler.

"I get it, this is a Native American thing," said Ezequiele.

Rambler shot a scowl at the politically correct buffoon and the way he talked.

"It shows we mean no harm," said Rambler.

"How do you serve warrants?" asked Agent Ezequiele.

"Depends," replied Rambler.

"On anything in particular?"

"Yes, on many things particular to any given case."

Rambler was becoming more annoyed with the sharp tongue the FBI agent used when responding to him. At that moment, a young girl stepped on the porch. She had long blondish-brown hair that hung almost to her waist. She appeared to be in her early twenties.

"That would be the homeowner," said Rambler.

Rambler stuck his hand out the window and waved. Ela returned the gesture.

"Okay, let's go see what she's got to say," said Rambler. "Please let me break the news to her about her mother."

"Maybe she already knows."

Agent Ezequiele's response was as cold as ice and dry as dust. Rambler had little doubt the FBI agent considered he might looking at the killer of Lily McGinty.

As the men approached Ela's front porch, two other women walked up behind Ela and stood like bodyguards. Both were in their early twenties and strutted with a dominant air about them. The one on Ela's right had a holstered .45 on her right hip. Rambler noted it but thought it to be nothing unusual. Ezequiele's radar went on red alert.

"Ela McGinty?" asked Rambler.

"Yes. You must be the tribal police chief?"

"Yes, ma'am. Rambler Braing."

She stuck out her hand and gave Rambler a good grip.

She pointed over her shoulder with her thumb to the two other women. "These are my friends, Raindrop and Poochie."

"Pleased to make your acquaintance," said Rambler, tipping his hat.

The young women smiled pleasantly, saying nothing.

"Your compadre doesn't look like one of your deputies, Chief Braing," said Ela. "He looks more like a federal agent."

At the ready, FBI Agent Ezequiele pulled out his billfold, flipped it open and displayed his federal agent identification badge. Ela McGinty took a step forward and snatched the ID from his hand. Shocked by her quick reaction, Ezequiele let his badge slip from his hand. She showed it to her friends. Ela politely handed it back to the agent.

"Looks legit, but anyone can fake anything these days. What do you want, Chief Braing?" asked Ela.

"When was the last time you saw your mother?"

"Is this about that little confrontation we had?" asked Ela.

"What confrontation was that?" asked Rambler.

"My mother and I had a little tiff, a dust up if you will, after the funeral. The issue began when my mother found out that I inherited the Klondyke 1 and all the power to start up the Klondyke 2. My mother was pissed off when she found out. As usual, she got drunk and we had a confrontation. A couple of Graham County deputies broke it up before it went too far south."

"Was anyone hurt?" asked Agent Ezequiele.

"Mostly just some bad feelings got stirred up. We're the McGintys after all."

"Was a report filed?" he continued.

"Talk to the sheriff's office."

Agent Ezequiele was about to ask another question when Rambler held up a hand, halting him in mid-sentence.

"May we talk in private, Ela?" asked Rambler. "Just the two of us?"

"You can say whatever you've got to say in front of my friends."

Rambler hemmed and hawed, seeking the right words to tell this beautiful young woman that her mother had been murdered.

"Just say it, Chief Braing. I think I know what you're about to say anyway. Likely something about the change in my late father's will not being valid. Your friend here is about to say it's a federal matter. Am I right?"

"I wish you were," said Rambler. "I would prefer if that were the news I had to give you."

Ela watched Rambler's face. She readily recognized darkness and doom.

"It's bad news, isn't it?" asked Ela.

"I'm afraid so," replied Rambler.

"You have the same look on your face that I've seen when someone passes on," said Ela. "Who died?"

"I am so terribly sorry to tell you that your mother is dead," said Rambler.

Ela didn't move a muscle, change her expression one iota or show any sense of emotion that Rambler could decipher.

"Did you hear me?" he asked.

Ela nodded, her face flushed and teeth gritted. Slowly she allowed tears to trickle down her cheeks. Her friends moved to her side, grabbed her by the arms and helped her to a porch chair. Minutes of silence passed. Finally, Ela spoke.

"Drug or alcohol overdose?" she coolly asked.

"It appears as though she was murdered."

Ela's head fell into her hands.

"She was so damn violent. It really doesn't surprise me," said Ela.

She placed her head back in her hands and began to cry. Her tears were interrupted by Agent Ezequiele.

"I'm sorry. I know this is a bad time, but we have to ask you a few questions."

"Can't it wait?" barked Poochie.

"No, I'm sorry, it can't," replied Ezequiele.

Ela quickly regained her composure.

"Go ahead. Ask away. What do you want to know?" asked Ela.

"I have concerns that since your father was murdered and now your mother..."

As he spoke, any indication of color in Ela's cheeks vanished.

"You think I'm next, don't you? That's what this is all about, isn't it?"

Ela turned to her cohorts and said, "Call my lawyer and tell him I need serious protection and I need it now."

Poochie pulled out her cell phone and walked a short distance away.

"We have no reason, based on anything we know right now, to believe you're in any danger," said Agent Ezequiele. "If you would like, I'm certain Police Chief Braing can have his men pass by your house with increased frequency."

"Christ Almighty," shouted Ela. "I'm a mile off the main road, hidden away in what used to be a drug lord's house. A drug lord's house that I bought at auction for pennies on the dollar. My father and mother have both been murdered. I need up close twenty-four seven protection."

"Perhaps we should step inside to talk," said Rambler.

"Yes, yes, let's do that," replied Ela.

Once inside the opulently furnished hippie pad, everyone took a seat.

"Let me assure you once again. We have no reason to believe you're in any specific danger," said Agent Ezequiele.

"Like I would trust the FBI," replied Ela. "You've been harassing ELM for years. I have no reason to trust you. For all I know you killed my parents."

"If we could ask you just a few questions without having any hostilities between us," interjected Rambler. "That would be most helpful."

"Agent Ezequiele, are you carrying a gun?" asked Ela.

"Yes," he replied.

"Then take it to your car. If you refuse, I know I am within my rights to ask you to leave my property."

"I'll do no such thing," responded Agent Ezequiele.

"I need to have my lawyer present," said Ela. "Or I say nothing."

"Whoa, this is getting a bit out of hand," said Rambler. "This is just an informational interview. We haven't informed you of your rights, so anything you say can't be held against you. You are entirely safe in talking to us."

"Don't do it," insisted Raindrop. "One of these guys is a fed, the other a cop. They can't be trusted."

"No police of any kind with guns in the house. Period. I will not bend on that," said Ela.

Fifteen minutes of intense negotiation followed. Ultimately the men could keep their guns but had to place them on a desk with the clips removed. The clips had to be emptied and placed on a second desk fifteen feet from the guns. Raindrop also placed her weapon on the desk.

Poochie re-entered the house and told Ela that four bodyguards would arrive within the hour. "Your lawyer advises against answering any of their questions," said Poochie.

"I can handle myself," replied Ela. "Okay, Chief Braing, Agent Ezequiele, what do you want to know?"

"Where were you last night?" asked Ezequiele.

"Here, with Poochie and Raindrop. We hardly went outside, except to drink a glass of wine on the porch."

Poochie and Raindrop nodded silently in agreement.

"Do you know your neighbors?" asked the agent.

"No. I haven't had the pleasure of meeting them yet."

Ezequiele pointed in the direction of the Skysong home.

"Have you walked the area between here and the next house over?"

"I have," replied Ela. "I wanted to check my property lines. I stopped when I came in sight of the neighbor's house. I didn't want to bother them."

"Your mother's body was found between your house and theirs."

Ela interrupted the agent.

"How exactly did she die?"

"Are you sure you want to know that? Hearing the details can be traumatic," said Rambler. "I can have a grief counselor here in thirty minutes if you want to wait."

"Thank you, Chief Braing. I don't need a counselor. I've been seeing counselors my whole life. I can handle whatever you tell me."

Ezequiele began to speak. He was instantly shushed by Rambler.

"She was found in a wadi between your neighbor's house and your own."

"Yes," replied Ela. Raindrop and Poochie sidled next to her.

"She…"

"My mother."

"Your mother was found hanged by a belt," said Rambler. "There is an autopsy being performed right now to see if she was injured before she was hanged."

"We couldn't tell by looking at her if she was tortured. We have reason to believe she was water tortured," said Ezequiele.

Rambler glowered at the FBI agent and his insensitivity.

"Water tortured? Like the military does to prisoners at Guantanamo?" asked Ela.

"We don't know for sure. It's just that some liquid, which appeared to be water, came out of her lungs when we moved her," said Rambler.

No tears came from Ela this time.

"Was it her own belt around her neck?" asked Ela.

"No. It was a man's belt," replied Rambler.

"Do you have any suspects?" asked Ela.

Rambler shot a hard glance at Ezequiele, hoping he had sense enough to keep his mouth shut and not mention the name of Sheriff Zeb Hanks. He spoke before the FBI agent had a chance to open his mouth.

"The investigation is just beginning," replied Rambler.

Ela exhaled heavily.

"What else do you need from me? This is insane. First my father. Now my mother. I can't help but feel I am next," said Ela.

"Has anyone threatened you?" asked Ezequiele.

"ELM gets threats every day. Large corporations hire goons and thugs to try and stop us," replied Ela.

Poochie and Raindrop once again showed agreement with passionate nodding.

"Have any threats mentioned the Klondyke mine or your parents?" asked Ezequiele.

"We would have forwarded death threats to the FBI and local authorities," answered Ela.

"Weren't you working to shut down the Klondyke Mine?" asked Ezequiele.

"Of course I was," replied Ela. "Mother Earth can't be continually destroyed in such an unnecessary and evil fashion."

"Are you going to continue your efforts to shut the Klondyke I mine down?" asked Ezequiele.

"I own half of it," replied Ela. "I can do with it whatever I damn well please. Which, by the way, happens to be exactly none of your damn business."

Ezequiele saw that he had a lot of homework to do before pursuing Ela any further.

"I would like you to stay around. If you're planning to leave the county or the Rez, please let me know where you're going," said Ezequiele.

"I'm waiting for my bodyguards. I'm not going anywhere until you can tell me who killed my mother," replied Ela.

Ezequiele and Rambler both handed Ela, Poochie and Raindrop their cards.

"If any of you think of something that might be useful in Lily's murder investigation, please don't hesitate to call either of us," said Rambler.

With that Ezequiele and Rambler picked up their weapons and ammunition and departed.

"Money don't sing, dance or walk, but it certainly talks," said Rambler.

"What?" replied Ezequiele. "What are you talking about?"

"Nothing," said Rambler. "Just thinking out loud."

30

SHERIFF'S OFFICE

Shelly Hamlin, computer expert and sometimes agnostic hacktivist, zipped along the back roads in her Porsche Panamera 4. She made the two-hour trip from Tucson to Safford in eighty-eight minutes. Helen greeted her at the door and showed her directly to Zeb's office.

"Shelly, I need your help again," said Zeb, noticing the maroon and gold highlights Shelly had added to the tips of her long hair.

"I'm totally independent now. My rates have gone up and my skill level has increased. I don't bargain with anyone on price," replied Shelly.

"Not an issue," replied Zeb. "I've got something I want you to do but no one can ever know about it."

"Sounds like fun," said Shelly. "What is it?"

Zeb slid a confidentiality agreement across his desk. Shelly read each and every word before inking her name to the paper.

"I want some background information on an FBI agent."

"What sort of information?" asked Shelly.

Zeb walked over to his door and shut it tightly. He came back to Shelly's side and whispered in her ear. She didn't balk or even act surprised by a single world Zeb said.

"I believe an FBI agent has a vendetta against me and I want to know why," said Zeb.

"I can't breach the current FBI firewall. They changed protocols only two weeks ago. They routinely but irregularly change firewall procedures and practices. I don't have the capacity to breach them today. I might by tomorrow if you want to pay me to use that route. It would be cheaper for you and quicker for me if you gave me his or her name, and I can work into his or her life through the back door."

"It's a man, so *his* life."

"Got it."

"None of this can ever, and I mean ever, be traced back to you or me, right?" asked Zeb.

"Not a chance. Do you have his email address?"

Zeb handed Shelly Agent Ezequiele's business card. Shelly opened her computer. Zeb watched over her shoulder, curious as to how this all worked.

"Mind if I ask what you are doing?" asked Zeb.

She swung her foot around and pulled a chair next to her without missing a keystroke. Zeb took a seat.

"I'm setting up a rootkit to spearfish Agent Ezequiele. Simultaneously, I'll be doxing him so whenever he uses his computer I can keystroke log him," explained Shelly.

"One more time, in English please," asked Zeb, his mind spinning at learning what was essentially a new language.

Shelly slowed her pace of speech. She was smart enough to realize that if she couldn't explain it to Zeb in a way he understood, she wasn't doing her job the right way.

"Ask questions if you don't understand something," said Shelly.

"What is a rootkit?" asked Zeb.

"Good question. It's the first thing I would have asked too. A rootkit is a collection of programs that gives me access to Ezequiele's computer network as though I'm the one controlling it. By installing the rootkit, I become a cracker. Got it?"

"I think so," said Zeb. "Sort of like breaking and entering."

"Precisely. You catch on quickly," said Shelly.

"Spearfish?' asked Zeb. "Like spearing a fish?"

Shelly spelled out the word for him. He'd heard of phishing but didn't really understand it.

"I'm using spear-phishing to obtain Agent Ezequiele's otherwise sensitive information such as usernames, passwords, credit card details. I go in looking like something his computer recognizes and likely ignores. Basically, I'm baiting him. I'll use his email and instant messaging to get what I want. That's the quickest and easiest way," explained Shelly. "Get it?"

"I do," replied Zeb. "The way you explain it, it makes sense. It's not unlike a sting operation in my business."

"Pay close enough attention and I might make a hacker out of you," said Shelly, half in jest.

"It wouldn't be a bad skill to learn," replied Zeb. "If I were new to the law enforcement business, I would certainly want to learn it."

"Want me to teach Kate or Black Bear?" asked Shelly.

"Not just yet. Let's see how all this shakes out first," replied Zeb.

Shelly nodded in agreement, realizing there was no sense in working herself out of a good paying gig. She liked Zeb, thought Kate was a fine person and found Black Bear somewhat sexy.

"Let's continue."

"Right," said Zeb, getting out a small book for notetaking.

"I'm acting as a fake administrator on his account and targeting him specifically. At the same time, I'm looking at anything and every-thing that's in public record or peripherally related to the public record. It includes documents that pertain to him, his life, his credit, yada, yada, yada. Basically, anything we can use against him. I will also be digging into his private background which could lead me to other reference sources that he keeps hidden. Ultimately, I want to track anytime he uses his computer, smartphone or any device and see what he's up to. Got it?"

"More or less. I see what you're doing, but I know I couldn't dupli-cate it."

"It took me a few years to get good at it. Just watch the information come in. Let me know if you see anything you think is important. Don't worry. What's important will be readily apparent. If you don't see the crucial information, I probably have a pretty good idea what it is."

"None of this can get traced back to your computer?" asked Zeb.

"I've got it set up to look like I'm a Russian hacker. I've routed everything through Amsterdam, Tehran, Singapore and Turkmenistan."

"Is any of this legal?" asked Zeb.

"The laws are pretty grey. Don't worry, I never leave electronic fingerprints behind," said Shelly.

Zeb didn't precisely understand the details of what Shelly was doing. In essence, the specifics of how she was doing what she was doing didn't matter that much to him. Zeb needed to know why Agent Jesus Ezequiele had it in for him and why he wanted to tag a murder on him. A federal agent trying to falsely pin a murder on a law enforcement official was usually personal. Since he didn't know Ezequiele, that seemed unlikely.

"Jesus Ezequiele," said Zeb, mostly to himself. "Out of the Tucson office."

Five minutes passed before Shelly spoke. "There is no Jesus Ezequiele who works on the regular payroll or has special agent status in either Phoenix or Tucson."

A rush of paranoia ran through Zeb. Was Ezequiele a dupe, a plant or something worse?

"I can check the national data base of FBI agents if you'd like?" said Shelly.

"Do it," said Zeb.

Fifteen agonizing minutes went by. Zeb's heart pounded with each tick of the clock.

"Here we go," said Shelly. "It's no wonder he didn't show up on the Tucson or Phoenix list of federal agents."

"How's that?" asked Zeb.

"He works out of the D.C. bureau. He is on special assignment.

There is an addendum in his file that states he is reporting directly to the D.C. office and that all information obtained on you is for a single set of eyes only. Interesting."

"Whose eyes want to see what he's found on me?" asked Zeb.

"I don't know yet. Whoever put in the request appears to have bulletproofed themselves. We're dealing with a professional here. I see what they've done. I don't know for certain if I can bypass what they've set up without crashing everything," said Shelly. "It could take days or weeks even."

"Let's get back to Ezequiele for the time being," said Zeb.

"Agent Ezequiele is too big of a muckity-muck to be doing field work. Take a look at this."

Shelly pointed to the computer screen. Agent Jesus Ezequiele's work history was laid out before their eyes. She had somehow tapped into his internal curriculum vitae. Ezequiele had been sitting behind a desk for the last five years working on international crime. Before that he had earned at least fifty citations for excellence in the field. His area of expertise was nabbing bad guys who worked on the inside of the legal system. Cops, sheriffs, lawyers, judges and even other FBI agents were on his trophy list.

"I guess we know why they sicced him on you," said Shelly.

"We know they use his skill set to get sheriffs and other law enforcement officials. What we don't know is why they sent him after me specifically," replied Zeb.

"Good point," said Shelly. "Look, he's got a motto on his letterhead,"

Zeb stared at it without saying a word. *Corruption is stopped by shedding light onto what was previously shadowed.*

"Hmmm," said Shelly. "This is odd."

"What?" asked Zeb.

"Here's a link to Echo Skysong's military record."

Zeb instantly recognized the date. It was the day after she saved everyone in the sheriff's office by killing Agent Rodriguez. Zeb silently stewed about Echo being caught up in all of this.

"Aha," said Shelly.

"Aha what?" asked Zeb.

"Rodriguez's ex-wife is Ezequiele's sister."

The information quelled Zeb's anger a bit. At least he understood why Ezequiele had a deep interest in the case. But the person directing Ezequiele was the real informant he was hoping to find.

"Blood's thicker than mud," said Zeb.

"Got that right," replied Shelly. "You better let Echo know about Rodriguez's ex-wife being Ezequiele's sister."

Zeb rapped his knuckles on the desk. He paced. His nervousness annoyed the daylights out of the computer hacker.

"Give me an hour to myself, and I'll gather a ton of information for you," said Shelly. "But before you go, take a quick gander at this."

Shelly pointed to some deleted spaces in Agent Ezequiele's records.

"There's nothing there to see. It's blank," said Zeb.

"Exactly."

"What does that mean?"

"Whomever is giving Agent Ezequiele his orders is very high up the ladder. They have set this up so there is no way to trace exactly where the order is coming from. I've got to hand it to the agency, this is the one thing they do well."

"Meaning?" asked Zeb.

"Obfuscation. When they manage to hide information from each other, they hide it from hackers as well. It will be impossible for me to tell you who is behind this. I'm sorry," said Shelly. "Because that is what I know you want to know."

"Keep at it. I feel certain you'll get me enough of what I need."

"No sweat."

"I'll get out of your tinted hair for a couple of hours."

"Didn't think you'd be the kind to notice a girl's hair," said Shelly.

"My late wife, Doreen, used to tint her hair. I always thought it was a kind of wild and crazy thing to do, but really I liked it."

"I had you pegged for bad boy from the start," joked Shelly.

Zeb smiled. He was feeling a nice, soft human connection with Shelly. He knew she had his best interests in mind.

"Do you think you will have time for a couple of other things?" asked Zeb.

"Depends."

"If you have time, would you check out Lily McGinty. She lived her life like an open book, even though she pretended to be hiding her wild behavior. I would really be interested in any secrets she was hiding."

"Roger that. It should be easy. I assume you're looking for anything that might implicate her in her husband's death or anything illegal she was up to?" asked Shelly.

"Whatever you find will be good. I'm looking for reasons she might have wanted her husband dead."

"Got it. What else?"

"There's a surveillance camera one block from my house, on Lemon Grove Avenue. I want you to check and see if there was any repetitive traffic turning onto Cactus River Road from Lemon Grove Avenue two days before and the day of Lily's murder."

"You remember my rates have doubled. You're racking up a pretty big bill here," said Shelly.

"No sweat," said Zeb with a smirk. "And, one more thing." Zeb stopped and wrote three dates on a piece of paper. "Check arrivals from D.C. on these dates and get the passenger manifests. Cross reference them with rental car companies. If someone listed Safford as their destination, I am particularly interested in that."

"Piece of cake," replied Shelly. "But you don't really believe a criminal is going to travel and rent a car under their own ID, do you?"

"I'm thinking that the person I'm looking for doesn't have a clue that I know who they might be," replied Zeb. "I'm counting on a stupid mistake. Everyone makes them."

"I don't," replied Shelly.

"You haven't yet, at least that I know of," replied Zeb. "Talk later."

"I'll have something for you by the time you're back," said Shelly.

Zeb grabbed his hat from the rack. He gripped the brim tightly in his hands as he walked down the hall to meet with his deputies. Somehow, the beat-up old hat served as a security blanket and quelled his paranoia about whomever was setting him up as Lily McGinty's murderer.

In the meeting room his deputies huddled around him.

"We've got a murderer to nab. I want each of you to go back and talk to your prime suspects."

"Sounds like a plan," said Jake.

"I got the search warrant for the McGinty mansion from Judge Gritz," added Zeb.

"I've been in the mansion a few times," said Kate. "If you want, I'll do the search."

"Great," said Zeb. "Lily's keys were found near the body in her purse."

"That's good, but I probably won't need them. I can pick any lock in the McGinty mansion," said Kate. "Getting at the private collections should be a piece of cake."

"The McGinty place is huge. It'll take hours to search it thoroughly. Kate, I'm sending Jake with you," said Zeb.

"That's your call, boss," replied Kate.

The expression on Kate's face turned dour. Zeb noticed but let it pass.

"I was on my way to see Toohey Blendah again," said Jake.

"Kate, you'll have to wait until Jake gets back to go out to the McGinty mansion. We'll meet back here later and put our heads together," said Zeb.

Kate was clearly unhappy with this order.

"Where are you headed, Zeb?" asked Jake.

"To have a little chat with Thorman Wright."

"Keep your head low," warned Black Bear. "Someone is out to get you."

Zeb snugged his hat on his head until it felt just right. A cool breeze brushed his skin as he walked out the door. He reached for the door handle of his truck just as an old man walking nearby stepped on a dried tree branch. The cracking sound startled Zeb and his hand found its way to his gun. The old man stopped dead in his tracks as he saw Zeb reaching for his weapon. He felt foolish for being so fearful. Something had to change and it had to change quickly. Everything hinged on finding out who killed Angus McGinty.

31

JAKE AND TOOHEY

J ake found Toohey Blendah exactly where he had last seen him, drinking warm beer on the beat up old sofa that sat in the open weather of his front porch. As Jake approached the inebriated homeowner, Toohey tossed him a beer. Jake snatched it out of the air like an All-Star third baseman nabbing a hot line drive.

"Nice grab," said Toohey.

"I don't drink anymore. You know that," said Jake.

"I must've forgotten that," slurred Toohey.

"What's the occasion?" asked Jake.

"Who needs one?" replied Toohey.

"You don't. That's for sure."

"You're right," said Toohey. "But today I have a reason. I see better days ahead because I outlived both Angus and Lily McGinty. Usen must be looking over me these days."

"He keeps an eye on children and fools," said Jake.

Toohey played deaf, pretending not to hear Jake's unsubtle slam.

"I take it you've heard about Lily."

Toohey cupped his ear with his hand.

"Drumbeats," he said. "Drumbeats that only Indians can hear."

"What've you heard?"

Toohey tipped his head to the side and held his hand above his head, making like someone hanging from a rope.

"Hanged by the neck until dead," said Toohey. "That's what the drummers are drumming."

"You wouldn't happen to know anything about it, would you?"

"Only that the instrument of death was a belt that belonged to the good sheriff of Graham County. What a shame. I always thought of him as a good, solid citizen and a righteous cop. Well, my opinion hasn't changed one bit," laughed Toohey.

"You think he killed Lily?"

Toohey shrugged his shoulders with the greatest of indifference.

"What difference does it make? She no longer walks among us. She can no longer steal from me what was rightfully mine."

"Did you kill her?" asked Jake.

"What good would that do me? I can't get what is owed me from the dead," said a suddenly temperate Toohey.

"Seems to me that if you hired a sharp lawyer you might be in the inheritance line right after Ela. Maybe even before her, if you could prove she wasn't really Angus's biological child," said Jake.

He waited for Toohey to chomp on the bait. Toohey was drunk, but he wasn't stupid. He nibbled around Jake's invitation to speak his mind.

"Who says Ela isn't the biological daughter of Angus McGinty?"

"Rumors are swirling around. I thought for sure you would have heard them, started them or sent up smoke signals about them," replied Jake.

Toohey stumbled to his feet and approached Jake.

"Jake, we're old drinking pals, aren't we?"

"We're former drinking buddies and I'd say we're still friends," said Jake.

"Come to think of it, Ela looks a lot more like her mother than her father. But Indian blood is strong and dominant, especially over Irish blood."

"Could be," said Jake. "So, what do you hear about Lily?"

"I heard she was screwing one of Zeb's deputies. Was it you, Jake? You must get plenty of opportunities to bang the rich women around town."

"You're not making sense, Toohey. You're drunk."

A hint of sentimentality tinged with the truth flowed from Toohey's mouth. It was as if the old drinking days had suddenly been resurrected. There was a time when Jake used the badge as a tool to bed women. Jake's mind wandered for a minute before Toohey brought up an odd subject.

"I've been drunk since my second tour at Gitmo. That hellhole fucking sucked the life right out of me," said Toohey.

"Want to talk about it?" asked Jake.

"You weren't there. You don't have a clue."

"You still in the reserves?" asked Jake.

"Hell no."

"Miss it?"

"Hell no. You know what they do to Indians in the Army at a place like that?"

"Not great duty, I take it?"

"I drove a goddamn gasoline truck. I'm trained to interview battle-field prisoners, and I end up driving a stinking gas truck. All because I'm an Indian. I'm smarter than seventy-five percent of those inter-rogators, but, no, give the Injun the keys to the gas truck and hope he doesn't fuck it up. It sucked and I smelled like gasoline and diesel fuel for two years."

"That's the Army. I served in the military police and did nothing but paperwork on drunken GI's. Fuck the Army," said Jake.

"Fuck the Army is exactly right. You never get to do what you know and are trained for."

Toohey rose and retrieved another warm beer. He plopped back down on the weathered sofa and opened the beer.

"Sure you don't want one?" he asked Jake.

"I've been riding the sober train too long to drink now," replied Jake.

"Your loss," said Toohey.

"I gotta run," said Jake. "Talk again soon?"

"Any time," replied Toohey. "You know where to find me."

Jake maneuvered close to Toohey's truck as he made his way to his own vehicle. He poked his nose through the window of the truck. After eying the floor of the back seat, he put his hand on the door handle. A half second later two bullets from .45 long barrel gun exploded in rapid succession. The first to exit the chamber of the gun whizzed by Jake's ear. The second bullet landed in the dirt ten feet to the side of his right foot. Jake put his hands in the air and turned around.

"What the hell, Toohey?" he asked.

"Nobody goes near my truck," growled the drunk.

But it was too late. Jake had already seen what Toohey seemed to be hiding. Five plastic, one-gallon jugs of water. Two of them were empty. Setting on the floor next to the jugs were two medium sized bath towels, just large enough to wrap around someone's head before you water tortured them.

Jake moved slowly away from Toohey's truck. Toohey was no fool. By the time Jake would be able to get a search warrant, the water jugs and towels would be long gone. But Jake had found a potential link to Lily's torturous death. The question he needed answered ASAP was how would Toohey have gotten hold of Zeb's boots and belt?

Jake turned and got into his car. Toohey had a crazed look in his eye as he kept the weapon pointed directly at Jake's head.

"Later then," said Jake, slowly backing out of the driveway.

"Later," replied Toohey, slowly lowering the weapon.

32

MCGINTY MANSION

Jake knew Kate was going to be upset at having to wait for him to do a search of the McGinty mansion. He was prepared for an earful from her, but she said nothing as he walked back into the sheriff's office. Kate motioned to Jake and they headed out the door.

Kate looked back inside the office as she held the door open for Jake. She didn't consider herself to be a radical feminist, but she needed to straighten out the thinking of the men she worked with. Pregnancy was not an illness. In fact, it was probably the greatest state of health a woman ever attained.

"Hop in, Jake. I'm driving," said Kate.

As they drove to the McGinty home, Kate was quiet. Finally, she spoke.

"Jake, do you think Zeb is thinking clearly these days?"

Jake curled his lip. He knew exactly where this conversation was headed.

"Yeah, he's all right. He's under a little more stress than usual because of the murders, but, overall, I'd say he's as clear as ever," replied Jake.

"Mmm-hmm," said Kate.

"Speak your mind," said Jake. "That mmm-hmm sounded like more than just a plain old mmm-hmm."

"Do you think Zeb sent you along because I'm pregnant?" asked Kate as they pulled into the long-arced drive of the McGinty digs.

"I'm going to be honest with you when I say maybe," replied Jake.

"Women have been having kids since time began..."

"Don't take it personally," replied Jake. "Zeb has never been a father or been through a pregnancy with a woman. If he sent me along because you're pregnant, believe me, he thinks he's being kind and helpful to you."

"What the hell is he going to do when I'm seven, eight, nine months pregnant? Tie me to a desk?"

Jake shrugged. "Why don't you worry about that when the time comes?"

"Do you think I need help doing this?" asked Kate.

"Nope, but I'm glad to assist. I always wanted to snoop around the McGinty place. Man, if the walls could only talk."

"Didn't know you were a voyeur at heart," said Kate. "I suppose you were a fan of *Lifestyles of the Rich and Famous*?"

"I was. How the other half lives can be mighty strange. God only knows what we'll find."

They got out of the car. Jake knocked on the door in case private security had been brought in by Ela. When no one answered, he watched as Kate unlocked the front door with the key found in Lily's purse. When they stepped inside, Jake's lower jaw dropped.

"Nice digs, huh?" noted Kate.

"My trailer house could fit in their foyer. Throw in my yard, which also serves as a horse pasture, and there would still be space left over in the main room."

"Lily liked to spend money."

"Well, I guess," replied Jake. "Where should we begin?"

Kate pulled a plastic bag from her pocket. It contained the 1909 SVDB with the umbra error.

"Let's try and match this for starters. I think that might be as good of a starting place as any. As I remember, the coin collection is over there," said Kate, pointing to a glass case.

"Go ahead, open it up," said Jake.

Kate gently placed Lily's set of keys on the glass case and removed her key picking set from a pocket. She opened the small leather case which held thirty or so small instruments of the trade.

"Where did you learn to pick locks?" asked Jake.

"Josh taught me when we were dating," replied Kate.

"Sounds like you guys know how to have a good time."

"He learned it from his dad who used some of the tools in his gun business. The smaller parts of some expensive guns are not that much different than the inside of a lock," replied Kate.

Kate eyed the lock and reached for a small tool.

"Why not see if one of Lily's keys works?" asked Jake.

"She told me she lost the key to the glass case a long time ago and had no idea where it was," replied Kate.

"She was a drunk. Drunks forget stuff all the time. Let's give the keys a try."

Kate reluctantly agreed. Jake grabbed the keys and handed them to Kate. The first one slipped in easily and opened the odd lock.

"See if you can find the light switch for the interior light," said Kate.

Jake nosed around and flipped a few switches before the glass case illuminated brightly. Kate and Jake both slipped on latex gloves. Together they carefully removed the roll marked "Umbra Defect 1909-S VDB Lincoln Wheat Cent".

"Grab a piece of clean paper from the printer," said Kate.

Jake looked around until Kate jutted her chin in the direction of a writing desk.

"Here," said Jake. "What's the plan?"

"I'm going to carefully open this roll and count them. But first I'm going to examine it to see if it has ever been opened," said Kate.

The waxy paper wrapping was intact at first glance.

"I doubt Angus McGinty would have purchased the roll sight unseen," said Jake. "He was all business."

Kate pointed with a small tweezers to one end of the roll. Indeed, it had been opened. A small disruption line in the waxy paper was evident. She pointed the defect in the wrapper out to Jake who now had donned his close vision glasses.

"I'm going to empty them onto the piece of paper and we'll count them. There should be fifty of them," said Kate.

She laid them out slowly and carefully so as not to further damage the packaging or harm the pennies. Her count numbered forty-nine. Jake double-checked her work. He also came up with forty-nine. They checked each coin for the umbra error. The misprint was readily apparent on all forty-nine pennies. Satisfied, Kate replaced them and closed the roll before placing it in an evidence bag.

"I think we can assume the missing penny was the one found in Angus's hand. But we don't know if Angus had removed it for some reason," said Kate.

"Or if Lily placed the coin in Angus's hand," said Jake.

"Or if the killer broke into the house, stole the coin and placed it in Angus's hand as part of some intricate plot to frame Lily."

Engrossed in their work, neither Kate nor Jake heard the front door quietly open.

"Hold it right there. Don't move or you're both dead. Put your hands over your heads. Do it now!"

Kate and Jake did as they were ordered.

"Slowly turn around. Keep your hands away from your bodies and above your heads where we can see them."

Kate turned around to see a pair of muscle heads. They looked like they split their time laying in the tanning booth and pumping iron at the gym. However, they were holding some impressive handguns.

"We have a search warrant," said Kate.

The pair exchanged a glance before the bigger of the two men jerked his head toward the front porch. The second man stepped just outside the front door and called out.

"It's safe to come in."

A few seconds later a car door slammed. Ela McGinty strolled into the house like it was her own, which, technically, it was.

"They said they had a search warrant," explained one of the men.

"Sheriff Hanks send you two?" asked Ela.

"Yes," said Kate.

"Where's the search warrant?"

Jake swiveled his hips and, keeping his hands over his head, directed a thumb toward his back pocket. "I've got it."

Ela ordered the smaller of the muscle heads to retrieve it for her. She read it word for word.

"It looks legitimate," she said.

Not knowing what Ela was capable of, Kate and Jake breathed a collective sigh of relief.

"How do I know you weren't thieving the place?" asked Ela. "After all, you do work for Sheriff Zeb Hanks, not exactly the most trustworthy man in the law business."

"Call Judge Gritz. His name is on the warrant," said Jake.

Ela stared at the judge's signature.

"Mind if we put our hands down. I've got a bum shoulder," said Jake. "Arthritis."

"Keep 'em up," said the larger of the muscle guys.

"Fuck you," said Jake.

Putting his arms at his side, he approached the larger of the men.

"Stop or I'll shoot," the muscle head said.

"Like hell you will," said Jake, continuing to move toward the man. "You haven't got the guts..."

He grabbed the gun away from the bigger man as Kate grabbed the gun from the smaller, second muscle head, now stunned by what he was watching.

"...or the knowhow."

Jake pointed the muscle head's gun directly at him and pulled the trigger. The man fainted dead away before Jake had a chance to explain the safety was on. The smaller muscle head looked at his fallen comrade and meekly raised his hands.

"Never mind with that," said Kate. "Wake up your friend."

"Why don't the three of you sit over there on the couch," added Jake.

The three moved to the couch and plopped down like petulant teenagers who had just been grounded.

"Give me your key to the glass case and any other locked cabinets you have keys for," demanded Kate.

Ela handed over her key.

"Have you used it lately?"

"No."

The abruptness of Ela's reply triggered Kate's internal truth detector. Ela's words sounded like a lie. Could Ela have taken the coin and planted it on her father? Had Ela killed her father? Had Ela killed her father because she hated him? Had she killed him in some strange kind of twisted Electra complex? Did she have anything to do with her mother's death? A wave of nausea swept over Kate. The two hired muscle men and Ela sat quietly, taking it all in.

"Maybe the three of you had better vamoose," said Jake.

"This is going to be my house. I'm staying," insisted Ela.

Jake held up the search warrant. "This suggests that we can search without being impeded in any way. You and your cohorts are impeding our progress."

He pointed to the door. The muscle heads stood to go. Ela remained steadfastly glued to the sofa.

"We don't want to force you out of your family home, but it's the law," said Kate. "Why don't you go sit in your car and let us finish. Give us an hour and then you can come back in. Okay?"

This time Ela listened to reason and headed out the door.

"Don't destroy anything," said Ela.

"We'll be professional about our search. I promise you that."

"Where do we begin?" asked Jake.

"With those," said Kate, pointing to a collection of mounted feathers.

"I recognize these as eagle feathers, clearly illegal for a private collection," said Jake.

"What about this one?" asked Kate. "Isn't it identical to the one found at Angus's murder site?" Kate picked up the hawk feather and handed it to Jake.

"Yup. It's a Cooper's hawk feather. Around here it's got a half dozen different names—Mexican hawk, big blue darter, chicken hawk, hen hawk, quail hawk, striker. I've even heard it called a swift hawk. Nothing illegal about having a feather from one, but it is interesting that it's identical to the one found with Angus McGinty's body."

"Do you think somebody broke in, took the penny and the hawk feather and planted them to make Lily look guilty?"

"Or maybe Lily gave them to the killer. It's even possible Lily killed Angus and planted them herself," replied Jake.

"You're right about one thing," said Kate.

"How's that?" asked Jake.

"If only these walls could talk."

33

ZEB AND THORMAN

Zeb gently rolled his fingers on the disc showing the fight between Thorman and Angus with the knives in Angus's office. Zeb assumed Angus had purposefully kept it as leverage should he need it against Thorman. Did Thorman even know about it? Based on the way he reacted earlier he must have suspected Angus had something on him. Certainly Thorman couldn't have forgotten the way they threatened each other with knives. Perhaps there were other incidences between the men. Zeb might be able to get Thorman to confess to those.

Arriving outside the federal building where Thorman worked, Zeb parked his truck, locked his sidearm in the glove compartment and eased his way into the building through the security detectors. When the security personnel at the detectors noticed he was a county sheriff, they couldn't have been more accommodating.

"Thorman Wright's office?" asked Zeb at the information desk.

"Are you expected?" asked the lady.

"He knows I'm coming to see him," replied Zeb, omitting the fact that no specific time had been set.

"Ninth floor. Office number nine seventy-eight. Do you want me to call his secretary and let them know you're on the way up?"

"Thanks, but that's not necessary. If I have to wait a few minutes, I'll wait."

"Suit yourself."

Zeb entered the elevator. The edgy feeling of claustrophobia surrounded him. He wondered how people in cities managed the anxiety of being so compressed by their surroundings. When the doors opened on the ninth floor, he breathed a sigh of relief. He found office 978 and walked into the waiting area. Zeb exchanged greetings with the administrative assistant who reminded him a bit of Helen. Fifteen minutes later he was escorted into Thorman's office. Thorman had been with the department long enough to acquire a coveted corner office with windows on two sides.

"Sheriff Hanks, have a seat," said Thorman.

Zeb took a seat directly across from Thorman.

"What can I do for you? I assume this has to do with Angus McGinty?"

"It does."

Thorman Wright paused and eyed Zeb reticently.

"Does it have to do with Lily McGinty?"

"You've heard she was murdered?" asked Zeb.

"Tribal police have contacted me. They also told me you're a suspect in her death," said Thorman.

"Mind if I ask who you talked to?" asked Zeb, suspecting but hoping it wasn't Rambler who was feeding information directly to Thorman.

"You can ask, but I can't tell you since you're a suspect," replied Thorman.

"Fair enough."

"Why would they contact you?" asked Zeb.

"Same answer as the last. I can't tell you because you are a suspect."

Thorman's response was a bit too smug for Zeb's liking.

Zeb flipped the disc of the knife fight between Angus and Thorman onto Thorman's desk.

"What's this?" asked Thorman.

"Have a look."

Thorman popped the disc into his laptop. He instantly recognized the situation.

"Angus tried to kill me," said Thorman.

"Looks like you returned the favor," answered Zeb.

"He was insane. He hated me."

"Why?" asked Zeb.

"I was a thorn in his side. I made him follow the rules and he hated following the rules."

"And?"

"And what?" asked Thorman.

"And what else?"

Thorman's face flushed red hot. He suspected Zeb knew he had slept with Lily. Thorman held his head in shame.

"I think you know, Sheriff Hanks."

"I do. You were shacking up with Lily periodically. Don't be ashamed. You weren't the only one."

"Fuck," said Thorman. "You aren't thinking I might have killed both Angus and Lily?"

"Your words, Thorman, not mine."

Thorman began to quiver.

"I didn't kill anyone."

"Neither did I," said Zeb. "Maybe we can help each other."

"What do you want from me?" asked Thorman.

"Just one question," said Zeb.

"Yes?"

"Who inside the government bureaucracy has been looking into the Klondyke I mine?"

Thorman hit a few keystrokes on his computer. Slowly he ran a finger down the screen. On the third page of information he stopped and raised his head in Zeb's direction.

"About ninety days ago the Senate Select Committee on Copper Mining asked for a list of violations committed over the last five years at the Klondyke I."

"Who inside the committee made the request?"

Thorman rose from his desk and shut his door.

"Some staffer. I suppose a mid-level bureaucrat looking for information to write a report."

"Do you have a name?"

"Lin Xe Pang."

Thorman spelled it out for Zeb who, in turn, wrote it down. Zeb stood to leave.

"That's it?" asked Thorman.

"Yes," replied Zeb.

"Then you don't think I killed Angus or Lily?"

"I doubt you have the balls to kill anyone."

"I don't. I really don't," replied Thorman.

"One more thing," said Zeb.

"Yes?"

"Did you use protection when you had sex with Lily?"

A confused look overcame Thorman's face.

"She said she was on the pill. She wasn't pregnant when she died, was she?"

"No, but she had multiple venereal diseases," said Zeb.

Thorman stared woefully at his crotch as Zeb exited the room. His junk had been extraordinarily itchy as of late. He picked up the phone and called his doctor for an appointment.

34

BLACK BEAR AND COWBOY SHANK

When Black Bear pulled up to Cowboy Bob Shank's house this time, he merely shouted up toward the bathroom window.

"Cowboy, got a minute?"

"Is that you, Deputy Black Bear?"

"Yup."

"You've got great timing."

"Well, I guess."

"Let yourself in. Beers in the fridge. Help yourself while I expel this hamster."

Black Bear sipped on a beer as he admired Cowboy's trophy case. One particular prize caught his eye. Halfway through the beer, the toilet flushed and a smiling Cowboy ambled down the stairs, beer in hand.

Black Bear glanced back at the trophy case, caught the date on a recent prize Cowboy had won, then turned toward Cowboy as he approached.

"I should put all my broken bones in there along with those trophies and belts," said Cowboy. "That would tell the whole story."

"I bet it would," replied Black Bear.

"What's up, chief?" asked Cowboy. "What brings you back my way? My good looks?"

"Just a couple of questions," replied Black Bear.

"Fire away."

"When was the last time you saw Lily McGinty?"

"Been a while."

"Care to narrow that down?" asked Black Bear.

"Why, is she looking for me?"

"Doubt it."

"Let's see." Cowboy chugged back a long pull on his beer. "Lily McGinty? Hmm? Been a while."

"You're repeating yourself. You stalling me?"

"No. She bought a saddle from me a few months back. I'd won it in a poker game. It was a woman's saddle. It was a 1572 Sheridan Western Trail Horse saddle to be exact. She gave me two grand for a fifteen-hundred-dollar saddle. I bet you know what the extra was for."

"You got a receipt?"

"You're kidding, right?"

"You haven't seen her since?"

"That answer ain't gonna change."

"Got that right," said Black Bear.

"What's that mean?"

"She's dead."

"Dead? As in no longer among the living?" asked Cowboy.

"Yup."

"Drugs or alcohol?"

"Belt."

"Somebody beat her to death?"

"Nope. She was hanged by the neck after she was water tortured."

"I'd betcha it was the same person that killed Angus," said Cowboy.

"What makes you say that?"

"They were joined at the hip in their nastiness. They weren't in love, but they hated real good together. If you pissed one of 'em off, you pissed the other one off. If one hated you, two hated you, if you catch my drift."

"Angus hated you for screwing around with his wife?"

"Don't think so. We did a threesome a couple of times. You know how weird rich folks are."

"Did you kill her?"

"You kidding me?"

"Nope."

"She was easy money for me. You don't kill the goose that lays the golden egg, do you?"

"Not unless you're awfully stupid."

"Well, there you go. I'm not stupid. I didn't kill her, and, for what it's worth, I didn't kill Angus either," replied Cowboy.

Black Bear took a drink. His beer was getting warm. He didn't mind warm beer as much as he did chasing down dead ends. Cowboy was definitely a dead end. He didn't kill anyone. He just didn't have enough reason or motive to do so. Black Bear set his beer on the edge of the table. He knew Cowboy would finish it off later.

"When's your next rodeo?" asked Black Bear.

"Two weeks. Wrangler Roughstock down in El Mira. Should be easy money in it for me."

Black Bear walked over to Cowboy and shook his hand.

"Good riding to you, Cowboy. I hope you bring home the gold belt."

"Thanks, chief."

35

ZEB'S OFFICE

*Z*eb called his team together. Something needed to be done and time was of the essence. His office was standing room only with Jake, Kate, Black Bear and Shelly all present.

"Well, what've you got?" asked Zeb.

"Cowboy Bob Shank doesn't have the motive or the opportunity. I rule him out for a lot of reasons. First of all, he had nothing to gain and everything to lose. When I was at his house, I noticed the date on a trophy he'd won in a rodeo over in Amarillo. It was the same date as Angus's death. I checked with the rodeo and his competition was at seven p.m. Seems like a decent alibi. Then I checked his work status at the mine around the days of Angus's murder. He was off the day before, day of and day after. Next, I had Shelly run a check on his credit card. He purchased gas in Amarillo around midnight on the date of the murder. About the worst you can say about him is that he has constipation issues and he's a sex maniac," said Black Bear. "I say cross him off the list."

"Good work, Black Bear," said Zeb, drawing a line through Cowboy Bob Shank on the list of suspects.

"I paid a little visit to Thorman Wright," began Zeb. "He's a petty, bureaucratic fool, but he's not a killer ..."

"What about the disc found at Angus's office?" asked Kate.

"He's basically a coward. He doesn't have what it takes to kill. I suspect he was just defending himself and feeling tough when he and Angus faced off," said Zeb. "He's a little man with a little bit of power. He's the only one who thinks he wears a lot of hat. Murder is not in his heart. I'm going to scratch him off the list. Besides, he was at his desk until six that day. Our resident computer expert hacked into his personal security system, and he arrived home at six-fifteen, ate some leftovers, watched a couple of daytime soap operas that he'd recorded on his Tivo and went to bed at ten after nine."

"Shelly is proving herself quite handy," said Kate. "I hope she never comes after me."

"She's expensive but worth it," said Zeb.

"What about Ela McGinty?" asked Black Bear.

"She had motive," said Kate.

"She had multiple motives," added Zeb. "One of them being a huge inheritance when both of her parents were dead. And, with her parents gone, she had a much greater ability to help ELM shut down the Klondyke I mine."

"She hated her mother," said Kate.

"My guess is that her father abused her," said Black Bear.

"They had a love-hate relationship," added Kate.

"She's a McGinty. That gives her the potential for a whole lot of craziness," added Jake.

"We have exactly nothing regarding her whereabouts on the night of the murder. I guess she's on the list," said Zeb. "Jake, what have you got?"

"Toohey Blendah," said Jake, "took a shot at me the other day."

"What was that all about?" asked Zeb.

"Toohey was just being Toohey. He was drunk."

"Why are you waiting until now to tell me?" asked Zeb.

"He wasn't trying to hit me. He just didn't like the fact that I was taking a peek inside his car."

"Yeah?" said Zeb. "What'd you see."

"You know he was stationed twice at Gitmo," said Jake.

"No, I didn't."

"Was he an interrogator?" asked Black Bear.

"Trained to be one, but he ended up driving a truck."

"The United States Army has never trusted the American Indian," said Black Bear.

"You don't know that," snapped Zeb.

"What'd you see in his car?" asked Kate.

"Gallon jugs of water and towels. When I was looking at that, he took a couple of shots at me or, rather, near me. He could have hit me had he wanted to. I took it as a warning."

"You think he was the one who waterboarded Lily?"

"He had reason to. He had something to gain with her death," said Jake.

"He still wouldn't own the mine. Ela would be in line ahead of him in terms of inheritance," said Kate.

"But he would have the satisfaction of seeing both Angus and Lily dead. He believed Angus screwed with him at work and Lily unjustly took his rightful inheritance," said Zeb.

"And if Ela shut the mines down, he just might feel some vindication from that," said Black Bear. "A little something going your way is better than a whole lot of nothing coming your way."

"He and Ela held no animosity toward each other. Maybe they had a deal?" said Jake.

"How so?" asked Black Bear.

"Who knows if Ela might see all those dollar signs, change her mind and placate her sense of justice by giving a piece of the pie to Toohey?" said Zeb.

"I could see that," said Kate.

Black Bear and Jake nodded in agreement with the theory.

"Do we all agree that Toohey and Ela are our main suspects?" asked Zeb.

"Yup," said Jake.

"Yes," added Kate.

"Looks that way to me," said Black Bear.

36

ELA AND TOOHEY

Toohey Blendah picked up his ringing cell phone. He didn't recognize the number. However, he was drunk enough to talk to anyone. He answered.

"Toohey?"

"Yeah, who's this?"

"Ela, Ela McGinty."

"Ela, I heard about your folks. Tough luck on you."

"Yeah, I guess," replied Ela.

"What's up? I haven't heard from you in years."

"I've been away."

"College over in California is what I heard."

"That's right. College over in California that is thankfully done," replied Ela.

"To each his own."

"Yeah, I hear you. Say, I have a small favor to ask of you," said Ela.

"What can I possibly do for you?"

"I need to do some thinking. I'm heading up to Lookout Peak. Your place is the closest house where I can safely leave my car. I was wondering if I could park in your driveway?"

"When?"

"I was thinking of walking up there around sundown," said Ela.

"Tonight?" asked Toohey.

"Yes, tonight. So I'd be putting my car there in the next half hour or so."

"Why not? Park it on the east side of the driveway, would you?"

"Sure. Is the trail headed up to Lookout Peak in good shape?" asked Ela.

"Haven't used it lately, so I don't know what to tell you about that," replied Toohey.

"Are you going to be home? I'll drop in and say hi," said Ela.

"Nah, I'm headed to the Copper Pit Blues Bar. Join me for one when you're done with your contemplating, if you like," suggested Toohey.

"I'll do that," replied Ela.

"Good. I'll hold a bar stool for you. And by the way..."

"Yeah?"

"The kids now call Lookout Peak Lover's Leap."

"Good to know, but I'm not in love and I'm not leaping."

Toohey chuckled as he ended the call. Ela had her mother's sardonic sense of humor. That was a good thing.

37

LOOKOUT POINT

Ela parked her car and locked it. She knocked on Toohey's door to say hello in case he hadn't already headed for the bar. When no one answered, she began her trek up the thousand-foot vertical incline that defined the southern rim of the Klondyke 1 copper mine. By the time she reached the highest elevation, the stars were out in full glory.

She gazed down at the mine, shut down because of the investigation into her father's death but well-lit by security lights. Ela closed her eyes and began to meditate. Her efforts were futile. How could she think of nothing when everything she thought she believed in was butting up against the reality of fabulous wealth?

As the stars continued to unfold, she began to talk aloud to herself. In turn, she answered her own questions.

"Ela, do you want to be rich?"

"Yes, but at what price?"

"The world needs copper. It always will."

"But I can't be responsible for destroying Mother Earth."

"But with all the federal laws on land reclamation, in twenty or thirty years this will all look like nothing was ever here."

She stood and made a sweeping gesture with her hand over the open pit below. She had power, real power. The choice was hers. She laid down and looked up at the stars. Closing her eyes, Ela drifted off for a moment. When she re-opened her eyes, someone was standing over her. When the person spoke, Ela initially thought that she was dreaming.

"Abby, is that you?"

Ela blinked her eyes rapidly. Was this real? How could it be?

"Should I call you Abby or would you prefer your real name, Ela?"

Ela jumped to her feet and stared into the eyes of the woman she knew as Charlotte. The very woman she had hired to kill her father. Ela's immediate reaction was to reach for her knife, but she realized she had left it in the car. Charlotte, a professional killer, recognized the gesture.

"I thought we had parted ways once and forever," said Ela.

"You thought so. Don't you remember I told you we'd meet again?"

Ela's mind shot back to that night in the Copper Pit Blues Bar. Indeed, Charlotte had said if she were a betting woman, she would have bet their paths would cross again. But Ela had insisted they were to never again lay eyes on each other.

"What do you want? More money? Are you blackmailing me?" asked Ela.

"No, nothing like that. You paid me for what you hired me for. It's all good," said Charlotte. "I just wanted one final conversation with you now that you're a rich woman."

"What do you want to talk about?" asked Ela.

Charlotte reached inside her coat. Ela imagined her pulling out a gun, but she merely handed Ela a business card. The business card was black. Written on it in gold numbers was a phone number. The numbers were surrounded by a white cloud. Ela breathed a sigh of relief.

"A woman in your position might find it important to know a woman like me at some point in the future," said Charlotte.

"I don't think so," replied Ela, handing Charlotte back her business card.

"You're certain?"

"I am. You did what I paid you for and now, for the last time, our business is forever concluded," said Ela.

"Even after the freebie I gave you?"

Ela stared blankly at the woman whom she knew to be a hired assassin. Then it dawned on her.

"You killed my mother."

"I did. First freebie in my all my years of business. I guess I was trying to win your heart," said Charlotte.

"She probably had it coming. Her heart was made of stone. Did you make her suffer?" asked Ela.

"Suffering is one of my trademarks," said Charlotte.

"And the others?"

"Others?" asked Charlotte.

"Other trademarks?" asked Ela.

A fraction of a second later Ela's body was hurling down the thousand-foot cliff into the open pit of the Klondyke 1 copper mine.

"The element of shock and awe mixed with a surprise factor," said Charlotte softly as Ela's body pounded off layered edges of hard rock.

Charlotte slipped her business card back into her pocket and opened her cell phone. She clicked ##50**. A man's voice answered on the second ring.

"Three for three," said Charlotte. "You can wire the money after you read the morning news."

"When are you headed back here?" asked the man.

"I think I'll take a couple of days in Mexico before I return," said Charlotte.

"It's always good to refresh the mind, body and spirit with a little time off. Get hold of me when you get back."

Charlotte turned off her phone, laid on the ground and stared up at the untold number of stars that floated overhead. Life was as it was supposed to be. Her star was rising.

38

ELA'S BODY

Helen answered the phone. Zeb had arrived at work very early. She was glad he was there to take this call.

"Zeb, this is Byrne Murphy. I've got another body on my hands. It's not good. In fact, it's horrible."

Helen hadn't bothered to hang up the phone. She knew something bad was up from the sound of Byrne's voice. She wanted in on every detail.

"Who is it?" asked Zeb.

"Ela McGinty. I found her at the bottom of Lookout Peak."

Helen gasped audibly. Zeb placed the phone against his chest and shouted to Helen.

"Get everyone in here right now. I don't care if they have the day off or have other plans, get them here ASAP!"

Helen hung up her end of the line and began making the calls.

"Don't touch the body," said Zeb.

"I've got the area roped off. I'm not letting anyone close. This is tragic, so tragic. My God, the entire McGinty family is dead. Ela was just a kid. She hadn't hurt anyone."

"I'll get Doc Yackley and we'll be there in fifteen minutes," said Zeb.

He ended the call and shouted out to Helen who was on the phone with Kate discussing quick cures for morning sickness.

"Get Shelly in here too. I'll give you a note to give her."

Zeb quickly jotted down a note for Shelly. It was simple and direct. Get everything she could find from Ela McGinty's cell phone for the last twenty-four hours. Then start digging into any bad people she might have contact with via ELM or in her personal life. He put the note in an envelope and scratched Shelly's name on it. He handed it to Helen and headed for the Town Talk where Doc would be having breakfast.

"Doc, I've got an emergency," said Zeb, sitting down at the counter next to Doc Yackley.

"What's up?"

Zeb leaned in and quietly pronounced, "Dead body at the mines."

"Who?" asked Doc.

"Ela McGinty."

"What happened?"

"She fell from the rim top near Lookout Peak and made it all the way to the bottom," explained Zeb.

Doc took one final slurp of his coffee and led Zeb out of the door.

"I'll drive my Caddy and follow you," said Doc. "I've got to call the office and tell them to cancel my morning."

Byrne Murphy was waiting for Zeb and Doc near the cordoned off body of Ela McGinty. Byrne had covered the body without disturbing it. Doc stepped over the safety tape and pulled back the cover. He stared at the young woman's bruised and battered dead body. Then he craned his ancient neck and looked up the thousand or so foot vertical incline to the top of Lookout Peak.

"What are you thinking, Doc?"

"I'm thinking about two things. One, why would a beautiful young woman with a fortune at her fingertips and her whole life ahead of her take a swan dive to end it all?"

"Maybe she had a little help," replied Zeb.

"I guess that just being a McGinty puts you on somebody's enemies list," added Doc.

"And the second thing?" asked Zeb.

"I was thinking about the day she was born. I delivered her. She had a red mark on her cheek. Lily was just a young woman off the Rez back then and not so sophisticated. She was certain it was some sort of curse. It was just a little beauty mark, but Lily had a hissy fit. She said her daughter was cursed just like she was. I will always remember that. A woman doesn't just go around saying something like that with her newborn in her arms. It still upsets me to remember it. And now this. Terrible. Just terrible."

In the near distance the crunching of the ambulance tires made a low din that echoed up the mine wall. Zeb immediately recognized the crew as the same man and woman who had picked up Sun Rey Russell's body.

"Sheriff Hanks," said the woman. "Who and what have we got here?"

"Ela McGinty. It appears she slipped from up there."

Zeb directed a finger at Lookout Peak.

"No shit," said the woman. "I just signed her ELM petition. I heard her talking a while back on Rez radio. She said she was going to close down the Klondyke 1. Think somebody pushed her?"

"The investigation is just beginning," replied Zeb.

"Somebody pushed her," said the driver. "She's a McGinty. For Chrissakes, everyone has a bone to pick with that family."

Zeb didn't think her crass words required a response.

"Take the body to the hospital morgue after Doc has had a little more time to look it over."

"Right."

"Doc, did you spot anything unusual, considering the fall, I mean?"

"Nope. She's good to go to the morgue. I'll have a closer look when I have all my equipment."

The ambulance personnel loaded the body into the back of their vehicle.

"I wonder who pushed her?" pondered the ambulance driver.

"Somebody that didn't like her much, I suppose," replied her assistant.

"I wonder how many times she bounced off the side of the rocks?"

"Quite a few. There were more broken bones than I've ever felt before."

"The high and the mighty fall harder than the rest of us," said the woman.

Her co-worker scratched his head. He didn't have a clue what she was talking about.

39

NEW INFORMATION

"Zeb, did you notice Ela's BMW i8 parked at Toohey Blendah's house?" asked Jake.

"Yup," replied Zeb. "I think we'd better have a little chat with him right now."

"If he's got something to hide, or even if not, he's likely armed," said Jake.

"Black Bear come with us. Kate, head back to the office. Find out what Shelly is working on and let me know," ordered Zeb.

"Are you keeping me out the action because of my pregnancy?" asked Kate.

"Nope," replied Zeb. "I need you to have Shelly figure out if there are any cameras that picked up Ela's car. I also want you to have her check and see if she can find any video footage of someone who might have been stalking my house on the day of and the day before Lily was murdered. If she can find any footage, she should dig deeper into it. I already have her working on some other things. She'll bring you up to date on what she's got. If you have any suggestions when you're working with her, give them to her. I know she'll listen. Just remember she's in such a different league than the rest of us when it comes to this stuff. I suspect anything we think of she's already ahead of us. When you find something out, get a hold of me."

Satisfied with Zeb's explanation, Kate headed to the office.

"I doubt Toohey is going to be helpful. More likely he's going to be pissed that we consider him a suspect in this murder too," said Jake.

"Tough. I'm going to arrest him if Ela's car is there. If nothing else, we'll nail him for shooting at you. We've got plenty of probable cause."

"Let's go," said Black Bear. "If he's seen any of the activity around here, he might have already skedaddled."

The three trucks, led by Zeb, took the lawmen to the bottom of Toohey's long driveway where Ela's stylish BMW was parked. Toohey's truck was parked next to it.

Zeb, Jake and Black Bear, guns drawn, approached Toohey's house.

"Jake, do you think Toohey will go down without a fight?" asked Zeb

"I doubt it," replied Jake. "If Toohey pushed Ela off the cliff, he has good reason to come out with guns blazing."

Zeb's two-way radio buzzed. It was Kate.

"Zeb, have you moved in on Toohey yet?"

"No, we're at the perimeter of his property," replied Zeb.

"Hold back. Shelly has something significant."

"What is it?"

"The mining company and the city both have cameras at the top of Lookout Point. Someone pushed Ela off the cliff. It definitely wasn't Toohey," said Kate.

"How do you know for sure?" asked Zeb.

"Because I'm looking directly at the footage. Even though it was dark out, it's obvious that it was a woman who pushed her," said Kate. "A woman with a tattoo on her right wrist."

"Can you make out the tattoo?"

"Shelly was able to zoom in really well. It looks like the same kilted dragon that was on the wrist of the person who killed Angus."

"You're sure of that?" asked Zeb.

"I've looked at it a half dozen times. I'm ninety percent certain and so is Shelly. She's doing some more enhancing of the videos to compare and using some computer program to overlay the images."

"Got it. Thanks."

Zeb, using silent hand signals, ordered Black Bear and Jake away from the perimeter of Toohey's house. Both men moved discreetly toward Zeb.

"What's up?" asked Jake.

"The MacMhuradaich clan tattoo showed up again. Kate and Shelly are looking at footage from Lookout Point that shows a woman pushing Ela off the cliff," Zeb informed him.

"How do you know for sure? It was dark out."

"The mine and the city both put video cameras on top of Lookout Point along with a single overhead light."

"When did the mine put that up there?" asked Black Bear.

"I'll have to ask Byrne."

"What did the video show?" asked Jake.

"We have an image of the kilted dragon on the wrist of the woman who pushed Ela," explained Zeb.

"We've got a female killer for two of our murders," said Black Bear. "Anyone want to bet she killed off the entire McGinty family?"

"Seems logical," replied Zeb.

"I know why the mine has a video feed from up there," said Jake.

"Why? Security?" asked Zeb.

"A kid fell halfway down from there about ten years back as I recall," said Jake. "I think there was a lawsuit that got settled out of court. Danforth-Roerg kept it all pretty hush-hush. I only heard about it a few years after it happened. The kid that got the settlement got into some other minor trouble involving alcohol and I picked him up. He told me about how he could afford a big shot attorney because he had this money from a falling accident up on Lookout Point. His dad had just died, so I gave him a break and drove him home. I never made any record of it. Seems like I probably should have."

"No big deal," said Zeb. "The city also put a camera up there.

They never told me about it. If we're lucky, we've got video footage of the woman shoving Ela over the edge from two different angles."

"We've got a fairly positive link between Ela and Angus's deaths."

"The MacMchuradaich clan allegedly has a thousand-year history of assassinations," said Zeb. "The killers are usually women, at least according to legend and lore."

"Why would the MacMchuradaich clan be hired to kill Ela, Angus and maybe even Lily?" asked Black Bear.

"We don't have anything specifically linking Lily's murder to the other two murders just yet," said Zeb.

"If these murders were assassinations, what could the motive be?" asked Black Bear.

"Control of the mines seems most likely," said Zeb.

"Who would have hired the MacMchuradaich clan?" asked Black Bear.

"Good question," said Zeb.

"Obviously someone who wanted the McGintys out of the picture," said Jake.

"That someone could likely be interested in buying the mine," said Black Bear.

"Or possibly inheriting it," said Zeb.

"You don't think Toohey hired the MacMchuradaich clan, if indeed it was the MacMchuradaich clan who did the killings, do you?" asked Jake.

"The cost of three hired kills is big money," said Black Bear.

"Where would Toohey have gotten that kind of money? asked Zeb.

"He's not the type. He simply doesn't have the smarts to pull that kind of thing off," added Jake.

"Who, besides Danforth-Roerg, has a vested interest in the mine?" asked Black Bear.

Everyone became silent. After several long minutes, Black Bear spoke.

"What?"

"Danforth-Roerg is a Scottish company. They owned the other

fifty-one percent of the mine. With the McGintys gone, they could buy the rest of the mine on the cheap, relatively speaking," said Zeb.

"But why kill the entire family?" asked Black Bear. "With Lily and Angus dead, Ela would have wanted to get rid of the mine."

"She would have wanted it closed," said Zeb.

"Who would have wanted the McGintys out of the picture and wanted to see you in jail as well?" asked Jake. "After all, someone went to a lot of trouble to make it look like you killed Lily."

Zeb tipped his hat back on his head. He really was having trouble imagining the connection.

"Let's have a friendly visit with Toohey. I want to find out what the water torture stuff in his car was all about.

"He'll probably deny it was ever there," said Jake.

"We'll never know unless we ask," replied Zeb.

40

TOOHEY

Jake and Zeb knocked on Toohey's door. Black Bear remained hidden but rested his rifle across the hood of the car, just in case Toohey was looking for trouble. Toohey didn't answer after multiple knocks.

"Toohey," shouted Jake. "You home?"

A minute or two later Toohey answered the door in stained, sagged-out underwear and mismatched socks.

"I feel like shit. Too much whiskey and not enough sex," said Toohey, pushing the screen door open.

Jake knew what to expect, a mess. Zeb knew people lived like this, but Toohey could only be classified as a messy hoarder.

"Beer?" asked Toohey, opening one for himself.

Zeb and Jake had the same answer, "No thanks."

"What can I do you gentlemen for? Let's try and make it brief. I need some sleep."

"Whose car is that in your driveway?" asked Zeb.

Toohey pulled back the curtain and looked out at the fancy car.

"Nice wheels. I didn't get a good look at it before. One of those fancy new beamers. It belongs to Ela McGinty. She parked it here last night. She said she had some thinking to do and was going up to

Lookout Peak. She must have stayed up there last night or found a lover in the sky," laughed Toohey.

"You talked to her?" asked Zeb.

"Hell yes. We go back a ways. You know we're second cousins. I was nice to her when her daddy wasn't."

"How was her demeanor when you saw her last night?" asked Zeb.

"Oh, I didn't see her. I just talked to her on the phone."

"What'd she have to say?"

"Just that she was headed up the hill to do some thinking. I asked her to meet me at the Copper Pit for a drink when she was done thinking, but she never showed up. I sort of got drunk and forgot about it."

"Did she mention what she was going up there to think about?" asked Jake.

"Not that I recall."

"Did she sound upset?"

"Not to me she didn't."

"Did you see anyone else go up there?" asked Zeb.

"I told you already that I didn't see Ela go up there. I didn't see anyone else go up there either," said Toohey.

"What time did you head over to the Copper Pit?"

"It wasn't dark yet. I suppose around six."

"Can anyone verify you were there?"

"Hell yes. Talk to Slippery, the bartender..."

"I know who he is," interrupted Jake.

"I sat at the bar all night except for a few trips to the men's room."

"Did you stay until closing?"

"I think so. Yeah, I remember hearing Slippery shout out for last call. I was pretty blasted by then," replied Toohey, rubbing his head with the beer bottle.

"Do you know anyone who might have wanted to harm Ela?"

"No one personally. She's been gone for most of the last ten or twelve years."

"Did you ever know her to be suicidal?"

It was obvious from the expression on his face that Toohey was searching his mind.

"What happened?" asked Toohey.

"Just answer the question," said Jake. "Was she suicidal?"

"No. I don't think she was the type."

"Do you know any of the other young women Ela hung around with?" asked Zeb.

"I saw her at the Copper Pit a while back. She was drinking and talking privately with another gal that was probably ten years older than Ela," said Toohey. "She was busy, so I didn't bother her. In fact, I'm sure she didn't even notice me."

"The woman she was drinking with, can you describe her?" asked Zeb.

"Like I said, probably early to mid-thirties, taller than most, fox-red hair. I remember that, long fox-red hair. She was drinking a mixed drink, not a beer. She kept her collar up, sort of like she didn't want anyone to recognize her," said Toohey.

"You always did have a good eye for details when it came to women," said Jake. "Think back, what else did you notice."

Toohey closed his eyes, tipped his head back and put his brain to work.

"Nothin'."

"You sure?" asked Zeb.

"Well, maybe one more thing. She cupped her drink glass, almost like she was keeping it warm. Made me think she was drinking straight whiskey. She had something, maybe a dark wrist band or a tattoo on her right wrist. It was too dark to tell which it was or what it was," said Toohey.

"The right wrist? How do you know that?" asked Zeb.

"When I looked at them from where I was sitting at the bar, her right wrist would have been facing me."

"You remember details pretty well," said Jake.

"I do when it comes to women," replied Toohey. "Is that about it?"

"For now," replied Zeb.

"Hope I was helpful. I feel bad about Ela dying. I liked her," said Toohey.

"It's a bad deal," said Zeb. "Dying young is never good."

"Guys like us, Jake, Zeb, we're too old to die young now. That's from a song I heard on the radio by Todd Snider. Kind of a catchy tune if you ask me."

"Say, can I ask you one more thing?" asked Zeb.

"Sure."

"Why'd you fire your gun at Jake last time he was here?"

"Sorry about that, Jake."

"It's all right. I know you weren't aiming to kill," replied Jake.

"So why did you shoot at him, twice?" asked Zeb.

"I'm behind on my car payments. I thought he came here to repossess it."

"No chance it had anything to do with what was on the floor of the back seat, was it?" asked Zeb.

"Don't know what you mean, Zeb."

"Five gallon jugs of water and couple of towels."

"Water is for the radiator. Towels are for drying off after I use the hot springs west of town. What makes you ask?"

"Just curious," replied Zeb. "Thanks for your time."

Zeb, Jake and Black Bear huddled in a circle by Zeb's truck.

"I don't think he killed Lily," said Jake.

"I don't think he killed Ela either," said Zeb. "And I think whoever killed Angus also killed Ela."

"You think it was the MacMchuradaich clan that did the hit on both of them, don't you?" asked Black Bear.

"Looks that way," said Zeb.

"And Lily?" asked Jake.

"I think she was killed and I, or maybe even Echo, was set up as a ruse in much the same way Ela may have been set up as a ruse using ELM in her father's death," said Zeb.

"Well, that begs two rather large questions," noted Black Bear. "Who would hire the MacMchuradaich clan and why."

"Remember that movie, *All the President's Men*?" asked Jake.

Zeb and Black Bear nodded.

"Remember what the character called Deep Throat told Woodward and Bernstein..."

"Follow the money," said Black Bear.

"Right," replied Jake. "Follow the money."

"What money are you talking about?" asked Zeb. "Everybody loses if Klondyke 1 closes. Danforth-Roerg loses big money. God only knows how the courts are going to settle out the forty-nine percent owned by the McGinty family. Ela had no heirs. Angus's will cut Lily out of the loop. So what money do we follow?"

"Whoever stands to gain if the mine closes, that's who," said Black Bear.

"That's some dark thinking, Black Bear," said Zeb.

"Only entity I know that operates that way is the government," said Black Bear.

"You might be a little prejudiced that way," said Jake.

"I know what I've seen. Question is why would the government want it shut down?" asked Black Bear.

"And put five hundred people out of work?" asked Jake.

"Someone with an agenda that would make them wealthy," replied Zeb. "I guess we had better find the money trail if we want to find the killer."

41

ZEB'S OFFICE

J ake, Kate, Black Bear and Zeb formed a semi-circle around Shelly as her fingers flew across the keyboard like nothing they had ever seen.

"Let's take these things one at a time," said Shelly. "Let's start with the last twenty-four hours on Ela McGinty's cell phone."

"Who'd she talk to?" asked Zeb.

"Her final call was to Toohey Blendah. It was a short call."

"Maybe Toohey was telling the truth about Ela. Maybe she did call him only to ask if she could park her car at his place while she walked up to Lookout Peak," said Jake.

"It seems to fit his story," said Zeb.

"She made one other call. It was to her home landline number," said Shelly.

"She must have been calling Raindrop or Poochie," said Black Bear. "They were the only other people living there."

"My guess is that she told them where she was going. The three of them are pretty tight," said Black Bear.

"That makes sense," said Zeb. "Anyone have anything else to offer on the phone calls?"

When no one immediately did, Shelly brought up what else she had found.

"When I read your notes on the MacMchuradaich clan of women killers, I did some digging. I found that three MacMchuradaich women live in the U.S. They're all directly involved with the clan's business. Breauana lives in New Jersey, Caitlyn in LA and Nesea just outside of DC. Breauana and Nesea are identical twins. They've all kept their ancestral name. All of them have arrest records. None of them have any convictions. One thing they have in common is the same tattoo on the right wrist. One of them, Neasa, is rumored to be an FBI snitch."

"Interesting," replied Zeb. "What do you have on her?"

"She's twenty-nine, twice divorced, one child that is being raised by her mother back home in Scotland. She took back her maiden name after her most recent divorce. The FBI file says she is considered 'troubled of mind' by the family. The file does not indicate that she is acting as an informant for them."

Zeb made a mental note of Nesea's name, that she might be an FBI snitch and that she was considered trouble by MacMchuradaich clan.

"I checked all flights coming in from the New York/New Jersey area, the LA area and D.C. on the day before Lily's death and Ela's death. I cross referenced that with onsite and offsite car rental locations in Tucson. Fortunately, there weren't that many flights."

"What did you find, anything?" asked Zeb.

"As a matter of fact I did. The security cameras at the airport showed a woman matching the description of the woman who had a drink with Ela at the Copper Pit Blues Bar a week before Angus's murder and the day before Lily's death."

"Makes sense," said Zeb. "A week to get to know the lay of the land, commit the murder and skedaddle out of town. The second time around she knew what she was up to."

"That's the way it looks," said Shelly. "I've also got even better footage of the same woman arriving the day before Lily's murder. The camera picked up a perfect image of the tattoo on her right hand."

"Good," said Zeb. "We know the tattooed woman was in Tucson. The question is did she come to Safford?"

"I further checked both on and offsite rental locations. I found footage of the same woman renting a red Jeep both times," said Shelly.

"Were you able to visualize the wrist tattoo either time?" asked Zeb.

"Not at the rental places. I was only able to obtain bad camera angles from inexpensive equipment. She pays cash for the rental itself and gives a cash deposit. I called and the deposit is only fifteen hundred dollars. I don't know how these secondary car rental places stay in business. You'd think they'd get their cars stolen all the time."

"I'd bet they're a front for drug money," said Black Bear.

"Not our problem," said Jake.

"When she left the car rental lot, could you tell where she went?" asked Zeb.

"Yes. It was practically no work at all to trace her movements. The I-ten has cameras every mile. Tucson has spent their federal home-land security money wisely. The city has a great video system that's easily integrated from camera to camera," said Shelly.

"Where did she go?"

"After she left the rental lot, she headed straight to a building in Old Tucson. It was her only stop. She parked on the street, fed the meter and was inside the building for roughly twenty minutes."

"Any idea who occupies the building?" asked Zeb.

"Mostly attorneys, but there is also a CPA firm, some PACs, a state senator's local office and a couple of dentists. State Senator Devon Dawbyns has his local office headquartered there."

Jake, Kate and Zeb shared a glance. Black Bear noticed the inter-action but had no idea what it meant. He knew Dawbyns had built his political career by being a deputy for Sheriff Hanks. But he knew little about the man himself. Shelly also caught their reactions and had a pretty good idea what it might mean.

"Any idea whose office she stopped at?" asked Zeb.

"I know exactly which office she stopped in." replied Shelly.

"Do tell," said Zeb.

"Let me give you a hint. She wasn't there to get her teeth cleaned, have her taxes done or make a political contribution," said Shelly.

"State Senator Dawbyns," said Black Bear. "What could he have to do with this?"

A single thought passed through the minds of Zeb, Jake and Kate.

"Are you thinking what I'm thinking?" asked Zeb.

"That Dawbyns was a middle man?" asked Kate.

"For whom?" asked Jake.

"I take it you guys think Senator Dawbyns is dirty?" said Black Bear.

"Let's just say he's the sort of fellow whose scruples are not above reproach," said Jake.

"Did you catch the woman on any cameras locally?" asked Zeb.

"Yes. She drove by this office three times on the morning before Lily's death. I caught a partial plate on the western most camera on the road headed to your place, Zeb. But, as you know, there are no cameras within a mile of your house."

"Was my vehicle parked at the office when she drove by?" asked Zeb.

"Yes," replied Shelly.

"She was casing the office to see if I was here."

"That makes sense," added Jake.

"I'd bet anything she broke into my house and stole my boots and belt, the ones involved in Lily's killing. She was setting me up."

"Why?" asked Black Bear.

"Whoever hired her wants me out of the picture," replied Zeb.

"Agent Ezequiel?" asked Kate.

"Thorman Wright?" asked Jake.

"Who holds the Sword of Damocles over your head?" asked Black Bear.

Zeb didn't like where his mind took him. The pieces of the puzzle were coming precariously together. Suddenly Lily's murder did appear to be about him. He needed to clear his mind and think it through logically. He dismissed his team and told them to get to work on what they now knew. When they left, he made a call to Echo.

"Watch your back," he warned her.

"From whom?"

"It could be anyone. A hired killer, I suspect. Likely a woman, thirty-ish, red hair."

The immediacy of the tension that comes with combat jolted through Echo.

"Okay. I'm ready. Do I need to know some background information?"

"I think it has to do with my past, but it's very likely more complicated than that. Just be hypervigilant for now."

"What's your next move?" asked Echo.

"I'm headed out to the Rez to talk to Rambler. I get the distinct impression he's being heavily pressured to keep me away from Lily's death scene. I need to find out why."

"You're a suspect in her murder," said Echo. "Isn't that reason enough?"

"Rambler knows I didn't do it. If someone wasn't breathing down his neck, he'd let me go over the scene of the crime with a fine-toothed comb."

"Who has Rambler on a leash?"

"Has to be the feds...I think."

42

RAMBLER'S OFFICE

Zeb removed his hat at the city limits and placed it on the truck seat. The sun beating through the windshield made him hot, sweaty and tense. Perhaps it was the anger he was feeling about the triple murders that wiped out an entire blood line. Maybe it was the distance Rambler was putting between their long-time friendship. Most certainly his rage was aimed at whoever was setting him up. The one factor he could deal with directly was his relationship with Rambler. Zeb punched on the accelerator.

The usual slow moving, semi-dozing Rez dogs peered through half-open eyes as Zeb pulled into a parking spot in front of Rambler's office. Zeb heard voices coming from inside.

Zeb walked into the office, not sure what to expect. Rambler's assistant told Zeb to take a seat. Listening closely, he heard his name mentioned more than once. Five minutes later Zeb heard the back door to Rambler's office slam loudly. He peered through a side window as four people stomped away. A minute later, flush-faced, Rambler walked into the outer office and grabbed a cold drink without so much as giving Zeb a nod. Zeb cleared his throat at the same moment Rambler's assistant spoke up.

"Sheriff Hanks is here to see you, Rambler."

Oddly, Zeb's presence seemed to calm the obviously upset Rambler.

"Come in, that is, if you're not here to complain about something and tell me what I can and cannot do," said Rambler.

Zeb stayed glued to his chair. Rambler looked over at him and noticed Zeb wasn't about to move. He laughed.

"What the hell, come in anyway."

"Tough day?" asked Zeb.

"Some days I could just take this job and shove it," replied Rambler.

"Politics?" asked Zeb.

"And then some," replied Rambler. "What can I do for you?"

"I didn't kill Lily," said Zeb. "But I might be on to why she's dead."

"Me too," replied Rambler. "What's your version of the story?"

"Money."

"I think we can agree on that," said Rambler.

"Who was that leaving your office just now?" asked Zeb. "Do they have something to do with the money?"

"You've got that right. Those were four of the five tribal council members. They are threatening my job if I don't make you look guilty."

"Why?" asked Zeb.

"Money."

"What's up?"

"The BIA, HUD, the Indian Trust, numerous congressional committees and unique private donors who give to special projects are threatening to take away half of the tribal budget unless this office can link you, even if only peripherally, to Lily's murder. It's not helping that your boots and belt were involved in the crime, or that Echo's family lives only a short distance from the crime scene."

"Someone wants my scalp, I take it?" asked Zeb.

"Got that right."

"Are they after Echo too?" asked Zeb.

"Only if it means getting you."

"Goddamn it. Who is behind this?"

"The usual suspects," said Rambler.

"And who are the usual suspects?"

"The great White fathers in Washington."

"Come on," said Zeb. "Don't talk hocus-pocus to me. You can't blame everything on politicians."

"Oh yes, I could but I'm not. This threat actually does come directly from D.C."

"Who wants so badly to see me go down?" asked Zeb.

"I was hoping you knew the answer to that one," replied Rambler.

"Agent Jesus Ezequiel might have a vendetta against me. In fact, I know he does. But I doubt he wields that kind of power inside the FBI," said Zeb.

"It could be him, but I doubt it," said Rambler. "He doesn't like you. That's for certain. He thinks you're guilty of something, but I don't think he's got enough proof to even come close to tying you to Lily's murder."

"There's a mine inspector, Thorman Wright, who hated the McGintys. He doesn't care for me all that much either, but I've got shit on him that I think would prevent him from acting against me," said Zeb.

"I don't know. He seems to be connected politically. At least that's the way he talks. I wouldn't cross him off the list just yet. Who else wants to see you go down hard?"

"Someone with a vendetta against Echo?" asked Zeb.

"That's a real shot in the dark," replied Rambler. "Who knows about what went down in Mexico?"

Zeb hesitated. He knew that Rambler knew he had killed Doreen's killer in Mexico. Rambler also was aware that Doreen's killer was connected to the upper rungs of a highly influential drug cartel. Could they have direct influence in the U.S. government? Maybe. He didn't know exactly how cross border favors worked. Then it dawned on him. Only two people in D.C. knew the full story of what happened in Mexico when Zeb pierced the beating heart of Doreen's killer, Carmelita Montoyuez, with the tip of an epee. Those two people were Elaine Coburn, Kate's mentor from her days at the FBI, and Senator Russell.

"I've got to run," said Zeb.

"Just one second," replied Rambler. "What do you know that you aren't telling me?"

"You don't want to know," said Zeb. "If I tell you, someone might come after you."

"I'm not afraid," stated Rambler.

Zeb slipped his hat back on his head and offered a final warning to his fellow lawman.

"You should be."

43

FOLLOW THE MONEY

Zeb's tires squealed and kicked up red dust as his truck jumped from the hardened dirt of the Rez road onto State Highway 70, headed back toward Safford. He tapped his two-way radio and contacted Helen.

"I need everyone at the office when I get there. No exceptions," explained Zeb.

"They'll be here," said Helen.

Zeb pulled his truck behind the office in his usual spot. He could see the others had already arrived.

"Everyone is in the conference room," said Helen.

Uncharacteristically, Zeb nodded to his receptionist/aunt without saying a word. Helen didn't care for the lack of manners.

"Zeb Hanks," she said, stopping the sheriff in his tracks. "You're better than that. You should always return a greeting."

"Yes, ma'am," replied Zeb. "I'm feeling rushed, but that's no excuse. Greetings Helen. How are you doing today?"

"I'm fine. Don't forget to mind your manners. Now you've got work to do. Get to it," said Helen.

Zeb smiled. Helen's words made him feel a little less tense as he entered the conference room where his cohorts awaited him.

"What's up?" asked Jake.

"Has Shelly left town?" asked Zeb.

"I just saw her over at the Town Talk," replied Kate. "They've got a special vegetarian menu for her. She eats every meal there when she's in town."

"Get her over here, please," said Zeb.

"I'll run over there and get her," said Black Bear.

The Town Talk was just around the corner. In less than four minutes Shelly joined the sheriff and his deputies.

"What's going on?" she asked.

"I think I know who's behind the murders of Angus, Lily and Ela McGinty," replied Zeb.

"Go on," insisted Jake.

"Kate, have you had any contact with Elaine Coburn lately?" asked Zeb.

"I called her to tell her I was pregnant."

"How did she seem?" asked Zeb.

"Seem? Elaine? Fine, I guess. Nothing out of the ordinary. We mostly talked about pregnancy. Why? How does she possibly figure into all of this?"

"She didn't bring up any past history between her and this office, did she?" asked Zeb.

Kate thought for a moment before answering. "No."

"Have any of you had contact with Senator Russell?" asked Zeb.

None of them had.

"What's this all about?" asked Black Bear.

"I just had a nice chat with Rambler. Unless he can deliver my head on a platter, the BIA, HUD, the Indian Trust, some congressional committees and private donors to special Indian projects are threatening to take away half of the tribal budget. The tribal council is putting almost unbearable heat on him. He stands to lose his job unless he can nail me for the murder of Lily McGinty."

"That points directly to Washington, D.C.," said Black Bear.

"My thoughts exactly," replied Zeb.

"The question is why," said Black Bear.

"No, you're dead wrong, Black Bear. The question is who," replied Zeb.

"My guess is that someone in D.C. figures you are the only one who can put the pieces of the puzzle together," said Jake. "Someone might be trying to kill two birds with one stone."

"What?" asked a puzzled Black Bear.

"Before your time," replied Jake. "Don't worry about it."

"If you say so," replied Black Bear. "But why keep me in the dark?"

No response was forthcoming. Everyone in the room knew there was no need for Black Bear to know about Zeb killing Carmelita Montoyuez.

"Shelly, I need some more inside baseball from you," said Zeb.

"What do you need?"

"I want to know what you can find out on Lin Xe Pang. He's a senatorial aide, I think. I suspect he writes reports for the Senate Select Committee on Copper Mining," said Zeb, pointing to the computer bag slung around her shoulder.

"I was in the middle of a cup of coffee..."

"I'll get you one," said Black Bear. "My guess is that this isn't meant for my ears or eyes."

"Don't get sarcastic with me. You're still the rookie around here," said Zeb. "But get everyone coffee and tea for me. Ask Helen if she wants a sweet treat."

In a flash Shelly was set to go. By the time Black Bear was out the door, she was on the senate staff page.

"The clock is running. Here we go," said Shelly. "Lin Xe Pang is a Harvard graduate who majored in International Relations and Economics. He minored in Creative Writing. His father is a billionaire who owns a half dozen Chinese copper companies."

"Makes him a natural fit for the job," said Kate.

"And a perfect inside man for his father's business," added Jake.

"Mr. Pang works for a highly trained pool of people who write the specifics into the final version of senate legislation. He is currently assigned to writing the definitive version of the copper mining bills that will go before Congress in this year's budget act," said Shelly.

"Makes perfect sense," said Zeb.

"How so?" asked Jake.

"Mr. Lin Xe Pang called Thorman Wright about three months ago. He asked for the records on any and all violations at the Klondyke 1 mine. Thorman gave me that information freely. As sure as dogs bark, I'd bet Mr. Pang was working at the behest of Senator Russell. Is there any way you can figure that out, Shelly?" asked Zeb.

"No sweat," said Shelly, pulling her multi-colored hair into a ponytail. "Reports have to go somewhere and they always leave an electronic trail. Give me one minute."

Shelly's fingers zipped across the keyboard at lightning speed as Black Bear returned with coffees and tea.

"Did you already give Helen her blueberry muffin?" asked Zeb

"How'd you know she wanted that?" asked Black Bear.

Before Zeb could answer, the frustrated deputy said, "Oh, never mind. It doesn't matter. I'm beginning to think I don't have a clue about half the shit that happens around here."

"You don't," replied Jake. "But if you stick around, you'll figure it out."

"Here we go," said Shelly. "The report was co-authored by another Harvard graduate, Silvio Rojas Soto, whose father just happens to be a major player in the copper mining business in Chile."

"Whoa. Bingo," said Jake. "Things are starting to link up and make sense."

"Who did the report go to?" asked Zeb.

"Let me check the electronic footprint they left behind. Hmm."

"Hmm?"

"You're not going to like this, Zeb."

"Give it to me straight," ordered Zeb.

"It didn't go to any committees or sub-committees. It went directly to Senator Russell, the Chinese ambassador, the Chilean ambassador and to the authors' fathers."

"Shit," said Zeb.

"Looks and smells like a conspiracy," said Black Bear.

"Good call," added Jake.

"No doubt, it does look like some people in the international copper industry are doing something collectively," said Kate.

"The summary of the report more or less damns the Klondyke as unsafe," said Shelly.

Everyone was thinking the same thought. Black Bear voiced it.

"Why would Senator Russell want the Klondyke mine closed down?"

"Follow the money," said Kate.

"What did you say?" asked Zeb.

"Follow the money. Shelly has already hacked into Senator Russell's offshore accounts. See if he received any money from the Chinese and Chilean copper interests, specifically those owned by the fathers of Lin Xe Pang and Silvio Rojas Soto," said Kate.

"Can you do that?" asked Zeb.

"Sure, but it's going to cost you. It won't be an easy process to link all of this together. Can you give me twenty-four hours?"

Zeb glanced at his wristwatch.

"Any chance of getting it quicker than that?" he asked.

"Even in the world of computer technology things only move so fast," replied Shelly.

"Okay. Twenty-four hours. We'll all meet here then."

Helen tapped on the conference room door before entering.

"Zeb, it's Senator Russell on line one. He wants to talk to you."

With his mind in conspiratorial mode, Zeb was certain his office had been bugged. He quickly shook off the thought. Paranoia had no place in solving a triple murder.

44

SENATOR RUSSELL

"Zeb, this is Senator Russell."

"Senator Russell, to what do I owe the honor of this phone call?" asked Zeb.

"I think you have a pretty good idea."

"I assume it concerns the murders of the McGintys," replied Zeb.

"It does. Do you have anything yet?"

"We're getting real close," replied Zeb.

"Real close to what?" asked Senator Russell. "Solving the murders or having decent suspects?"

Zeb paused. How much should he tell Senator Russell? The senator was not only one of two people in D.C. that could link him to the killing of Carmelita Montoyuez, but he headed the copper mining committee and was on the numerous committees that held fiscal power over the San Carlos tribe. Knowing politicians as he did, Zeb assumed the worst. His words hedged his bet.

"We're getting closer to knowing what happened and to linking the three murders to the same killer," said Zeb.

"Is the killer someone from the area?" asked Senator Russell.

Zeb had no desire to give away his hand. An easy lie slipped from his tongue.

"We think so."

"Get him and get him fast," said Senator Russell. "I'm flying into Tucson. I'll be in Safford the day after tomorrow. I'm meeting with the top executives from Danforth-Roerg. I'd like you to join us for supper at the Top of the Mountain Steakhouse. Feel free to bring your new girlfriend, Echo, with you."

Zeb wondered exactly how much Senator Russell knew about Echo. Anything was too much. He would have access to her military records. Zeb also knew that if Shelly could hack into anyone's information, the senator certainly had people who could do the same.

"You buying?" asked Zeb.

"Of course. This is official government business," replied Senator Russell. "Can you be there at eight?"

"I'll be there," replied Zeb.

"And Miss Skysong?"

"I don't think she would want to miss a chance to meet a US Senator," replied Zeb.

"Good. Then it's all set. Dinner at eight on the Top of the Mountain, Friday night. I'll see you then. Have something for me on these murders."

Zeb didn't much care for the command coming from the senator. He didn't reply before the senator abruptly hung up. Zeb pressed 2 on his cell. Echo answered.

"Do you want to have supper with Senator Russell and the big dogs from Danforth-Roerg Friday night at eight?" asked Zeb.

"I can think of better ways to spend my time," replied Echo.

"I need your eyes and ears on this," said Zeb.

"Maybe what I meant to say was, I can't think of a single thing I'd rather do," said Echo.

"I love you," said Zeb.

"I love you, too," responded Echo.

45

MONEY TALKS

Zeb arrived early at the office. True to her word, Shelly had worked through the night. Zeb eyed a half dozen empty coffee cups and noticed a pot of fresh brew.

"Too much of that will kill you," said Zeb, pointing to the freshly brewing coffee.

"Tell me about it. You can't buy a decent cup of coffee in this town after midnight," retorted Shelly.

"You want me to grab you something from the Town Talk? You want to take a break for breakfast? It's on me," said Zeb.

"My time clock ticks either way, but I am getting hungry."

"Let's go," said Zeb. "The blueberry pancakes are killer."

The pair walked silently across and down the street to the Town Talk Diner.

"It would have been quicker to walk kitty corner style instead of walking in the crosswalks," said Shelly.

"I never jaywalk," replied Zeb. "I'd have to give myself a ticket. I'm a bit like Barney Fife that way."

"You are a stickler for the law, aren't you?" asked Shelly.

"Well, I guess..."

"You don't need to BS me, Sheriff Hanks. I took a ten-minute break, on my own time, around three a.m. I checked to see if Senator Russell had been keeping an eye on you. I figure he knows I do work for you. If he knows that, he will look into me. I checked that out too. He's got a lot more on you than he does on me."

"What exactly do you know?" asked Zeb.

"Everything Senator Russell knows about you."

"Something bothering you about what you know?" asked Zeb.

"Yes."

"Now's the time to ask," said Zeb.

"How on earth did you work your way into the upper echelon of a drug cartel without them doing a deep background check on you. It would have been so simple to figure out who you really were," said Shelly.

Zeb looked down. He didn't know how much Senator Russell had written in his private accounting of what happened in Mexico. That made it difficult to answer Shelly's question.

"You have me at an advantage," said Zeb. "I don't know what you know about Mexico."

"Carmelita Montoyuez, if she really did kill Doreen, then she had it coming. I don't hold you up to any higher standard than I would hold myself to. I've never been married. I thought I was in love once with this game freak in college, but he turned out to be a lazy bum. Still, I can understand how the pain and suffering of loss leads to the desire for revenge," said Shelly.

"Then you know all there is to know," said Zeb.

"I'll keep what I know between us," said Shelly.

"I was hoping that was how you'd see it," replied Zeb.

"Subject is dropped," said Shelly. "Let's have some breakfast."

The pair chose a seat far away from the other customers. Zeb ordered a stack of blueberry pancakes for each of them, coffee for Shelly and chamomile tea for himself.

"Are you clear minded after being up all night?" asked Zeb.

"Clearer than most people ever are," replied Shelly. "I'll sleep tonight."

"What did you find out?" asked Zeb.

"Lots. Maybe too much."

"Meaning?"

"Meaning that when you deal with people who have the kind of power Senator Russell has, there is no telling what might happen if and when you spill the beans on him," replied Shelly.

"You're not obliged to tell me anything that you think could endanger your life," said Zeb.

"If I tell you what I've found, my life could hang in the balance. So could yours," said Shelly. "But there's no doubt in my mind what's the right thing to do."

"Let's hear it," said Zeb.

"Senator Russell is playing both sides to his advantage," said Shelly.

"That's his M.O.," replied Zeb. "He's operated that way ever since I've dealt with him."

"He's playing the Chinese and Chilean copper industries against American interests, and he's taking money from all three," said Shelly.

"What kind of money are we talking here?" asked Zeb.

"Almost two million from the Chinese and just over a million from the Chileans. All that money is off the books. On the books, he's received just under a quarter of a million from Danforth-Roerg and Angus McGinty."

"That makes for rather strange bedfellows," said Zeb.

"He's already officially told Danforth-Roerg that the water it takes to run the Klondyke I is gone for the next two years. Then, magically, somehow the spigots will be turned back on."

"How is he going to pull that off?" asked Zeb.

"He's using his influence in the BIA and several committees he's on. He's threatened to cut funding in half to the San Carlos Reservation if they don't stop supplying the mines with water. That is an across the board cut including health agencies, schools, roads, bridges, food stamps. You get the idea."

"That explains a lot," said Zeb. "When I was talking to Rambler Braing, Chief of Police on the San Carlos, he was being pressured by the tribal council to pin the murder of Lily McGinty on me. Russell doesn't want me getting to the bottom of all of this."

"There's no doubt Senator Russell would like to see you out of the picture. More than one memo in his personal file points to finding a way to pin the death of Carmelita Montoyuez on you while at the same time keeping him out of the picture," said Shelly.

"At least he's smart enough to be concerned that if I go down and I'm still alive and talking, he goes down too," said Zeb.

"I would be watching my back if I were you," said Shelly. "He's got connections to some very bad people. From looking at his private records, I think he's hired a professional killer. It's all code talk in his notes, but it really couldn't be anything else."

"Does it appear he wants me dead imminently?"

"You're on the short list. So were Angus McGinty and Lily McGinty. That would make my answer to your question, yes, he wants you dead sooner rather than later," replied Shelly

"But Ela wasn't on the short list?" asked Zeb.

"Not that I could see. Perhaps he thought her connection with ELM would cause her to shut down the mines. It's just conjecture. I have no proof she was on the hit list. Plus, he's dealing with Danforth-Roerg."

"I'm pretty sure Danforth-Roerg is going to get some nice federal benefits for temporarily closing down the mine," said Zeb.

"It all makes sense from the criminal point of view, doesn't it?" said Shelly.

"It does," replied Zeb. "Senator Russell gets rich by taking big money from Chinese and Chilean copper interests. He gets some graft from Danforth-Roerg as well. He holds the Apache Nation hostage by threatening their funding. He has an entire family knocked off to remove any influence they have on the situation. He can dish out political favors to whomever he wants. In the end, he controls the purse strings."

"He's a psychopath," said Shelly. "And a sociopath."

"Proof that the apple doesn't fall from the tree," said Zeb.

"His son, Sun Rey Russell? Is that who you are referring to?"

"Yes. I kept Sun Rey out of jail and handed him over to his father for treatment. He had numerous mental and psychosocial disorders. The treatment failed and Sun Rey is dead."

"I know," said Shelly.

"Senator Russell invited me to dinner tomorrow night with some executives from Danforth-Roerg," said Zeb.

"Far be it from me to tell you how to do your job, Sheriff Hanks. But if I were you, I'd be carrying a gun," said Shelly.

Zeb looked over at the seemingly innocent young woman with the giant brain and multi-colored hair and smiled.

"I always carry a gun," said Zeb. "Or two."

46

MEXICAN STAND OFF

E cho, dressed to the nines, stood in front of the full-length mirror and checked herself out in the way that all women do when they want to make certain they look their best. Tying his dress shoes, Zeb glanced over his shoulder and noticed how stunningly beautiful she really was.

"Are you wearing that outfit to impress Senator Russell or me?" he asked.

Echo turned to Zeb and slowly pulled back the slit on her skirt, showing off a smooth left thigh. She paused. Zeb smiled from ear-to-ear.

"It's all for you, Zeb, honey." She lifted her skirt to her knees, revealing a small, self-defense 9mm handgun strapped to the inside of her lower right calf. "This is for Senator Russell."

Zeb chuckled, stood up, walked over and planted a kiss on Echo's lips.

"You're the best backup a man could have."

"Let's hope I don't need to use it," replied Echo.

"You won't. This should be a very civilized dinner."

"You ready to go?" asked Echo.

"Yup, and I'm hungry too," joked Zeb.

On the drive to the Top of the Mountain Steakhouse, Echo wanted to know what the plan was.

"This isn't a war mission," replied Zeb. "We're going to have to play it by ear."

"I've been in the field often enough to know that once the mission starts the plan is out the window," replied Echo. "I'd like to know what to expect."

"I've told you everything I know. Senator Russell has no limits on what he's willing to do or capable of doing."

"What about the professional killers on his speed dial? You don't think he'd have you hit at the restaurant in front of Danforth-Roerg executives, do you?" asked Echo.

"I've got enough on him, and he's got enough on me, that I doubt killing me tonight will be his first option."

Echo felt military mission tautness in her mind and body.

"I'm ready for anything," she said.

The car lot attendant took the keys to Zeb's truck after holding the door open for Echo.

"Sheriff Hanks, the rest of Senator Russell's party is in the Elk Room," said the attendant.

Zeb tipped the young man ten dollars.

"The Elk Room looks out over the valley toward Safford. It's very intimate with floor to ceiling glass windows," explained Zeb.

"Good place for a sniper shot," said Echo.

"I wouldn't worry about that," said Zeb as they entered the restaurant.

The maître d' showed them to the Elk Room. The president of Danforth-Roerg, his wife and another couple beckoned Zeb and Echo to the table.

"Sheriff Hanks, I'm Duncan MacDougal and this is my wife, Anne. This is my Chief of American Operations, David Sullivan and his wife, Mary."

Zeb introduced himself and Echo to the others. The maître d' slid back the chair for the ladies and everyone took a seat.

"I'm afraid Senator Russell is out glad handing the other patrons of the restaurant," said Duncan.

As the waiter poured wine, Senator Russell whisked himself into the room.

"Zeb, Echo, thanks for joining us," he said.

"Our pleasure," replied Zeb.

Dinner chat was cordial and superficial. Once dessert had been announced, Anne MacDougal suggested the women leave the boys to talk. With that, the men headed to a smaller private room with a fireplace.

Duncan MacDougal began the conversation.

"Senator Russell, Sheriff Hanks, with the untimely and unfortunate deaths of Angus, Lily and Ela McGinty, we have some serious timing problems at the mine. Although the McGintys owned forty-nine percent of the mine, our by-laws do not allow us to move forward with any major projects without a sixty percent majority of the voting shares. Since Danforth-Roerg owns fifty-one percent and the other forty-nine percent has no one to place their vote, we're stuck in limbo. We can't move forward with Klondyke 2. If we can't do that, the expenses from Klondyke 1 are going to become overwhelming. We're anticipating at least a two-year legal battle over the McGinty estate as several people and the tribal council have laid claims to the forty-nine percent the McGintys held."

"What does this have to do with me?" asked Zeb.

"I had our research team look into crime statistics the last time there was an extended shut down of the mines."

"The strike of 2002-03," replied Zeb.

"Precisely. There was a thirty percent increase in non-violent crime and a twelve percent increase in violent crime in Graham County during that two-year period. It was even higher than that on the San Carlos Reservation," said Duncan.

"Due to loss of tax dollars from the mine and its workers, the sheriff's department had to cut one full time and one quarter time job," said Senator Russell.

"I remember," said Zeb.

"I don't want you to get caught in that situation again," said Senator Russell. "I am going to try and get federal funds so you can keep your staff intact."

"That's good, but why would you anticipate a loss of tax dollars of that magnitude?" asked Zeb.

"Because we're closing the mines indefinitely starting next week. We're laying off two hundred fifty workers immediately and another two hundred over the next three months as we shut down," said Duncan.

"I want Graham County to remain safe," said a smugly satisfied Senator Russell.

"Is the federal government helping with the costs of closing down the mines?" asked Zeb.

Senator Russell and Duncan MacDougal exchanged a wary glance.

"We shall be providing some aid in the form of tax credits. If you're talking about unemployment insurance, the state will pick that up with the help of the federal government," said the senator. "It's a joint program."

Zeb started putting it all together. The copper mines would close temporarily, two years from the sounds of it, and likely still make a profit based on federal tax credits. In the meantime, copper would be easily imported from China and Chile. The Chinese and Chileans had paid off Senator Russell to make that happen. After that, the process would start all over again, and Senator Russell would continue to rake it in from all sides. Meanwhile, the good citizens of Graham County would suffer from increased unemployment, decreased income and loss of local business. One question stuck in Zeb's craw. Was it necessary to kill off the McGintys to get this done?

"Just wanted to give you a heads up," said MacDougal.

Duncan MacDougal stood, reached out for Zeb's hand and shook it firmly before heading out the door.

"Zeb, stick around for a few minutes. We need to talk," said Senator Russell. "Cigar? It's a Cohiba Behike."

"No thanks," replied Zeb.

Senator Russell lit his $450 cigar with a gold lighter.

"Zeb, I can see from the look in your eyes that something is bothering you. What is it? The death of Angus McGinty? I doubt it. No one seems to miss him. Lily? Oh, that's right, you're still a suspect. We can't talk about that one. Ela, now that's a sad story. I never imagined anything like that would happen."

"You're a heartless bastard," said Zeb.

Senator Russell puffed a circle of thick smoke at Zeb's face. Zeb swiped it away.

"It's the way the world works, Zeb. As a killer you should know that. I'd hate to see what happened down in Mexico catch up with you."

"It won't," said Zeb.

Senator Russell looked puzzled as Zeb took out a pen and began writing. On a piece of paper, he wrote two words—Nesea MacMhuradaich.

Senator Russell looked stunned, then calmly puffed away on his cigar for a few minutes before placing it on the edge of his plate.

"What should that name mean to me?" he asked.

"I'm going to place a warrant for her arrest in the murders of all three of the McGintys. I have enough proof to put her away. I know she's tough, but my guess is she'll give up a US Senator for her freedom.

Senator Russell drew in so close to Zeb that the smell of the cigar almost made Zeb vomit.

"If I go down, you go down and everyone around you, including that lovely Pocahontas you brought to dinner, her family and your Aunt Helen. And that's just to name a few."

Senator Russell picked up his cigar and drew in hard to get it going again. Zeb stared at the white ashy end of the Cohiba Behike as it glowed red once again.

"I can't just let this go," said Zeb. "Three unexplained murders from a prominent family in Graham County just can't happen."

"How does life in a Mexican jail sound to you?" asked Senator Russell.

"I can link Nesea MacMhuradaich directly to you. How does life in a maximum-security prison sound?" asked Zeb.

Senator Russell's face turned red and he coughed deeply, spewing bits of cigar tobacco across the table. As a man not unfamiliar with tricky situations, he quickly composed himself.

"There are no problems that don't have solutions of some kind," said the senator.

As Senator Russell reached inside his coat, Zeb already had drawn his .38 and was pointing it directly at the fat man's belly. Two quick shots would cause a belly wound that would lead to a painful death. Zeb gently held his first finger against the cold steel. Senator Russell pulled a picture from his pocket. He plopped it in front of Zeb.

"Put your weapon away, Zeb. I'm too old to die young. Besides, what's the point in killing an old man anyway? Shoot me now and you go to jail. I go to hell where I would end up waiting for you. I'm offering you a way out of this mess and a promise that I will never do one thing that will put you in a Mexican jail."

Zeb knew he had no choice but to deal with the devil face to face. He kept his finger on the trigger, just in case this was where it all ended. He glanced at the picture. It was two youngish looking, red-haired women. They looked to be twins.

The senator seemed to have read his mind.

"They're absolutely identical twins, right down to their freckles and moles. You're looking at Nesea and Breauana MacMhuradaich."

Zeb studied their images. With the evidence he had, it would be impossible to tell which one did the killings. The only thing that separated the twins were fingerprints, of which none had been found. This information would, with the help of a sharp attorney, no doubt lead to a hung jury if it even made it to trial.

"Somebody has to pay," said Zeb.

The fat man chortled as he responded. "Yes, someone always has to pay."

Senator Russell puffed heavily on his cigar, blew out the smoke and reached for his snifter of brandy. He inhaled the essence of the drink, tipped his head back and swallowed deeply. Zeb could almost see the wheels grinding inside the powerful senator's head.

"Who pays and what is the cost are the two things that matter," said Zeb.

"It appears we have an old-fashioned Mexican standoff, don't we, Sheriff Hanks," said Senator Russell.

"It can't end this way, Senator. Some sort of justice has to be served."

"Even if that so-called justice means you spent the rest of your born days in a Mexican jail. I don't think a southern Arizona sheriff would be looked upon too favorably in a border town prison."

Zeb saw the injustice of it all and felt it right down to his bones. He would end up in some Mexican jail holding the shit end of the stick. Senator Russell would end up in some club fed and likely serve very little time. Zeb's heart quickened.

"There has to be some solution," said Zeb.

"I might have an answer. You might not like it, but it will keep us both out of prison," said Senator Russell. "I'll have to make a few phone calls first. Let's meet tomorrow morning at your office. Nine o'clock work for you?"

Zeb nodded.

There was a knock on the door.

"Enter," boomed out Senator Russell.

As Echo opened the door, she was afraid what she might find. Her love for Zeb, her ethereal Apache skills and years of experience told her she had to get Zeb the hell out of there. One look into Zeb's eyes confirmed that.

"I'm not feeling so well, Zeb. Do you mind if we call it a night?" asked Echo.

"Our work is done," said Senator Russell. "Take your lovely girl-friend home. I will see you tomorrow."

47
_____

BAD CHOICES

A restless night's sleep erupted into a flood of nightmares. Zeb dreamed of being trapped in a cave, in a dark, blind alley, underwater and even buried up to his neck in desert sand. Ultimately, it was a nightmare of him staring at himself behind bars in a filthy, south of the border jail that woke him. His moaning had also stolen Echo from an uneasy slumber. She reached over and rubbed Zeb's leg.

"Zeb, you're drenched."

"Bad dreams," he replied, wiping his face on the pillow.

"It's your meeting with Senator Russell, isn't it?"

"Probably. I don't know. I don't have a good feeling about what has to be done," replied Zeb.

"Sometimes every choice is a bad one," said Echo. "The real question is can you live with your choice?"

The previous night Zeb and Echo had talked from the time they left the restaurant until quarter to three in the morning. By the time they were done, Zeb felt he had opened his heart, mind and spirit to Echo in a way he never had to anyone else. War had at once softened and hardened the woman he loved. Her thoughts were practical. No matter what, he had to survive, not only for his own sake but for those around him. That was his first duty. He also had to be able to live with himself. She planted the seed of how time could work in his favor if he let it. Or, of how it might work against him if he allowed fear to control his mind.

Zeb took a long hot shower to wake himself to full alertness. Echo went downstairs to make breakfast. His food was on the table when he walked down the stairs fully dressed. In the background, the television was playing the morning show on a station out of Phoenix. Echo was reminded of the mood that overcame men and women as they ate a meal before a mission that carried with it real elements of danger.

"You okay, honey?" asked Echo.

"I don't much care for my options, to tell you the truth," replied Zeb. "I have to live with myself if I let Senator Russell walk away unscathed."

"You could win the battle and lose the war," said Echo. "That wouldn't be good. Remember what I said about long-term thinking when it comes to Senator Russell."

"Three people were murdered. His hands are smack dab in the middle of all of it."

"He's got you cornered. If he goes down, you go down. Sometimes life isn't fair," said Echo. "I've seen it a hundred times. Somehow life goes on. Justice isn't always served on a golden platter."

"Like I said, I have to live with myself."

"Nothing is going to bring back the dead," said Echo.

Zeb circled his fork through what was left of his half-eaten breakfast. He drank what remained of his fresh squeezed orange juice and got up from the table. Echo walked him to the door. She hugged him tightly and rubbed her foot along the top of his boot to see if he was carrying a second gun. Satisfied, she handed him his hat.

"You're not thinking of shooting Senator Russell in your office, are you?"

"Only if it would be considered self-defense."

"I have a .38 I brought back from the war. It isn't traceable. You could plant it on him," said Echo.

"Thanks, but no thanks."

"Please," she pleaded. "Just in case."

"I've already got it covered," replied Zeb.

She stepped back and eyed Zeb up and down. Killing was sometimes the only answer. Most of the time a better strategy could be found if one was patient enough. Echo worried about Zeb's stamina. Could he remain unflappable toward the senator? His short fuse could be his undoing.

"My field commander in Afghanistan once told me that to survive in this world we need to hold our most ardent of enemies the closest, that is, if we want to live to fight another day."

Zeb studied Echo's face as tears rolled down her cheeks. She was his lover. She was his friend. She was his reason to live to see another day.

Soberly, Zeb walked to his truck. Echo watched each step. He waved and smiled as he watched his lover staring back at him.

On the road to work the Sheriff of Graham County took a detour. He drove to the graveyard, directly to Doreen's grave. He rested against the hardened, plastic-covered motorcycle that served as her headstone. He thought of how he felt when she was so cruelly taken from him. He thought about his absolute need to avenge her death and how it had changed him. He thought about the note Doreen had left behind with Kate, telling Zeb that he must share his love with another when she was gone. He thought about spending the rest of his life in a Mexican jail and what that would do to Echo.

As his mind pondered the imponderable, Jake and Song Bird arrived at the grave site. Zeb had asked them to meet him to discuss his meeting with Russell.

"Trouble lurks all around you," said Song Bird. "Don't become lost in its fog."

"You appear a little on the testy side this morning," said Jake. "You never do your best work when I see that look on our face."

"As you know, Senator Russell is responsible for the deaths of all three of the McGintys," said Zeb. "My information was illegally obtained. If I charge him, he will bring me down for what happened in Mexico and likely walk away unscathed."

"Now is not the time to bring him down," said Jake. "We'll find another opportunity. Life may be short but the road is long. There will be other chances to get the bastard."

"He is too high profile of a Washington White man for you to do anything directly against him," said Song Bird. "God's plan, Usen's plan, is better than whatever you are considering. You must remember that patience is a virtue."

"How many times did Song Bird and I try and teach you that as a boy and as a man?" asked Jake.

Zeb merely nodded. His mind was moving a million miles an hour and standing still at the same time.

"Thanks for the advice. I'll try and heed it," said Zeb.

He glanced at his watch. It was time to go to work and face the music. Jake wished him good luck. Song Bird blessed him with burning sage.

"We've got your back, regardless of what happens," said Jake.

"You will be protected from evil," added Song Bird.

"Good morning, Zeb," said Helen. "Senator Russell called."

"Yes," replied Zeb, half hoping the senator had cancelled the meeting.

"He has to catch a plane earlier than he thought. He'll be here in five minutes."

"Thanks, Helen."

"What's bothering you?" asked Helen. "I rarely see that long, hang-dog look on your face."

"Rough night's sleep," replied Zeb. "I think I ate supper too late."

"You should know better, what with that touchy stomach of yours."

"Yes, I should be more careful," replied Zeb.

Entering his office, Zeb noticed an envelope addressed to him sitting in the center of his desk. Instantly recognizing Shelly's handwriting, he opened the envelope. Shelly's note was short and direct. At the bottom of the envelope was an Arizona state flag lapel pin. Zeb examined it briefly, took it out and placed it on his desk. He read the note three times, folded it and put it back in the envelope. He placed the envelope in his top drawer next to his 9mm Glock. He placed the Arizona flag pin on top of the letter, next to the Glock.

Two minutes later Helen knocked on Zeb's office door. Right behind her was Senator Russell.

"My time is limited," said Senator Russell. "Let's get this over with."

"The sooner this whole thing is off my plate the better," said Zeb.

"I know you want to see me dead, possibly even kill me yourself," said Senator Russell.

Zeb stared and said nothing.

"Trust me when I tell you that I understand the situation from your point of view. Things did get out of hand. This all could have been done without Ela dying, maybe even without Lily getting killed. However, things turned out the way they did, and there is no undoing them at this point," said Senator Russell.

"I do think you should pay for what you set in motion, Senator Russell," said Zeb. "You're just as guilty as the killer."

"And, it is my belief you should pay for your crimes as well, Sheriff Zeb Hanks," said Senator Russell.

"Let's skip the formalities. All of us have done bad things," said Zeb. "Some day we all will pay the piper."

"Maybe you and I can balance the universal score card by sacrificing Nesea MacMhuradaich," said Senator Russell.

"Which one of the sisters actually did the killings of the McGinty family?" asked Zeb.

"Does it matter? They are both professional killers," replied Senator Russell. "We need a sacrificial lamb. It would be good to put one of them away. I have a solution that should work for you, me and the general public."

"What do you have in mind?" asked Zeb.

"Nesea is out of control and acting on her own. The MacMhuradaich family wants her out the family business. From what I've been told, she's lost her mind. They're willing to sacrifice her if you have the evidence," said Senator Russell.

"I have enough to place her at Angus's crime scene," said Zeb.

"The FBI, working with Tribal Chief Rambler Braing, has already found evidence placing her at Lily's death site," said Senator Russell.

"When were you going to let me know about that?" asked Zeb.

"I just did."

"What about Ela?" asked Zeb. "She didn't have to die."

"You've got the evidence," said Senator Russell.

"But not the reason why."

"Jealousy, envy, hatred, spurned love or maybe Nesea going for a trifecta? Who knows. We'll probably never get the truth."

"You're probably right," replied Zeb, lying with each word.

Senator Russell stood and reached his hand across Zeb's desk. Reluctantly, Zeb shook it, feeling the soft mushiness of the politician's hand.

"We're good then?" asked Senator Russell.

"I have a little parting gift for you," said Zeb, opening the top drawer of his desk.

"Will I have to report it as income?" The senator's voice was jovial, confident and flush with victory.

"I think this one will slip by the IRS," replied Zeb.

Zeb reached into the desk, fingered the Glock, but let his hands come to rest on the Arizona state flag pin.

"I couldn't help but notice you always wear one of these," said Zeb, holding up the pin. "I also couldn't help but notice yours is bent and worn. Consider this a gift."

Senator Russell removed his old flag pin and tossed it in the trash. Zeb handed him the new one, which he slipped onto his lapel.

"Very nice gesture, Zeb. Highly appreciated. I wear the American flag and the Arizona flag every day. Thank you."

"It's an honor, Senator Russell," said Zeb. His voice dripped with sarcasm.

"I'll be getting in touch with you in a few days when Nesea returns. I already have a plan for her arrest."

"Good," said Zeb.

Little did Senator Russell know that Shelly had planted a microphone in the upper left hand corner and hidden a micro-camera behind the tip of the flag pin's golden star. Now Senator Russell's words and actions would be his own downfall.

Zeb thought of the simple sentences Shelly had written to him in her note. A realization came to him. Her words were nothing more than detailed instructions. By following them to the letter, he would have a plan that might just allow him to control Senator Russell.

The note read: "Zeb, give Senator Russell this Arizona flag pin. It has audio and video capability. I need three weeks to scrub everything that incriminates you from Senator Russell's computers. He will never know how it happened. None of this comes cheaply. Mostly importantly destroy this letter."

Now two things had to happen. Senator Russell had to hang himself with his words and actions. That certainly wouldn't be a problem. And, Nesea MacMhuradaich needed to be arrested. Senator Russell had assured him that would not be an issue.

48

FIVE DAYS LATER

"K ate, how are you feeling today?" asked Zeb.

"Fine. Thanks for asking. My morning sickness seems to have passed," replied Kate.

"What's your schedule like for this afternoon?"

"Paperwork, paperwork and more paperwork, hopefully with a coffee break in there somewhere."

Zeb glanced at his watch. It was 1:30.

"Want to give that paperwork to Black Bear? He needs the practice," said Zeb.

Kate sighed and grinned. "Not a problem."

"I've got a task for you," said Zeb.

"Anything is better than paperwork."

"I want you to run out to the Rez and go through Ela's house one last time," said Zeb.

"Have you cleared this with Rambler?"

"Yup."

"What am I looking for?" asked Kate.

"Nothing in particular. I want closure. I want one last set of eyes to run through Ela's house. I want to know if anything there ties her to her parents' deaths," replied Zeb.

"Sure you don't want to send a babysitter with me?"

Zeb smiled at her caustic remark.

"No, I think you can handle this solo. It's one-thirty. You can be there by quarter after two. Since we've already been through it and so have the feds and Rambler, it shouldn't take you more than an hour. You can be home by four o'clock."

Kate got in her truck, heading toward the Rez. She was finally feeling like she thought a pregnant woman should feel... happy.

Zeb handed off half of Kate's paperwork to Black Bear and finished the rest himself. At 5 p.m., just as Helen was packing up to leave, the phone rang. Helen answered and stuck her head into Zeb's office.

"It's Senator Russell," she said.

"Good, I've been waiting for his call," replied Zeb. "Put him through and go home and enjoy your evening."

Helen smiled.

"This is Sheriff Hanks."

"Zeb, Senator Russell. We've got a problem."

"We?" asked Zeb.

"Yes, we, you and I have a problem."

"What sort of problem?" asked Zeb, knowing it could be anything.

"Nesea MacMhuradaich didn't go to Mexico like she said she was going to. She didn't return here either. She was going to contact me, but she's disappeared. My people can't even track her phone. She's in the wind."

"Fuck," mumbled Zeb. "You said you had this under control."

"Obviously, I have a little issue. I just thought you should know... in case..."

"In case what?" growled Zeb.

"In case she never left your area," replied the senator.

"Why the hell would she stick around here. She has to know how dangerous that is," snarled Zeb.

"Don't get huffy, Zeb. All problems..."

"Have solutions. I know your quips."

"I just wanted you to be aware of the situation. I'll keep you informed. I've got a late meeting. I'll keep in touch. You do the same. Goodbye."

No sooner had Zeb hung up the office phone when his cell phone rang. It was Josh Diamond, Kate's husband.

"Josh, what's up, what's new?"

"Not much. I've been trying for the last hour and a half to reach Kate. She's not answering her cell phone. I even tried her two-way. Is she still at the office?"

"No. I sent her out to check on something regarding Ela McGinty. I thought she'd have been back by now. I'll track her down and have her get back to you," said Zeb.

"Should I be worried?" asked Josh.

"Kate's a big girl. She can take care of herself," said Zeb. "You know that."

"I know, it's just that with her pregnancy, I'm a little overly protective."

Zeb chuckled. "She thinks we're all being a little overly protective. That kid of yours is going to have a whole bunch of people watching over it."

Josh felt at ease after talking to Zeb.

"Thanks. Have her call me when you track her down. I'm making my special spaghetti dinner for her. She's been craving tomato sauce when she isn't gagging on it. She started calling it gravy after watching the *Sopranos*."

"She'll be home for dinner, and I think she'll lap up your gravy. She told me her morning sickness was gone. Later."

"Later. Thanks again, Zeb."

49

TROUBLE

K ate didn't answer her cell phone or the two-way radio. Ela's home phone rang through to an answering machine. A lightbulb lit up in Zeb's brain. He called Echo

"When are you going to be home for supper? I'm missing you," said Echo.

"You're sweet. I hope to be home soon," replied Zeb. "Can you do me a favor?"

"Anything."

"I sent Kate out to Ela's house for a final run though. I can't get ahold of her. Would you call your parents and send them over there to see if Kate's truck is there?" asked Zeb. "I need to know if she's still there. There shouldn't be anyone else at the house. If they see something odd, have them call back right away."

"You've just made their day," said Echo. "Nothing two retired Marines like more than a mission. I'll call right now. You should have an answer in ten minutes."

"Thanks, Echo. You're the best."

"How about an I love you?"

"I love you," said Zeb.

"Backatcha, Sheriff," laughed Echo.

Eight minutes passed. Zeb's cell phone rang.

"Recon accomplished," said Echo.

"Was she there?" asked Zeb.

"My dad said a Graham County Sheriff's Office vehicle is parked in front of the house. A red Jeep is parked about a quarter mile from the house. It's half hidden by trees and overgrowth. No movement is noted."

"Shit," said Zeb.

"What?" asked Echo.

"Possible trouble."

"My dad and mother are both armed and awaiting further instructions."

"Call them back. Tell them I'm on my way with Deputy Black Bear. Do they have binoculars with them?"

"Of course. This is a recon mission."

"Have them keep an eye on things. Black Bear and I will hurry out there. Tell them not to approach the house. They're civilians and I don't want them getting involved in case anything goes south."

"I'm already in my car. I'm going with you. I'll be there in two minutes," said Echo. "I want to protect my parents as well as Kate."

Zeb knew there was zero chance of telling her no and having her follow his orders.

"Step on it. We're leaving here in two minutes, with or without you."

Zeb quickly brought Black Bear up to speed. The two of them were just stepping into Zeb's truck when Echo came wheeling into the parking lot at full speed. She hopped out of her vehicle and jumped into the back seat of Zeb's truck.

"Let's rock and roll," she said.

Zeb squealed his tires as he turned onto State Highway 70. The high-speed trip to the reservation was not fast enough as far as Zeb was concerned. He had a sick feeling that Kate was in serious trouble.

50

HOSTAGE

Z eb drove through the gate that marked the end of the long drive to Ela's house. He parked halfway up the driveway. He handed Black Bear a rifle, grabbed one for himself and handed Echo a .45.

"Where are your parents?" asked Zeb.

Echo pointed to the northwest where the brush was thick and the ground sloped into a wadi.

"Over there. They told me exactly where they are. I can see them. Their horses are tied to a tree about a hundred feet behind them. There's a good horse trail between their property and this one."

"Your eyes are better than mine. Let's head to them and get some real-time information."

Zeb, Black Bear and Echo crept through a wadi, keeping out of sight from any views Ela's house afforded of the area. They reached Echo's parents in a matter of minutes.

"What have you got?" asked Zeb.

"Nothing. No movement inside the house as far as I can tell. I crept in closer and had a decent look from fifty yards out, but the curtains are all drawn. What's the plan?" asked Echo's father.

"Black Bear and I will approach the house from the east side.

Cover us. Find a good vantage point from a hundred feet out. Keep your movements to a minimum. I think I know who the red Jeep belongs to. It's a woman. Her name is Nesea MacMhuradaich. Consider her armed and dangerous. I don't want to provoke her. That would be trouble. My deputy is very likely in there with her, if she isn't dead."

"Yes, sir," replied Echo and her parents in unison.

Black Bear and Zeb began creeping through the underbrush as Echo and her parents moved to three separate vantage points. The oncoming dusk gave them an edge.

"You're endangering your girlfriend and her parents. They're civilians," said Black Bear.

"They've all got more experience in this type of situation than we do," said Zeb.

At the perimeter of the property, Zeb stopped, turned and checked out the positions of Echo and her parents. They had chosen well. All escape routes from the house were covered. Zeb called Black Bear to his side. He pointed to a window where the curtains were open slightly on the bottom.

"Move north and come in low toward that window. I'll come in from the south. We should be able to do that without being seen."

Black Bear slid away silently. When both had reached the edge of the house, Zeb signaled Black Bear to the window.

"I'm going to take a peek in the window. If I get my head shot off, well, then it's in your hands," said Zeb.

Zeb peeked through the window. A single light lit the living room. He didn't like what he saw. Kate's hands were bound behind her with duct tape. Her ankles were strapped together with rope. Her mouth was covered with duct tape as well. Nesea MacMhuradaich was sitting across from Kate on a couch, watching television and casually eating a sandwich. On an end table next to the couch were two handguns. One was a .38, the other a .22, an assassin's weapon for up close killing. Every fifteen or so seconds Nesea glanced out the window she sat in front of. Zeb signaled Black Bear with a nod of his head. He and Black Bear moved away from the house.

"We've got a situation," said Zeb. "A bad one."

Using hand signals, Zeb called everyone to his side.

"We've got a hostage situation. Kate is bound and tied to a chair in the living room. Nesea is watching TV and having something to eat. She has two handguns next to her. I didn't see any long guns, but I'm sure she has some in the house. I want everyone in place, covering all exits. I'm going to take a shot through the closed window and hope to injure her," said Zeb. "It seems like the only way to get Nesea and keep Kate safe."

Echo's father waited until Zeb laid out his plan before speaking.

"That won't work," he said.

"Why not?"

"I worked with the crew that put in the windows. The original owner, the drug lord, put in bulletproof glass throughout the house."

"Is there any other way in?" asked Zeb.

"Did you check all the doors and the garage door?" asked Echo's father.

"I suspect time is running out for Kate," said Zeb. "If Nesea sees any of us, she won't hesitate to put a bullet in Kate's head."

"I've got an idea," offered Echo.

"Let's hear it," said Zeb.

"In Afghanistan I knocked on many an unfriendly door. I'm an expert at diffusing scared, excited and angry people. If I could get her to open the door, Zeb, you could place yourself in position to get a shot at her," said Echo.

Before Zeb had a chance to respond, Echo's mother spoke up.

"No! It's not going to happen that way. I sweated out three years while you were over there in that hellhole. I refuse to allow you to put yourself in harm's way."

"Mom, do you have a better idea?" asked Echo.

"I do. Your plan is good, but you're the wrong person for it. I'll do it," said Echo's mother.

A silent battle of wills, spoken through their eyes and body language, ensued between mother and daughter. Echo's father broke the silence.

"Zeb, my wife is combat trained and an expert in avoiding conflict. I trust she can get the door open and give you enough time to get a shot at this Nesea woman."

Zeb eyed Echo and her mother.

"What if something happens to you?" pleaded Echo.

"Now you know how I felt every single day for three years. Since you made it out safely, I know I will."

"Zeb, she's not trained to do this and she's not deputized. You have to follow the law, at least a little bit," said Black Bear. "Let me do it."

"You're in uniform," said Zeb.

"I could take off my shirt," said Black Bear.

"And your pants?" asked Zeb.

"Please, Zeb, let me do it," said Echo. "You know that I can."

Zeb had already lost one love in his life. His mind was made up. He looked at Echo's mother and decided to deputize her. Everyone else was quiet. Echo and Black Bear did not like what was about to happen.

"Here's the plan."

Zeb took a stick and drew a quick layout of the house, its entry points and where everyone should locate themselves. The plan was simple. Echo's mother would ride her horse on the horse trail that came out of the brush just south of Ela's house. She would make just enough noise so as not to surprise Nesea. She would wait, sitting atop her horse a couple of hundred feet back from the house. She would place herself in plain sight so that Nesea would easily see her as she glanced out the window. Since the windows were bulletproof, there was no chance of Echo's mother getting shot from the inside. Zeb would hide in some low-lying brush a hundred yards from the front door. Black Bear would be twenty-five feet directly south of Zeb. Both men carried 30.06 rifles.

"Does everyone know what to do?" asked Zeb.

Echo and her parents nodded.

"Shoot to kill?" asked Black Bear.

"Your call. Depends on the danger level to Kate."

It took ten minutes for everyone to get in place. Dusk was starting to make an appearance. Zeb signaled Echo's mother to ride her horse up the trail and into position. Minutes felt like hours. Echo's mother was in place for five minutes, but nothing was happening. Was the plan a bad one? Was Nesea simply ignoring them?

Echo's mother was about to call out to the house when her horse spotted one of the wild horses that roamed the Rez. Her horse let out a loud whinny.

Inside the house, Nesea cut loose the bindings from Kate's hands and removed the tape from her mouth.

"Do you know that woman?" asked Nesea.

"I believe it's one of the neighbors. Out here people stop by when they pass through on the horse trail that's just south of the house. She probably just wants to acknowledge she's passing through on your property. It's a gesture of kindness," explained Kate.

"Does she know you?"

"She might have seen me in town," lied Kate. She recognized Echo's mother immediately.

"Will she recognize your face?" asked Nesea.

"I doubt it."

Kate was formulating a plan in her head. If it worked, she and her baby would live. If it didn't, they both would die and so might Echo's mother. Kate prayed Zeb was behind all of this.

"Okay. Answer the door and stick your head out and say hello. Make it quick and get it over with fast," commanded Nesea. "Screw it up and you're both dead. Don't forget for one second that I'm right behind you."

Kate looked down at her bound feet. There was no chance of running. Fortunately, the door opened outward. She opened it far enough to allow her head to poke through. She felt the cold metal of a gun in her ribs, right about the level where she imagined her unborn child was lying in her womb.

"Hello," shouted Kate.

"Ya'ateh," responded Echo's mother.

"What'd she say?" whispered Nesea.

"She greeted me."

"I am using the horse trail. I wanted you to know. Several others will be passing by soon. They are right behind me."

Kate's heart raced. Echo's mother was giving her a signal that she was not alone and that others were right behind her. It was time to execute her plan. Her life depended on it.

"That's fine," replied Kate, her heart beating faster.

"Get rid of her," growled Nesea.

"My phone is ringing," said Kate. "Use the trail. Your friends are welcome to use it too. Goodbye."

As the word 'goodbye' pursed through her lips, Kate shoved her shoulder into the door, opening it wider, and fell to the ground. Before Nesea could figure out what happened, two kill shots came flying toward her at 3000 feet per second. The first hit her in the neck, twisting her body. The second blew through her skull. She fell backward into the house.

Kate removed the bindings on her feet, got up and took off running along the side of the house. Seconds later Zeb, Black Bear, Echo and her parents closed in on the house. Echo and her mother ran to aid Kate. Zeb, Black Bear and Echo's father approached the dead body of Nesea MacMhuradaich with caution.

"She's dead," said Black Bear.

Zeb kicked the weapon away from the dead woman's hand.

"Call the ambulance and let's get her body out of here. I'll call Rambler to get permission to move the body off the Rez. It's time to call it a day."

THE GOOD GUYS

S helly pressed the thumb drive that contained all the incriminating evidence against Senator Russell into Zeb's palm.

"Senator Russell made a foolish mistake thinking his burner phone was safe when he made the call to the head of the MacMhuradaich clan," said Shelly.

"The Arizona flag pin with the mini-cam and recording device worked better than I could have imagined," said Zeb. "We've got all of Senator Russell's private and public data, including his dealings with Chile and China and his nefarious dealings with the Apache Nation," said Zeb.

"Don't forget we have a perfect trail following his money to and from overseas accounts," added Shelly.

"Follow the money," they chimed in one voice.

"Speaking of which," said Zeb.

Zeb reached into his back pocket and handed Shelly a check for services rendered. She handed it back to him.

"When it comes to dealing with politicos, drug dealers and plain old bad asses I want non-traceable cash. A check from your account to me is traceable. We want to minimize the potential for connections that could lead to bad outcomes for either of us."

"Got it," said Zeb. "I'll have the cash for you later today."

"Thanks," said Shelly. "Everything on the thumb drive appears to have come from legitimate, anonymous sources. By the way, when are you going to hand it over to the FBI?"

"I don't know that I'm going to give it to them," said Zeb.

"What?" asked Shelly. "Why not?"

"In dealing with Senator Russell, I need an ace in the hole. At some point in time, the information you were able to obtain could be significantly more valuable."

Shelly nodded with a newfound respect for the way Sheriff Zeb Hanks dealt with the most difficult of situations.

"Can I buy you a cup of coffee at the Town Talk?" asked Zeb. "We're having a little get together."

"You bet. The caffeine level in my blood is starting to get a little low," replied Shelly.

Zeb and Shelly walked across the street and into the Town Talk. Jimmy Song Bird, Jake, Kate, looking more pregnant by the day, and her husband, Josh, were seated in the back of the cafe. Sawyer Black Bear was conspicuous by his absence. When everyone was seated and coffee and tea were served, Zeb made an announcement. He held his tea cup toward Shelly.

"None of this would have happened without you," said Zeb. "Like it or not, you're one of us now."

Jake lifted his coffee cup and made a toast.

"The circle is larger by one," he said.

"I'm honored to be in the circle," said Shelly.

"It's definitely an odd group of characters," joked Jake.

"But, we're always the good guys," said Kate.

"At least in our own minds," added Zeb.

Song Bird winked at the pale-skinned, red-haired waitress passing by the table.

"We are the good guys," said Song Bird. "Maybe the last of a breed."

THE END

ALSO BY MARK REPS

ZEB HANKS MYSTERY SERIES

NATIVE BLOOD

HOLES IN THE SKY

ADIÓS ÁNGEL

NATIVE JUSTICE

NATIVE BONES

NATIVE WARRIOR

NATIVE EARTH

NATIVE DESTINY

NATIVE TROUBLE

NATIVE ROOTS (PREQUEL NOVELLA)

THE ZEB HANKS MYSTERY SERIES 1-3

AUDIOBOOK

NATIVE BLOOD

HOLES IN THE SKY

ADIÓS ÁNGEL

OTHER BOOKS

BUTTERFLY (WITH PUI CHOMNAK)

HEARTLAND HEROES

ABOUT THE AUTHOR

Mark Reps has been a writer and storyteller his whole life. Born in small-town southeastern Minnesota, he trained as a mathematician and chiropractor but never lost his love of telling or writing a good story. As an avid desert wilderness hiker, Mark spends a great deal of time roaming the desert and other terrains of southeastern Arizona. A chance meeting with an old time colorful sheriff led him to develop the Zeb Hanks character and the world that surrounds him.

To learn more, check out his website www.markreps.com, his AllAuthor profile, or any of the profiles below. To join his mailing list for new release information and more click here.

BB bookbub.com/authors/mark-reps

facebook.com/ZebHanks

twitter.com/markreps1

INTERVIEW WITH THE AUTHOR

Mark Reps, author of ZEB HANKS: Small Town Sheriff Big Time Trouble series is being interviewed by Lisa Vehrenkamp.

Lisa: We were talking about Zeb's flawed character and the people who influenced him. You imply his father was a bad influence, or at least not a positive one.

Mark: Zeb's father physically and emotionally abused him throughout his life. His father favored his brother, who turned out to be a criminal. His father also abused Zeb's mother.

L: What sort of relationship did Zeb have with his mother?

M: His mother tried to protect him while protecting herself. She exposed him to different things that personally helped her and inadvertently broadened the tracks of his mind.

L: Can you give me an example?

M: The Hanks' family appeared to be typical Mormons. Mrs. Hanks withdrew from Mormonism at times and sought religion through tent ministries. She even went as far as taking Zeb to snake handling ceremonies and got him involved with that end of the religious experience. This influenced Zeb a great deal.

L: I imagine it would. What else did his mother do to protect Zeb?

M: She allowed her sister, Helen Nazelrod, to keep Zeb for extended periods of his youth when things were particularly bad at home. Helen became very protective of Zeb.

L: Is this the same Helen Nazelrod who is Zeb's secretary?

M: Yes. She still protects him, as you well know if you've read the series. He keeps an eye out for her as well. They maintain a very close relationship and have a funny little thing between them. She snoops and listens in to his official business at the sheriff's office, and he tries to minimize that, except when it might benefit him solving a case. Helen is a busy body in a good way.

L: Who else had a large influence on Zeb's way of thinking, his actions, his being, his soul, his spirit, etc.?

M: When Zeb reached the point in his life where he began making his own decisions, Apache Medicine Man Jimmy Song Bird entered his life and took him under his wing.

L: Can you tell us a little about the relationship between Zeb and Medicine Man Jimmy Song Bird?

M: Song Bird is one of those people you would call an ancient soul. He was blessed to be born wise. He has used the gift of spirit as a medicine man. He first noticed Zeb as a young kid riding his bike around town. Jimmy Song Bird could immediately tell Zeb had an injured spirit. Through a series of events, including Zeb's first understanding of crime, they become closer. Song Bird is Zeb's constant teacher. Over decades Song Bird continues to teach Zeb about the world, Native American traditions, especially Apache ways, astronomy and life in general. He is the perfect mentor for Zeb.

L: The perfect mentor? What does that mean?

M: Zeb is a man, just a man, but he is also the sheriff. His job and his life are full of mistakes, regrets and errors. At the same time, he's an excellent law man who helps many people. Because Song Bird understands his own imperfections and that existence is more than just the world we live in and see every day, he helps Zeb work through his own mistakes and imperfections. He makes no harsh demands on Zeb, but tries to teach him the best ways, which can sometimes be harsh.

L: Is Song Bird meant to be magical?

M: It's complicated. He knows many things of this world and other worlds, but he doesn't view any knowledge he has as magical. He sees the world through practical eyes and wants to help Zeb see the world as it really is. He doesn't force his consciousness on Zeb, nor does he want Zeb to mimic his. Song Bird tries to help Zeb recognize his own consciousness and conscience.

L: How did Zeb and Song Bird begin and establish their lifelong relationship?

M: The beginning of their relationship has not yet been fully explored in the books but was the subject of the novella NATIVE ROOTS. I can tell you that Song Bird saw Zeb riding his bike late one night and witnessed a troubled soul. In that book, the readers have a chance to see the roots of what brought Zeb to where he is today.

L: You also mention Jake, former county sheriff and now one of Zeb's deputies, as an influencer of Zeb.

M: Yes, Jake Dablo taught Zeb how to be a law man. Before the series began, Zeb was originally a deputy to Jake. Jake couldn't solve the ritualistic murder of his granddaughter, which is the basis of the story for book 1, NATIVE BLOOD. This drove him to drink. He became a drunk, quit his duties as sheriff and Zeb took over and eventually won the next election. By the time NATIVE BLOOD occurs, Jake has sobered up and ends up working as Zeb's deputy.

L: How has Jake influenced Zeb, other than Zeb working as his deputy?

M: Much of this is also explained NATIVE ROOTS, which goes back to Zeb's childhood. The crime that Zeb witnesses involves both Song Bird and Jake. What happens on a 4th of July when Zeb is around 10 years old dramatically changes his life as well as his brother's life. Jake and Song Bird are longtime friends, dating back to their youths. Both have a keen interest in astronomy which is a common bond for teaching Zeb. Both men recognize that Zeb and his brother are not being properly raised by their father and, as is typical in a small town, just sort of naturally step in to help Zeb learn how to become a good person.

L: Do Jake and Song Bird instruct Zeb in the same manner?

M: No, not really. Both men have their own beliefs, mannerisms and way of doing things. Song Bird, an Apache, sees the world through that set of eyes. Jake, a local small town guy who has never left town except for a stint in the army, has the local White way of viewing the world. In his youth, Jake was a rough and tumble character. In middle age he was a drunk, and now he has mellowed into the more experienced law man who has seen the world from different sides. He has an eclectic view of the world that is decidedly different than

Song Bird's, yet both men join together throughout the entirety of Zeb's life and certainly in all of the books in the series to influence Zeb.

Lisa: Mark, I understand you recently spend some time in Graham County researching for your series.

Mark: Yes, in April (2017) I had a great time in and around Safford, AZ, on the San Carlos Reservation and Graham County in general.

L: Did you have a specific purpose in mind during the visit?

M: I'm always looking around the area to find out new things, rediscover old things and meet people. This time I spent considerable time at the Graham County Sheriff's Office. I met with many of the staff who have a great sense of perspective on the area as most of them are lifelong residents. I managed to get photographs of all the Graham County Sheriffs dating back to 1912 when Arizona became the 48th state.

L: Did anything in particular jump out at you regarding the sheriffs?

M: Graham County has had only one female sheriff. She took over for her husband when he died while in office.

L: What is your favorite reason for visiting Graham County?

M: I have many. The people are great, open and easy to talk to. The food is spectacular. My favorite restaurant food is the chimichanga at the El Coronado restaurant. I could eat one at every meal. The sheriff's office staff are incredibly helpful, as are the people at the Chamber of Commerce and the courthouse. Everywhere I went people were warm and welcoming. There are several places in town that have been operating for decades and provide excellent mineral baths and massages. The hiking in the area is phenomenal. I enjoy everything I do when I visit.

L: Any final words?

M: Please enjoy reading the ZEB HANKS: Small Town Sheriff Big Time Trouble series.

NATIVE DESTINY - CHAPTER 1

Olga Mae Hooper Feathers sat silently in front of her campfire and listened to the world surrounding her. One hundred two years of living had begun to express itself with heightened perception. As unexpected as it was for an improvement in her senses at such an advanced age, she knew it was coming. It had been foretold.

She listened, not like in the old days when she pressed her ear to the earth, but rather through the echoes and vibrations that rode on the air. Horse hooves beating on the hardened desert dirt, the time of day and family interactions of the recent past signaled to her all that she needed to know. Her deceitful grandson and her equally dishonest nephew were on their way to pay her yet another visit.

In the prior decade they had been but ghosts of memory in her life. But in the past six weeks they had gone far out of their way to visit her a dozen times. At first, their collective cunning had almost fooled her. Olga Mae felt like a foolish old woman for nearly being bamboozled by her own flesh and blood.

The first time her grandson and nephew stopped by, they brought her gifts. This alone should have aroused her suspicion. Her grandson, Cle Feathers, had just enough of the old ways in him to bring her the things she needed and could not provide for herself. The good side of him would do her a favor by saving her the long trip into Safford. In truth, the old ways **did** not compel him. He was driven by greed and desire. He was also under the spell of his cousin, Dram Hooper. Dram's powerful influence over Cle proved to Olga Mae that Cle was born with a disproportionate amount of coyote in him. In that respect he was not unlike his father and his father's father. Her nephew's seed had fallen on even fallower ground. The demon that dwelt in his soul had removed all harmony from both nature and the Creator of all things.

On that first visit, before she understood their motivation, they had all laughed and remembered what she had thought of as the good old times. Cle had spent much of his youth helping his favorite grand-mother tend sheep and goats. He made her laugh when he told big stories about his love for sheepherding and how the goats had tricked him many times. Tears trickled down her sun-beaten cheeks when he fondly reminisced about playing for hours on end with her beloved border collie. Back in those days, the collie was named Shep. Shep, like in shepherd, he had reminded her, as if she needed reminding. He covered her in a veil of happy memories that softened her soul as he recalled how every night she would sing him and Shep to sleep with the songs from the times that were no more. Shep would snuggle up close and keep him warm. He told her she was the perfect grandma. Even at that first visit, she should have recognized he was larding her up like a piece of stale bread. But how could a grandmother allow herself to imagine just how crooked her grandson's heart had become? She could not allow herself to believe the treachery that Cle and Dram carried in their minds. Such is the spirit of a grandmother.

She continued listening to the approaching hoofbeats. The fire at her feet burned brightly. She stirred the cookpot. Cle knew she ate just after the sun slipped below the horizon. He would make certain to arrive at exactly that moment. Could this be the the night Cle and Dram would confront her?

Cle Feathers and Dram Hooper dismounted. They quietly tied

their horses next to Olga Mae's horse. Olga Mae's hypersensitive ears heard the men dismount. Her hearing sharpened as Cle and Dram, ever so softly, brushed the trail dirt from their new Levi jeans. When Cle had taken to wearing fancy Mexican shirts and skintight jeans, she thought maybe he had joined a gang. Surely he must be too old for that? She did not want to believe a man of his age would make such a foolish decision. Dram, on the other hand, had always acted like a gangster. The sound of their boots crunching the earth spoke volumes with each step.

Not only did Olga Mae hear Cle coming, but she turned her head just enough to watch him slide through the dusky darkness. She also witnessed Dram lurking behind, watching each move like a nocturnal mountain lion stalking its prey. Cle slipped up behind his grandmother. He placed his hands over her aging but still nearly perfect eyes. His fingers carried a foul odor, like a man who did not keep himself clean. Cle whispered the traditional name for grandmother in her ear as he pronounced his love for her.

"Shiwóyé. Siln'zhoo."

"It is a good boy who loves his grandmother."

As Olga Mae spoke, she lightly ran her ancient fingers across his hands as if to cleanse them of their vileness.

"I missed you, Shiwóyé."

"You missed me and wanted to come and see me again. That is very nice of you, but I saw you only a week ago. How could you come to miss me so quickly? You are practically here every week for these last two moons."

"Maybe I just want to be near you," said Cle. "There is so much you can teach me. I want to learn from you what no one else has ever heard."

Indeed, there was much to teach this man, her grandson. She knew many things that very few others had knowledge of. But Cle's words were little more than a lie. She might be old, but she was not stupid. Olga Mae knew exactly what Cle wanted. She would die a dozen deaths before she revealed her secrets to him. In fact, even if she told him, the information would do him no good at all. The magic of hidden knowledge did not work that way.

As he had in the past several months, Cle attempted to reason with her. Lately he had approached her more directly, dismissing most of the small talk. Olga Mae suspected Cle's thieving cousin, Dram, had more than a little to do with Cle's ambitions. Likely Dram was the devious schemer behind their conniving ways.

"Shiwóyé, why do you not tell me where the Apache gold is? You do not need it. I can make a nice life for myself, my family and even those yet unborn. Have you not been keeping the secret of the Apache gold so our family can prosper? Is that not what you want?"

Olga Mae ignored Cle's pleadings. She did not respond to his piteous supplications. What would be the point? The Apache had long ago taken back from the Spaniards what rightfully belonged to the People to begin with. Her job was to protect its location and pass the secret of the Apache gold, along with an infinite number of other confidentialities, to the next Knowledge Keeper. The next in line to hold the ancient knowledge would not be her grandson. Only a woman who could be trusted to hold the many mysteries of time and history. The knowledge would be transferred to a woman with special abilities. A woman who had unknowingly, but with great persistence, spent a lifetime preparing to take Olga Mae's place. The Knowledge was and always had been passed down from one female Knowledge Keeper to the next. That was the design since the beginning of time of the People. For the Human Beings who lived on this planet, it was an eternal way.

"There is no such thing as Apache gold. Your talk is nothing but nonsense. I will speak no more of it. You should never waste another single breath in asking me."

Cle lowered his head to hide his anger. He could feel the heat of Dram's demanding ways burning a hole in his back. Cle knew the direct approach would be no more effective than any of the surreptitious methods he had tried on his other visits. He was down to his final option.

Cle reached into his pockets. His right jeans pocket held a small bottle of poison. In the other, the antidote. Both had been given to him by Dram. Nervously, he rolled each through sweaty fingers. Dram had given him explicit orders. Dram had told Cle the poison would put her in so much pain that she would feel as though her entire body was burning in the fires of hell. Because of the agony the poison would induce, she would be compelled to tell them where to find the Apache gold. After she talked, Cle could quickly administer the antidote, and all would be well. A simple plan which Dram assured him could not fail.

Olga Mae turned away to grab some herbs for the stewpot. Cle removed the lid of the poison bottle. He held it over the food. Instinctively, he pulled back before dropping the venom into the stew.

In the next instant, as though she knew precisely what he was up to, his grandmother made a sudden turn and stared at the pot. Olga Mae gazed into her grandson's eyes without saying a word. Her heart sang a song of sadness. Her grandson was unaware she suspected Dram called the shots. Intuition told her she was about to be sacrificed. She had lived a long time. If this was to be her destiny, such was the will of the Creator. Her heart felt calm. Her mind remained clear. Her spirit was free.

"You are men. After that long ride, you two must be hungry," said Olga Mae.

"I am very hungry," said Cle. "I love everything you cook."

She bit her lip. Her grandson was also a liar. He was never pleased with anything. He never had been. Cle had always wanted what he could not have, even when it came to food. This was especially true when it came to the gold.

Olga Mae dipped the serving spoon into the cookpot. She filled a bowl of mutton stew for her grandson. She gently handed it to him before filling a second bowl for Dram. Lastly, she filled one for herself. Honoring proper form, they waited for her to take the first bite. She did so without casting her eyes upon her wayward grandson and evil nephew. A moment later she heard the ill-mannered slurping of a ravenous young man devouring mutton stew. Cle ate like a man with deep hunger. If death would come tonight, it would visit both her and her grandson. Dram stirred the mutton stew in his bowl. He ate not a single bite.

After finishing his stew, Cle told his grandmother he needed to ride back to town. He had to work in the morning at the radio station. He spoke of his love for the job. Cle explained that he could record the sounds of a fox, a bear, a horse or even a hawk and make a person believe each animal was nearby. Olga Mae wondered why anyone would do such a thing and how it would serve the Creator.

"You could leave early in the morning," said the old woman.

"No, I must go now."

"Yes, we must go," added Dram.

Dram stood, turned and walked toward his horse without saying a word. To Cle, Dram's anger was palpable and directed at him.

Cle Feathers kissed Olga Mae Hooper Feathers goodbye. He pressed his lips against each of her cheeks, an unusual but respectful gesture he rarely performed. Olga Mae shook her head ever so slightly. The boy was such a fool.

READ NATIVE DESTINY NOW

Made in the USA
Monee, IL
24 June 2023

37190073R00174